She had been through this before and was sure she could never survive a second time...

Julia woke to the light touch of Sofia's hand. As she came to from her groggy, drug-induced sleep, she saw that her bare-breasted masseuse had put on her bikini top by now.

"Come, it's time to get dressed for dinner. You must look your most beautiful, Julia. For Anton. I have never seen him so taken with anyone before. No wonder, you are a gorgeous woman."

Julia was not quite sure what this all meant, but as she had drifted off to sleep, she had thought that the best avenue for her to survive this ordeal would be to cooperate with Polyakov and his crew, even though he no doubt had some nefarious plans for her. Was he intending her for his son? Or did he himself want to have sex with her again, the creep? Either way, the thought repulsed her. She was still traumatized from the terrible experience in Ozersk the previous night with Hetzel and the arms merchant.

The alternative to not cooperating that he had hinted at seemed even more terrible, though—and if what Sofia said was indeed right, and if she...she went with Anton...she might at least not have to suffer the advances of any of these despicable, debauched older men. Polyakov, or the pervert Hetzel. Or, for that matter, that awful Brother Peter. Ugh. Or all three, plus the guards, which is what Polyakov had implied. She shuddered at the hellish thought. And, hopefully, Anton would at least not hurt or torture her, if he was as taken with her as Sofia had suggested. But still, being forced to submit to her rapist's son, who was also the grandson of Beria and her aunt, was a very grim prospect indeed.

Crime novelist, Greg Martens, and his wife, former Interpol agent Anne Rossiter, are once again called back to Vienna by Anne's former boss at Interpol because Julia Saparova has disappeared a second time. Afraid that the same evil men, Sergei and Boris Polyakov, Julia's own cousins, are behind her disappearance, Greg and Anne reenter the seedy underworld of the Russian mafia, sex-trafficking, black market arms dealing, and international terrorism, in hopes of rescuing Julia. But this time, their enemies are expecting them, and Anne stumbles into a trap, joining Julia in depraved captivity. Now the two women's only hope is that Greg and their friends in Interpol can locate and rescue them before it's too late—not only for them, but for the world at large…

KUDOS for *Twisted Fates*

In *Twisted Fates* by Geza Tatrallyay, Greg Martens and his wife Anne are once again on a mission to rescue their friend Julia from the clutches of her evil cousins, powerful Russian men with ties to the underworld. Kidnapped and brutalized, Julia's only hope is that Greg and Anne can find and rescue her. But things do not go as planned, and soon Anne has been captured as well. Now it is up to Greg and his friends at Interpol to locate them before the two women disappear forever. Intense, suspenseful, intriguing, and fast paced, this is an excellent addition/conclusion to the trilogy. Once you pick it up, you will have a hard time putting it down. A really good read. ~ *Taylor Jones, The Review Team of Taylor Jones & Regan Murphy*

Twisted Fates by Geza Tatrallyay is the third and final book in his "Twisted" trilogy, the story of three friends and their struggle to bring an evil man and his associates to justice. Greg Marten, his wife Anne, and their Russian friend Julia Saparova have tangled more than once with Sergei Polyakov, a Russian arms dealer and human trafficker, who has kidnapped Julia more than once, since part of her job is to monitor nuclear material at various sites in Russia. Sergei hopes to use Julia to steal nuclear material to sell to international terrorists. He has tried it before and failed, but this time he is determined to succeed, and he doesn't care who he has to destroy to accomplish his goals. *Twisted Fates* is down-to-earth, gritty, and very intense, definitely not for the faint of heart. I thought Tatrallyay handled the subject of the consequences of rape and brutality for the victims with both sensitivity and compassion, while still telling a realistic and compelling story. It will grab you by the throat. ~

Regan Murphy, The Review Team of Taylor Jones & Regan Murphy

ACKNOWLEDGMENTS

I would like to thank the team at Black Opal Books—Lauri, Faith, and Jack—for their belief in my work, for all their help along the way, and for the many improvements they suggested to make this a better book.

My wife, for accompanying me on life's journey. Without her love, patience, and support, the "Twisted" trilogy would not have been conceived and written.

Other works by Geza

Arctic Meltdown

Twisted Reasons

Twisted Traffick

Cello's Tears

For the Children

The Expo Affair

Sighs and Murmurs

Sophie, My Dear

A Wanderer's Evensong

Dawn Dreams

Echoes

Autumnal Question

Let's Give Business An Incentive It Understands

Portfolio Pollution

Café Scene

Ember Eyes

Twisted Fates

Geza Tatrallyay

A Black Opal Books Publication

GENRE: CRIME THRILLER/SUSPENSE

TWISTED FATES
Copyright © 2018 by Geza Tatrallyay
Cover Design by Jackson Cover Designs
All cover art copyright © 2018
All Rights Reserved
Print ISBN: 978-1-626949-39-3

First Publication: JUNE 2018

Published by Black Opal Books **http://www.blackopalbooks.com**

DEDICATION

*To all the women and men who devote their lives to
bringing terrorists and merchants of evil to justice*

"For all the cruelty and hardship of our world, we are not mere prisoners of fate. Our actions matter and can bend history in the direction of justice."

~ Barack Obama, Nobel Lecture, Dec. 10, 2009

Summer 2065

Preface

Andrew put the book down and pulled one dangling leg up underneath him. Staring at Julia for a moment, the gangly fifteen-year-old asked, "Grandma, is it true? Were you really a stripper?"

The two were sitting on the porch of the family house in Vermont overlooking Lake Champlain in one direction and the beautiful Green Mountains in the other: he with one leg still hanging over the side into the flower garden teeming with Bee Bomb and Brown-Eyed Susan, she sitting in a white wicker rocking chair. The late afternoon sun reflected off the pond, bathing the two in its warm, golden glow.

Just then, Anne came through the door. "Mother, can I get you something? Greg is making your favorite drink. The Vermont Vertigo—"

"You know what your son asked me just now?" Julia asked, chuckling, instead of answering. "He asked if I really was a stripper in my youth, Anne! Imagine that—me, his grandmother."

"Andrew!" Anne exclaimed, wanting to scold her son, but not finishing, since she knew that the question was legitimate, and she was not sure where she should go with it. Fortunately, she was rescued by the ringing of the phone inside.

"But that's what Grandpa wrote in his book! That you danced and took your clothes off in that…that bar in…Vienna."

"Mom, the phone." Lily, Andrew's sister, appeared in the doorway. "It's for you. The Farmers' Market…"

꿍

"Well, Andrew—" Left alone with her grandson, after a long silence Julia launched into an answer to his question. "—when I first came to the West from Russia, that was the only way I could support myself. I was an illegal immigrant in Austria. So, yes, I did some exotic dancing, as it was called."

"What's this? Grandma is telling you about her youth? Your grandmother certainly was a beautiful young lady," Greg said with a smile, appearing through the screen door with two glasses of his signature concoction: one part maple syrup, two parts freshly squeezed lime juice, three parts dark rum, and lots of crushed ice. "She still is. And she certainly knew how to dance, she did." He handed one of the drinks to Julia, taking a sip from the other. "Hmm. Very good, even if I do say so myself. But more than that, Andrew, she was a very smart lady, your grandma. And she worked very hard. She's a nuclear physicist after all. The exotic dancing—that she did just to make enough to live on until she got a proper job."

"And there was nothing more to it than that, I can assure you. I had a boyfriend then, you know." And looking lovingly up at her husband, Julia added, "Your grandfather's best friend, as a matter of fact."

"Grandma!" Lily interjected, shocked, too, by these revelations. "So, you were a stripper, and then you ran off with Grandpa? And left his best friend." It all seemed a little too much for the teenagers.

"Yes. It was my friend from school, Adam Kallay. He was Grandma's boyfriend, way back then. But he—he died well before your grandmother and I got together," Greg said, glancing at Julia. Adam and he had grown up together in Cleveland in Hungarian-American families that had known each other in the old country. They had shared a room at Harvard, fenced together for the college team, and Greg had tried to disentangle his friend from the first sordid nuclear heist affair when he went to visit him in Vienna several years earlier. He hoped the questions would end there.

But they did not. "How did this friend…this Adam Kallay…die?" Andrew asked, suspicions aroused.

"He was shot. In a heist. You know, some terrorists wanted to get their hands on some nuclear material." Again, Greg hoped there would be no more questions. "It's all in the book you're reading, Andrew, *Twisted Reasons*. Right toward the end."

"You will see that your grandpa and some other friends played a very important role in making sure the highly enriched uranium did not get into the wrong hands," Julia explained. "He helped prevent a major atomic blast that could have killed several hundred thousand people. You should be very proud of him."

"And your grandmother, too. She was involved as well."

"I guess I need to finish the story, Grandpa," Andrew said, overwhelmed and sullen, as he buried his head in the book again.

Julia gave Greg a loving smile as he sat down beside her and took her hand in his.

Summer 2019

Chapter 1

Greg was glad to be back in Vienna. The Imperial Capital was his favorite city: it held fond memories for him, but he also relished its vibrant and changing present. For one, this was where he had met and fallen in love with his beautiful wife, Anne, who was now sitting beside him in the cab from the airport, checking her emails after the two-hour morning flight from London where they had been visiting Anne's brother after a three day stay with her parents in Cornwall.

Vienna was where he had first become entangled in the international intrigue that he had, after that—surpriseingly to him—come to thrive on, and now, with his quiet academic life in Vermont, sorely missed. This was all in large part thanks to Anne, who had been working for Interpol at the time. But there were painful memories mixed in: the suspicion of, and disillusionment with, his erstwhile best friend, Adam Kallay, had started here. Yes, the messy first attempt by some Russian arms merchants to steal some nuclear material from Mayak—the former secret city where Stalin and Beria had developed the Soviet atomic bomb—that his friend had drawn him into. And that had 'resulted' in Adam's death: Greg had never really ly told anyone how he had pulled the trigger of the pistol killing his friend as he was taunting him, ready to get away with enough highly enriched uranium for half a bomb.

On the positive side, yes, it was because of Adam that he had met Anne, who had been Kallay's contact at Interpol. And also Julia Saparova, the beautiful physicist who had taken Adam's job at the International Atomic Energy Agency, in charge of monitoring security at the former Soviet nuclear sites. In fact, Anne and he were really looking forward to spending some time with her over the weekend. She was flying back to give a report to the IAEA's top brass, and when she had heard that they would be in Vienna, had made arrangements to stay in town. Although she had said on the phone that she normally liked to get back to Ozersk to spend her free days with her sick mother when work took her there.

Another positive: Vienna had been the source—directly or indirectly—of so much of the material for Greg's writing ever since. In fact, his three most recent successes were all somehow linked to his times in Vienna. First had come the bestseller biography *cum* memoir about his Hungarian grandparents, *András and Lily*. Then *Twisted Reasons*, the story of the "Adam affair," his second highly acclaimed 'novel' after *Wintertime,* the one he had written straight out of college. And most recently, *Katerina, Beria's Slave*, the true story of Julia's aunt, picked up by a major New York house. Just before leaving on this trip, he had finally finished and sent off to his publisher, *Twisted Traffick,* the next novel in the 'Twisted' trilogy: the story of human trafficking and the second heist attempt by those merchants of evil that he and Anne had helped foil. *Twisted Fates* would be the third book in the series, all of which were basically thrillers based on real life.

Thinking about the past—and really, the reason that

he was back in the Imperial Capital this time—brought back another Viennese memory. One that had been unpleasant and nerve-racking then, but with time, had acquired a somewhat humorous patina. It was of that embarrassing moment at the meeting of the Austrian Literary Society, where he had been exposed in the act of impersonating a more famous author with a very similar name, Gareth Martens. And by none other than Billy Crawford, an old acquaintance from summer camp days, who—as he had found out during the "Kallay Affair"—was now an internationally sought-after terrorist. But that was all now well behind him, and, justifiably, he was proud of the fact that based on his newly acquired renown as a writer, he had been invited back by the Austrian Literary Society to give another lecture. This time, though, since he had written in both genres, he was asked to talk on the continuum between memoir and fiction in modern literature, which he knew he would have no problems with since it had been the topic of many articles he had written. However, this time it was not that busybody imbecile, Crabbe, who had sent Greg the all-expenses-paid invitation, but the newly elected head of the Society, the dowager Frau von Hitzinger whom he vaguely remembered meeting way back then.

Greg returned to the present from his musings about the past just as the taxi pulled up outside the Sacher. He loved to stay in this beautiful hotel, and it helped that, as before, the Society's meeting was to be held here the very next day, Friday. The Hotel Sacher was right across from the Staatsoper, and, as he got out of the cab, Greg resolved to ask the receptionist to get them two tickets to whatever was being performed at the world's most famous opera house. He was an avid lover of the genre, having grown up with it as a child in Cleveland, where, at the insistence of his Hungarian grandmother, Omi, there had always been classical music playing in their home. Fortunately, Anne too, was a keen opera buff, although her tastes were not as eclectic as Greg's and tended toward the more often played romantic pieces.

"Tonight at the Staatsoper, Mr. Martens," the receptionist answered Greg's question, "let me see…there is a new production of *Siegfried*, you know, the third opera in Wagner's Ring Cycle. A great production. Wonderful, I have seen it myself. With Jonas Kauffman and Svetlana Kokova. Tickets are hard to get, but I am sure we can manage. And tomorrow, there is a performance of…let's see…Dmitry Shostakovich's *Lady Macbeth of Mtsensk.* As another possibility, there is also *The Merry Widow* at the Volksoper today and tomorrow. Perhaps that is more to your liking, Mr. Martens?"

Greg glanced over at Anne, who was standing several meters away with the bags, busy looking through a pamphlet on what to do in Vienna that week, then back at the receptionist, and on an impulse, said, "No, please, see if you can get us two tickets for the Wagner for tonight. That would be terrific." He loved the German composer, and although he knew that the Ring wasn't exactly Anne's "cup of tea," she would certainly prefer it to the Shostakovich. Although he remembered that she had adored Julian Barnes' wonderful little novel about the composer where the opera had been mentioned. He himself had never seen it performed but had always been intrigued by the work, especially since it had caused Shostakovich so many problems with Stalin and his régime. In fact, an article attributed to Stalin himself had dubbed it "Muddle Instead of Music," he remembered from the book. Also, the complicated story of adultery, scheming and murder spoke to him as an author. He was sorely tempted, but no, Wagner was definitely a better choice, Greg decided. In any case, he knew his wife would be pleased just to go out in their favorite city and make a romantic evening of it, especially with dinner at Julius Meinl after the opera, as on their very first date. Yes, it was indeed something to look forward to. He would break the news to her when they got up to the room.

Why not—maybe that would result in a little loving before we wander out to see the sights, Greg thought, liking his plan very much.

Chapter 2

Julia smiled to herself as she got off the little bus that shuttled workers to and fro between the Mayak Nuclear Facility and the center of Ozersk. She was pleased that she had managed to put the finishing touches on the presentation she would be making on Friday, the day after tomorrow, to her big boss, the Director General, and other senior officials of the International Atomic Energy Agency, on progress with security at Mayak and nuclear sites in Russia in general. But even more so, because tomorrow she would be flying to Vienna, the city she now called home—although she was spending a lot of time in Ozersk with her mother these days—and where she would see some old friends.

Yes, she was particularly looking forward to catching up with Anne and Greg, who would be in town and had promised to spend most of the weekend with her. She remembered, too, that she and her friend Maria had those opera tickets to the Saturday evening performance at the Staatsoper's of Dmitry Shostakovich's *Lady Macbeth of Mtsensk,* an opera that had intrigued her since her youth, and one that was not played very often. Perhaps Anne and Greg could get tickets as well. They were opera buffs, so that seemed like an excellent plan. Yes, it was all of these things, but above all, she was in a good mood because it was a gorgeous late afternoon, and, as she walked down the path crossing Lenin Park, she soaked up the warmth of the sun's rays peeking around the statue of Ivan Kurchatov, the father of the Soviet bomb.

Julia thought of the time she had met with Mikhail Glinkov, the Mayak security guard, under the statue on an equally beautiful day several years earlier to seek his help to defeat a second planned heist of nuclear material by declining to cooperate with the arms merchants Sergei Polyakov and Andreas Hetzel who were trying to blackmail him. She shuddered at the thought of the abuse and rape Nadia, Glinkov's daughter, and she had suffered at the hands of these men, who were also evil human traffickers and deeply involved in the international sex trade. They had tried to use Nadia and her to steal some nuclear material then, but fortunately, on that occasion, her former Interpol friends and she had been able to foil the attempt.

Julia was glad that episode was well behind her now, although the trauma had lasted for a long time and occasionally she still had nightmares about it. She wondered what had happened to the criminals: she knew Sergei Polyakov had managed to escape, and a severely incapacitated Hetzel—her particular abuser—had been taken into custody…

But what then? She just hoped they were both securely locked up somewhere.

Coming to the other side of the park, Julia crossed the road, walked a few steps down the street running away from the green, then turned into the alleyway leading to her mother's apartment, which was where she always stayed when she came to Ozersk. She looked forward to spending time in the evening with her Mamochka, particularly because she would be gone on the weekend and she didn't know how many more such occasions there would be. Her mother was suffering from cancer, and they had recently been told after a grueling session of chemotherapy Julia had arranged for her at the Rudolfinerklinik in Vienna that she had not much time left. But, as she took her keys out, she reminded herself that this apartment was really too small for the two of them, and she needed to start looking for a bigger place where they could be together comfortably when she was working at Mayak, now that Mamochka was permanently back in Russia after the treatments had run their course.

It was at that very moment, when she was just about to put the key in the lock, that two huge men, both armed with a knife and a pistol, appeared from out of nowhere on either side of her. Julia stopped, quickly turned and wanted to run, but the smaller one of her two assailants grabbed her arm and twisted it behind her back, saying, "Gospodja Sarapova, you are coming with us. The boss wants to speak with you." They slapped handcuffs on her wrists, and quickly shoved her into the back of a waiting black KIA SUV. The two thugs climbed in on either side of her and did not waste any time in tying a blindfold across her eyes.

Julia could not believe that this was happening to her again. The fear, though, was not the panic of the last time she was captured, but an intense anxiety that nevertheless still allowed her to think rationally about what the next steps might be.

Above all, she knew she had to maintain her ability to think clearly if she was going to survive a second kidnapping by these monsters—if, as she feared, they were the same criminals as before. They did know her name, and she did hear them refer to someone as "boss," just like the last time, so there was a strong likelihood.

☙❧

The vehicle finally came to a halt, after twisting and turning, stopping and starting on city streets, and then driving through what—from the clicks and grinding noises—Julia was convinced was an electric gate. The doors of the SUV opened. She was pulled out of the back seat and shoved along and up some stairs. She heard a doorbell ring, then a large door opened and closed, and she was tugged along a corridor by the two thugs. When they stopped, one of them said, "Here she is, boss, just as you ordered."

"Thank you, Ivan. You may leave us now."

Was that cold, hard voice Polyakov's? The terror welled up again, tangible in its intensity.

The guard released her, and, standing there in a dark void, she felt the approaching presence of the man she dreaded was the Russian merchant of evil, as Ivan and his colleague left, shutting the door behind them. Instinctively, she recoiled and stepped backward until she bumped against some furniture…a table, a desk?

A man's hand stroked her shoulder length blond hair, while another hand brushed her breasts, and as she cringed, she heard the voice again: "Andreas, she is as gorgeous as ever, isn't she, our little Julia?" And then the hand whisked her blindfold off, and to her horror, Julia saw that indeed she was face to face with the two men she feared and loathed the most in the world: Sergei Polyakov and Andreas Hetzel.

The Russian had not changed much, she quickly ascertained. Perhaps he was a little older and balder, and his face sterner and even more evil looking, but he still seemed fit as ever, and despite his shortness of stature, was still a commanding presence. She had last seen Polyakov in Georgia, during the first heist attempt, when he had taken her and her friend Anne, prisoner. And—she struggled with the memory—viciously raped Anne in front of her. The pervert Hetzel, on the other hand, she had had a more recent and even more terrible encounter with: he had tricked her to come to the Revuebar Rasputin in Vienna, where she had earlier worked as an exotic dancer, kidnapped her and serially sexually abused her, just as he did Nadia, Glinkov's teenage daughter. Hetzel had definitely lost weight since then—and perhaps, she thought, this was linked to the terrible revenge Anne had wrought on him, on her and Nadia's behalf, blowing his genitalia away with a well-aimed shot—probably becoming wrinkly and wizened and gray as a result of some hormonal imbalance, with his hair turning white.

"Do you know why you are here, my lovely?" Polyakov asked, stroking her face and then letting his hands roam along her curves. And when, recoiling, she didn't answer, he continued: "Tell her, Andreas. Tell her. I am sure she is just dying to know, the little cunt." He moved his right hand down to between her legs, lifting her short dress.

Hetzel looked at Julia with his bulging frog eyes, approached her, and slapped her across the face. "Because you are the source of all our problems, you bitch. First, you refuse my very generous offers of marriage, and then you escape and double-cross us."

"Yes, my dear, you are in real trouble," Polyakov added, shoving her down on the table and stroking her pubic area. "You helped prevent a very important business transaction from taking place and got some of my men killed in the process. So now, you are going to set things right, aren't you?"

"You better believe it. But the only way she can even come close to setting things right with me is if we make the slut suffer. After all—"

"Now, now, Andreas. First, she is going to help us get at least fifty pounds of highly enriched uranium out from Mayak. No, in fact, she will bring it out herself. No fooling around. And no double-crossing this time, you little bitch," Polyakov continued, as he reached under her skirt and inside her panties. "Yes, my dear. And then Andreas, we will get her to deliver her partners in crime—that's a good one, you've got to admit, Andreas, 'partners in crime'—to us, so we can pay them back for what they have done to us. That cocksucker, Greg Martens and—and your friend, Julia, the beautiful Anne, that stupid Interpol agent…what was her name? The one I had so much fun with. In Poti—remember, you witnessed it all, my dear? Don't tell me you didn't enjoy watching! I know you are loving this, too, my lovely, aren't you?" And then, as an afterthought, "Anne Rossiter, wasn't that the cunt's name?"

"Now the bitch is married to that dickhead, Martens." This from Hetzel. "I can hardly wait to get my hands on her—"

"Yes, of course, Andreas, I know. Well, my dear, you are going to help us get to them. And then you will have the pleasure of watching them die a slow death for what they did. But first, the uranium, you will help us get that. If you don't want to suffer the same fate as your friends will."

"Yes, first the uranium," Hetzel, the toady, added.

"But, Andreas, enough for now," Polyakov pulled his hand away, licking the fingers, and tugged Julia to her feet. "Why don't you have Ivan take this whore downstairs? Lock her up for now. We've got work to do, you and I. We can have fun with her later."

Chapter 3

Greg did indeed find the *Siegfried* to be a *tour de force*. He loved Wagner's thrilling, expansive music, and Svetlana Kokova and Jonas Kauffman were magnificent as Brünhilde and Siegfried, and Bryn Terfel as Wotan. Also, the staging, the orchestra, the lighting he found…well, all to be first class. As the curtain went down on the first act, he resolved to see when *Götterdämmerung*—the fourth and last opera in the cycle—would be performed, on the off chance that Anne and he might still be in Europe.

Filing out behind the mix of aging, formally dressed Viennese, and younger, more casually attired tourists, he asked Anne what she thought of the opera. Her answer was, "Not much, my dear. I thought…I guess I just don't like Wagner. It puts me to sleep. And the stupid story of the Norse gods…it's so over the top. Ugh."

"Sorry, my love. I must say, you sound a bit like Rossini." Greg gave a little laugh, leading up to his punch line. "He was the one who said 'Wagner has lovely moments but awful quarters of an hour.' Yeah, and D.H. Lawrence, whose comment, 'I love Italian opera—it's so reckless. Damn Wagner and his bellowings at Fate and death,' also reminds me of you, my dear."

"Ha, ha ha…"

"I must say though, I am enjoying it. And I still love you. In any case, this was the only option for tonight," Greg said as his excuse, having anticipated the reaction.

They made their way up the beautiful marble staircase to the lavish "Schwind" foyer, which takes its name from the frescoes by Martin Schwind of scenes from operas. The room was packed, the noise was deafening, and there was already a queue at the bar. Greg glanced around, and seeing the crowd, said to his wife, "Why don't you just wait here by this pillar, Anne, and I'll get us two glasses of *Sekt*. I'll be right back, dear…"

Anne said, "Okay," as Greg released her hand, giving her a peck on the cheek, and hurried over to the lineup. Looking back, he could not help but consider himself to be the luckiest man alive, with a partner as beautiful and loving as Anne. Although they had been married for several years now, he was still head over heels in love with his wife.

Greg was just ordering the two glasses of the bubbly, when he did a double take, as he saw a balding, short, stocky man in a ceremonial military uniform approach his wife and say something to her. It was when he saw his wife's face turn glum and angry, that he knew who it was: Boris Polyakov, he was certain. It was *déjá vu*, just like the last time. The FSB Deputy Director had somehow known they would be here. He must have his spies everywhere.

Greg grabbed the glasses handed to him by the barman, and, not waiting for his change from the twenty Euro note, rushed back to Anne, just as he saw the Russian intelligence operative peel away from her and disappear into the crowd without so much as looking back. His wife had turned pale and was visibly shaken.

Greg handed her one of the flutes. "Anne…Polyakov? Boris, the twin brother? Again?" as he put his arm around her waist.

"Yes, the bastard." Anne gulped the contents down and handed the glass back to Greg as she steadied herself against the pillar.

"What did he say?"

"Something like, 'Well, well, well, if it isn't the beautiful Anne Rossiter! Here again at the Staatsoper. I wouldn't have thought though that Wagner was your style. But I do hope you won't leave during the intermission like you did the last time. Remember, after *Bluebeard's Castle*. And just before *Iolanta,* my favorite Tchaikovsky opera. How tactless of you.' So, Greg, the jerk did remember our last encounter. And he finished off by threatening us. He said: 'In any case, I am so glad you and your sorry excuse for a husband are back in Vienna. You have just made it that much easier for us to pay the two of you back for all the grief you have caused us. Just you wait.'"

The bell started to ring just then, indicating the end of the break.

"Damn him! And the entire Russian intelligence network. They are in cahoots with his brother's evil trading activities, I am sure," Greg said, finishing his bubbly and putting the two glasses on one of the tall tables strung around the hall. But to himself, he said, *This is surreal. It can't be happening again. The Deputy Director of the FSB menacing us the same way he did several years ago, at the opera in Vienna. Am I living a nightmare?*

"I will tell my former Interpol colleagues when I meet with them tomorrow," Anne said as she followed him down the beautiful marble staircase to the ground floor. "They need to know that these bastards have threatened us again."

"We need to be on our guard, Anne."

"Actually, could this mean that the Polyakovs are trying again?" Anne mused. "To carry off another heist, I mean—"

"Let's not go there. Let's put this behind us, and have a nice evening. Like we planned."

They made their way back to their parterre row eleven, center seats, when all of a sudden, Anne, who had been looking at the audience all around, trying to see if she could catch sight of the hated FSB Deputy Director, suddenly grabbed her husband's arm. "Greg, hold on. Isn't that the Labrecques up there? Look, there, in the balcony! Nicholas and Marie Christine."

"Yes, I think you're right, Anne. Fancy that. The world's entire intelligence community seems to be interested in this opera. Let's try and catch up with the French couple after the performance. Even though you are supposed to meet with Nicholas tomorrow."

∾

When the opera was over, and the curtain calls finished, Anne and Greg were itching for the members of the audience on either side of them to get up from their seats and file out quickly, however, by the time they got to the lobby and searched for their friends and the Russian operative, they were nowhere to be seen. Nor did they have any luck out in front of the Staatsoper. The illusive FSB chief and their French friends were all long since gone.

It was as they were walking along Augustinerstrasse toward the Graben where the restaurant was located that Greg finally thought to check his cellphone for messages. He was surprised to see several calls from a 7 35130 area code, which he thought he remembered from previous experience was Ozersk, the city adjacent to Mayak.

"Hmm. Anne, it seems someone was calling during the opera. From a seven, three, five, one, three, zero number. Ozersk, I think. Do you think it might have been Julia? Perhaps—"

"That would be strange. We haven't heard from her for a while, and she usually gets in touch by email. Plus, she would likely be phoning from an Austrian cell number. In any case, we are seeing her over the weekend."

"I hope she's not canceling—"

"Strange coincidence that this call came so close to the threat from Boris Polyakov." Anne could not get the FSB officer out of her mind. "Could they have been connected?"

"Hmm…Interesting. But more likely not. Just chance."

"Whoever it was, called right after seven p.m., just as the opera started. Let's see, in Chelyabinsk Oblast that would be after eleven p.m."

"That's pretty late, isn't it? It must have been something important then. Or it could just be a wrong number."

"Let's hope if it is Julia, she's okay."

"Maybe you should try to call the number back, Greg. What do you think?"

"I'm not sure. It's now ten-twenty p.m. here," Greg said, glancing again at his phone. "Two-twenty in the morning there. That's extremely late."

"And we do have a lovely dinner to look forward to—you're right, Greg, let's call first thing tomorrow. There is nothing we could do now anyway."

Chapter 4

Julia must have fallen into a deep sleep in the darkness of the cold and damp cellar. She woke with a start to loud voices and clanging, and light seeping into the room where that man Ivan had shoved her to the cold earthen floor. Now she recognized his voice again as he opened the lock on what she saw was a barred cage door, yelling, "Come on, bitch, the boss wants you upstairs. He is ready to have some fun, no doubt. I sure can't blame him."

Her terror rose to a fever pitch again, as the thug pulled her to her feet, and tugged her along a corridor, then up some stairs and into a cozy looking room full of antiques where Polyakov and Hetzel were sitting on a couch, brandy snifters in one hand, cigars in the other.

"Well, well," the Russian arms merchant said, "our entertainment is finally here."

"This is definitely going to be an amusing evening, I can tell!" The pervert Hetzel could scarcely contain himself.

Julia dreaded what the two meant.

"Come over here, my dear. Come, sit between my friend, Andreas, and me." Polyakov put his cigar in the big crystal ashtray on the coffee table and patted the red velvet couch between him and Hetzel.

When she didn't move, Polyakov said, "Ivan, for fuck's sake, bring the slut over here, will you? And then you can leave."

"Yes, boss," the guard answered, shoving Julia forward to sit on the sofa between the two gangsters.

"Oh, and before you go," Polyakov continued, "take her bloody handcuffs off. She won't be needing them anymore. We may want her to use her hands." He cackled at his own sick insinuation.

Ivan reached behind Julia, manhandling her as he released her from her shackles.

"Well done, Ivan," Polyakov said as he watched. "And now, good night. Please close the door behind you."

When it was just the three of them, Polyakov asked, "How about a drink, my dear? Cognac? Champagne? What would you like?"

And when Julia, trying to hold herself together, did not answer, he grabbed her by the chin, and saying, as he raised his brandy snifter to her mouth, "I am sure you will like this!" even as he poured as much of the Cognac as he could down her throat. Julia coughed, and most of the golden liquid streamed down the front of her dress and into her cleavage.

"Well, well, well. We won't let this expensive nectar go to waste, will we, my lovely?" Polyakov said, eyeing Julia's cognac-soaked torso lasciviously. He pushed her down into Hetzel's lap, at the same time pulling her dress off her shoulders, and, as she squirmed, he licked the brandy from her neck, cleavage, and breasts.

"Andreas, why don't you have a taste? She sure is delicious, your little Julia," Polyakov said to his friend—who was now pinning Julia's arms above her head—as the Russian proceeded to pull her dress up over her waist. Hetzel attacked her breasts with glee, ripping her bra off, licking and biting, while the Russian brute tugged at her panties with one hand, unzipping the dress with his other.

Julia squirmed, trying to free herself, and cried out, "Please, please, no!" but to no avail.

Then Polyakov said with a perverse chuckle, "I think I would like some more of that delicious Rémy Martin Napoléon," and, even as Julia could not help but sob as she tried to protect herself from her attackers, he took the bottle, poured a good slug onto her bared pubic area, and then proceeded to lick it up with loud slurping sounds. "Wow, you are indeed very, very tasty, my dear," he said. Then spreading her legs with his hands and moving his head back, he continued, "Andreas, why don't you have a lick down here too?"

Hetzel was more than happy to do as he was told, as Julia saw Polyakov start to undo his trousers. *Oh, please, God no! Don't let him do this.* Her terror was multiplied exponentially by the fact that he had seen this man viciously rape Anne in Poti, and also that she knew from the files they had found in Porto Montenegro that this beast was—quite incredibly to her—in fact, her maternal cousin, the bastard son of Katerina, her mother's older sister and that monster who had kept her as his sex slave, the former Deputy Premier of the Soviet Union, Lavrenti Beria.

"Okay, Andreas, hold the slut down," the Russian arms merchant said. "Remember, I am doing this for you, old man. Since you no longer can, my friend." And with a crazed laugh, he shoved his hardened penis into Julia's by now well-lubricated vagina, as Hetzel helped hold her down and gawked with lust-filled eyes, pawing her breasts and enjoying her humiliation.

When the Russian finished his horrible task, he proceeded to wipe himself with Julia's discarded panties. Julia shuddered and curled up in the fetal position, sobbing quietly, as she heard Hetzel say, "Is this the time to give her the shot, Sergei?"

"Probably as good as any, since we need her to play ball tomorrow. And she won't show any resistance now, I am sure. Have you got it ready?"

"Yes, of course." And he went over to a sideboard where he opened a drawer and pulled out a needle and a vial, handing it to Polyakov.

"This should do it," the Russian said, sticking the needle in the ampoule and then holding it up to the light to make sure it was full. "It's what we used to use during the Chechen Wars to get prisoners to talk. They would be totally pliable after a dose like this. No will to fight whatsoever. And it lasts a good twenty-four hours, so it should be enough." He jabbed the needle into Julia's left buttock. She screamed and jerked spastically before resuming her curled position amid violent sobs.

"Good. We're on then."

"Get Ivan to take the bitch away for now," Polyakov said, picking up her Cognac-soaked dress from the floor and throwing it at her. "She'll be useless for the next few hours anyway. Let's all get some sleep. Tomorrow is a big day."

Chapter 5

Elena was worried. Julia was still not back, and it was after eleven p.m. Her daughter was usually at home by six at the latest, and she had expressly called before leaving her office at Mayak, happy that she would be able to come home early to spend time with her Mamochka since she would be gone for the rest of the week. Not keeping her word was very unlike her Julia, but it was mainly because she had disappeared once before in a similar vein, kidnapped by some terrible criminals—merchants of evil, sex traffickers, arms traders—of the worst kind, that Elena now felt especially agitated.

There was also that feeling she had as soon as she entered the apartment when she got back from shopping earlier in the afternoon that someone had been just there. It was weird, eerie: nothing of hers had been taken—or at least nothing that was immediately obvious—but despite her age, she was astute enough to know that some things had been moved or were out of place, if ever so slightly. And she was wondering where her daughter's ablutions kit was—for sure, Julia wouldn't have taken it with her to the office? There was also that lingering, musty odor of a male presence—yes, some man had been in the apartment, she was certain.

Elena took down her rusty little tin box where she kept all her papers, and she looked for the one she had written Greg's phone number on, the last time they had met, in New York, at the launch party for his bestselling book about her older sister, *Katerina, Beria's Slave.* She had enjoyed the collaboration, and they had developed a liking and respect for each other. Moreover, Greg Martens and his wife, Anne—she had been an Interpol agent before, which had no doubt helped—had tracked Julia down the last time she disappeared. They had found her, rescued her, and brought her daughter back to her. Elena was sure she could trust them to do so again. And there was no one else she could ask.

She found the note neatly filed in the red Soviet era tea holder and dialed the Vermont cell number.

The cell rang and rang, and eventually, she was switched to voicemail. "This is Greg Martens. I cannot answer the phone right now. Please leave a message, and I will get back to you as soon as I can. Thank you."

Elena tried a few more times, without success. She had no one else she could ask for help. Even so, she did not want to leave a message. So she went to bed and cried herself to sleep.

ℰ✺ℰ

Julia's mother woke up early, just after five a.m. She counted back and came to the conclusion that with the time difference of ten hours between Ozersk and Vermont, it would be just seven p.m. there. A good time to call, right around dinner.

It was on the eighth ring that someone finally answered. "Hello, hello?"

She immediately recognized the somewhat groggy male voice that seemed close enough to be coming from someone in the same room. Although he did seem to be a bit out of breath.

"This is Greg Martens here."

"Gospodin Martens, I am so glad to have reached you."

"Aah, Gospodja Saparova, how nice to hear from you." Elena sensed some surprise in the voice at the other end. "I hope everything is all right. Ahem. You have been receiving the royalty payments I take it," Greg continued.

"Yes, thank you. But Gospodin Martens, that is not why I am calling. By the way, I am sorry, are you—are you in bed?"

"Yes, Gospodja Saparova. Anne and I are actually in Vienna. It is just after one in the morning. But never mind, please, what is wrong?"

"Gospodin Martens, I am sorry. But Julia—my Julia—has disappeared again, and I don't know what to do." The old lady clearly had trouble holding back the tears.

"What? Not again!"

"Yes. She did not come home yesterday, even though she called just before leaving the office to say she would be back early. Almost twelve hours ago, she was supposed to be home. I am sure she has been kidnapped. I just know it."

"Gospodja Saparova, she could—"

"There was also someone in my apartment earlier yesterday, I am certain. I don't think they took anything, but I am afraid. Very afraid for my daughter. Please, please will you help us?"

"Where are you now, Gospodja Saparova?"

"Back home, in Ozersk."

"Gospodja Saparova, thank you for letting me know about his. Stay in your apartment, please. Anne and I will make a few phone calls to see what we can find out and call you back. It may take a few hours though since it is still night here. Don't worry, we will find Julia."

"Thank you, Gospodin Martens. You are the best of friends to my daughter. And to me, too."

"Of course."

"Gospodin Martens, I was coming to Vienna tomorrow with Julia, anyway. I will proceed with those plans. I want to be there when you find my daughter. Besides, it is not safe here, if a man can just come into the apartment. I am very afraid."

"But we don't know where Julia is, Gospodja Saparova. She could still be in Russia—"

"Never mind. Vienna is much more central. I will be in Julia's apartment if you need me. I will feel safer there. I have a key."

There was no arguing with her, once the old lady had made up her mind.

Chapter 6

"That was Julia's mother, as you could no doubt guess," Greg said to Anne.

He had just turned the lights off, looking forward to what would come next after the opera and a wonderful meal at Julius Meinl, when the call from the old lady had come—needless to say, deflating the ambiance. Much to Greg's disappointment.

Although what Elena Saparova had said certainly got the adrenalin pumping.

"She was very upset. Her daughter did not come home as expected, and she suspects foul play again," he continued, turning the light off and settling into the pleasure of embracing his naked wife under the sheets.

"Julia might have just gone for a drink with a colleague," Anne said, straddling her husband's knee and gently taking his penis in her hand. "And met up with a man." She nudged her face against Greg's. "Surely."

"Yes, but she called her mother just before leaving the office, saying she was on her way and would be home shortly." He could feel himself hardening. "Ahem…four or five hours later, Elena started suspecting the worst. Which was when she first tried to reach us."

"Hmm…" Anne mumbled, nibbling on her husband's chest. "We were at the opera then, weren't we? That was the call—"

"Yes, I believe so. You know very well, Anne, with Julia's job, she is a prime target. As was Adam," Greg said, giving his wife a kiss on the top of her head, as she rhythmically caressed his member between thumb and forefinger. "And it's not as if this is the first time."

"Umm…" Anne murmured. Acquiescence or pleasure, Greg was not sure. Or both?

"Plus, Elena was sure that someone had forced entry into her place earlier."

"I guess you're right, Greg," Anne agreed, starting to undulate slowly against Greg's knee. "That is…umm …terrible…Umm. Wonderful."

"You heard me tell her we would make a few calls in the morning and get back to her once we know something. She told me that she was going to come to Vienna with Julia tomorrow. She intends to proceed with those plans because she wants to be here when we find Julia. She will stay at Julia's, She is very afraid, and does not feel safe in her apartment after the intrusion."

"Yes, my love. But right now…umm…I want you to…umm…forget about Elena. I want you to make love to me."

ତ∕ତ∕ତ

Fifteen minutes and a satiating orgasm later, Anne said. "You know Greg, that in the morning I was going to go by my former Interpol office anyway. To say hello, and to see everyone. But with all that is going on here, you had better come too, and we can get them to do some digging. The Boris Polyakov encounter, then this phone call…it is all rather concerning."

"Sure. I think you are right."

"Just thinking aloud, Greg. Perhaps on the way, we should go by Julia's apartment here in Vienna. Before her mother gets here and disturbs any possible evidence. You never know, she may have decided to come back a day early, although I am sure she would have told her mother about a change in her plans. In any case, that way, we may have some answers."

"Sounds good."

"I can try and get Haffner—you know, Lieutenant Haffner, my old contact with the Austrian police—to join us. Just to add heft and legitimacy."

"Yes, that would be good. And he could help us get a warrant if we don't get anywhere. Although by then, Julia's mother will be here, no doubt."

"Then after the meeting at Interpol, I—or both of us—and maybe Labrecque can go over and talk to the IAEA to find out what we can from Julia's colleagues."

"Good idea, Anne. Also, I was just thinking, the Revuebar Rasputin that's where it all happened before…but I guess there is no real point in sending anyone there, since the Austrian police have supposedly closed the strip joint down," Greg mused, adding, "But we can have Nicholas or someone check it out, later. Just in case."

"Yes, best to have them verify that the club no longer exists," Anne agreed. "You never know with these gangsters."

"And for God's sake, we need to talk to Demeter about Boris Polyakov—Interpol should be tracking his movements when he is here in Vienna. He's got to be one of the most important Russian intelligence officials now, so I don't understand why they wouldn't—"

"He must be on their watch list. I will bring that up tomorrow."

"Anne, I can call Charles Levinson, the American government rep at Mayak, and get him to do some checking around there." He looked at the time on his phone before continuing. "In fact…already in just a few hours. I'll try at five our time. That will be nine a.m. there. I had better set the alarm, though." He picked up his phone and did just that before continuing, "I can ask him if he has seen Julia recently. And to do what he can to get the Russians to tighten security at the facility."

"Good point. Because if it is Polyakov and crew again who kidnapped Julia, this could be the prelude to another heist."

"Yes, that's what I fear."

"I will also get Demeter to see if he can have Interpol in Russia monitor air traffic from Chelyabinsk and adjacent airports. If Julia was, in fact, kidnapped, whoever did it, may try to move her somewhere else."

"Yeah, you're right, Anne."

"Greg, I am very worried, about Julia. If what happened the last time happened again—you know, the abuse—it could kill her. And her mother, too."

"That's what I fear too, my dear. We need to move fast."

Chapter 7

Julia woke to rough shaking and the groping of a man's hands. She was terribly cold. During the night she had put her wet, flimsy little dress back on, but that was all that was between her and the damp earthen floor of her prison deep in the cellar of the Siberian villa. She felt bruised and sore all over, her breasts were like sacks of lead, and when she moved to try to get up, nausea overwhelmed her. Her brain, too, seemed to be frozen—was it from the cold or the drugs or the trauma she had suffered, or all of these, she did not know. When she finally opened her eyes, the hazy image of a man's face with a naked light bulb hanging from the ceiling behind it was what greeted her.

"Come on, you bitch! Time to get going." It was the thug they called Ivan, come to get her.

What horrors do these monsters have in store for me next?

Ivan pulled her to her feet, saying, "The boss wants you cleaned up, and dressed. Ready to go to work. Come."

Ivan dragged Julia to a bedroom with an en suite bathroom, where, on the king-size bed, she was surprised to see one of her summer work dresses, along with clean underwear and the wash kit with her make-up in it. They must have broken into her mother's apartment yesterday to get all this gear, she thought to herself.

And what did these pigs do to my mother? Suddenly, the terror overwhelmed Julia again.

"You wash up fast, put makeup on, and get dressed," Ivan said, shoving her toward the bathroom. "Boss wants you to go to work." He sat down on the bed, stretching himself out, settling in comfortably to gawk at her. In fact, when Julia went hesitantly into the bathroom and tried to close the door, the thug said, "No, no. You leave the door open. Boss say I have to see what you are doing all the time."

The shower revived her somewhat after the trauma of the night before, and she was glad to wash away from her wounded and aching body the smells and cells of the two evil men who had so brutally manhandled her. She felt sick all over, and there were bites and bruises on her thighs and breasts, which felt tingly and sensitive from abuse, and heavier than usual. She remembered the horror of the rape—her monster of a cousin defiling her—and a terrible thought entered her mind: *what if he impregnated me with his seed? What then?* She tried to put it out of her mind. The physical hurt would heal over time, she knew, but would the psychological and emotional terror ever subside? Would the horrific memories ever go away? And worse still—it was clearly not over yet: as she came back out into the bedroom with a towel wrapped around her, Julia again wondered what these gangsters intended with her next.

"Could I at least have some privacy please?" she asked the guard.

"No," Ivan answered. "Boss say to stay with you all the time. Not let you out of sight."

As if she could escape, being in what seemed to be

Polyakov's local headquarters. Some kind of a villa, she thought to herself. And then she wondered: could this be the same mansion by the lake where that pervert Beria had held and abused her aunt, Katerina, during Stalinist times? The one that Efim Pleshkov, her grandfather, had written about in that letter he had left for her grandmother? Could Beria's illegitimate son, Sergei Polyakov, have somehow reclaimed the estate for his own evil purposes? It was all so, so surreal…

Julia sighed and then proceeded to get dressed as discreetly as she could, while the thug leered at her, watching every move. When she was finished, he grabbed her by the arm and said, "Okay, we go now. You come with me."

❧❦❧

Their black limousine was at the main gate of Mayak at eight o'clock sharp, well before the main traffic of workers arrived. Ivan handed the security guard the two passes—the one they had extracted from Julia's wallet after her capture, and the ID card that she surmised was some kind of a fake one for him. Julia vaguely knew she should probably try to give some distress signal to the guard, but with her hazy thinking, she could not figure out what and how. Moreover, before she had been shoved into the back seat of the car beside Ivan, Sergei Polyakov had grabbed her by the chin, pinning her against the vehicle, and told her exactly how she was to act. Otherwise, they would torture and kill her mother and then her too, he had said.

With the drug Hetzel had injected the night before at this point at its most effective, Julia was much too terror-stricken and compliant to disobey, so she did not dare utter a word as the guard quickly looked at their papers and waved them through and into the nuclear complex.

The driver took them to one of the warehouses where Julia knew there was still work being done on securing and cataloging the radioactive material held at Mayak. The black KIA SUV from the evening before was parked in front, and Polyakov and Hetzel were already there at the entrance, talking to several Mayak officials Julia recognized from behind the tinted windows of the limo. She discreetly pressed the button on the door to open the window a crack so she would hear what was being said.

Or was that…Boris Polyakov, the other twin? Certainly, the FSB officer's uniform suggested that. Whichever one it was, it was obvious that all the locals deferred to him with great respect. If it was Sergei, he was no doubt in clothes borrowed from his brother, the Deputy Director. Ivan got out, and Julia heard Polyakov tell him to go get a large briefcase from inside the warehouse and put it on the seat beside her. *It must be Sergei*, Julia concluded. *It has to be.*

After the big thug plunked the case down, the arms merchant climbed in and putting the trench coat he was carrying on top of the briefcase, said to the driver, "Okay. We exit through the East Gate. And you, Julia, you had better behave, if you know what's good for you."

Could this oversized briefcase contain stolen nuclear material? The highly enriched uranium they had talked about last night that they would have her bring out of the complex? *God help us…*

With Polyakov dressed in his twin brother's FSB Deputy Director's uniform and Julia Saparova, the IAEA representative who regularly passed through this way for work, both traveling in the same black limo registered to the intelligence services, the guards took the easy decision to forego the usual thorough search of an exiting vehicle. They did not even cursorily pass the radiation detectors around the car and its trunk. So the arms merchants were waved through, with Julia their prisoner, and circa fifty pounds of highly enriched uranium in the briefcase under a trench coat between her and Polyakov.

Once they were several kilometers away from the gate, Polyakov patted her on the thigh and said, "That was very good, Julia. Don't try any funny stuff, my dear, and we'll just get on fine. You can go to sleep, now, if you please, while I work. Get some rest." The two cars were on the highway toward Chelyabinsk in no time at all, with the other vehicle following, Julia thought, carrying Hetzel.

ⱷↃⱸↄ

After a couple of hours, during which Polyakov was on the phone a lot and going through some papers while Julia dozed off, she woke just as the vehicles turned off the main highway to follow signs for Shagol Airport. Julia remembered that this was a military base—Sergei Polyakov seemed to have impeccable access everywhere in official Russia. It also came into her mind that it had been right around here that her Aunt Katerina had spent a few months in a since disappeared gulag, dying in childbirth as she brought her twins, Sergei and Boris, the illegitimate sons of Lavrenti Beria, into the world. It was around here that she had come several years ago to try and find any traces of her Aunt and the gulag where she had disappeared.

Minutes later, they pulled up at a gate where their papers were examined, the two soldiers at the guard post snapping to attention as they passed through. The driver drove them straight to an unmarked small jet sitting on the tarmac, with its engines running and stairs alongside.

"Well, Julia, this is your lucky day, my dear. You have done so well today, that as your reward, I will take you to vacationland on my brand new plane," Polyakov said smiling, as he opened the car door on his side. "Follow me. We're going to the beach."

Just then, the other car pulled up, and Hetzel and another guard climbed out. Ivan grabbed the large metallic briefcase from the backseat, and they all followed the arms merchant and Julia up the stairs to the aircraft.

At the top Polyakov was met by two beautiful hostesses, both of whom he greeted with a hug and kisses. One took his coat and briefcase, and Polyakov told the other one to escort Julia to a seat in the back. As the driver of the other car—the thug, whom Polyakov addressed as Igor—shoved her past a fully stocked bar and a table laid for two, Julia was astounded by the luxuriousness of the jet's inside. The hostess took them down the aisle to a little sitting area, and the guard shoved her down into a revolving armchair, and secured her seat belt, before sitting down beside her. Ivan passed by with the large briefcase, stowing it in the rear galley, and then took the leather chair across from her.

Polyakov came down the side aisle. "Settle in, my dear. We will be flying to my place in Greece on my new Falcon Eight X. I want you to meet someone special there. Yes, and after your hard work today—and yesterday—you will enjoy a little well-deserved rest and relaxation at my villa for a while. It is in a beautiful spot—" She recoiled as he stroked her chin and continued. "—and we will all have such a good time, won't we? Enjoy the trip."

Chapter 8

It seemed to Greg that he had just finally fallen asleep when he heard his phone alarm buzz. He reached over to turn it off, and lying back on his pillow, searched for the number he had for Julia's office at Mayak. It was just after nine a.m. Ozersk time, but the call went straight through to her secretary. He did not tell her the reason for his call nor did he leave a message for Julia, but asked the assistant to connect him to Charles Levinson, the American he had met during the earlier heist affair. Levinson was working with Julia and the IAEA on behalf of the US government to help secure Russia's nuclear arsenal.

He was still not in his office either.

Greg settled back beside Anne but was not able to fall asleep, thinking about everything that was going on. It was an hour and a half or so later that the American rep finally called him back, just as he was contemplating getting out of bed. "Greg, I was glad to get your message. So good to hear from you. What's new? Are you coming to visit?"

"Charles, Julia Saparova has gone missing again. She disappeared after leaving work for home early yesterday in Ozersk. Her mother called to tell us. When did you see her last?"

"Why, Greg, I was with her just yesterday. She poked her head in around three-thirty. I remember because I had just finished a conference call. But I'll go across right now and check in her office. She's usually in by this time when she's here."

"Great. Thanks, Charles."

Levinson called back within five minutes. "Julia's secretary says she left around five yesterday and was going to come in early this morning before catching a plane from Balandino to fly to Vienna. She is supposed to give her quarterly presentation to the high brass at the IAEA on progress here and elsewhere in Russia tomorrow."

"I guess she might have gone straight to Chelyabinsk after work. But it would be weird to call her mother like that to say that she was coming home and then simply not come," Greg mused.

"Well, Julia was going to pick up the final printout of her presentation this morning. But she hasn't come in, according to the assistant."

"Charles, will you check with security at the gates, to see if they recall seeing her leave yesterday? More importantly, have them keep an eye out for her this morning, both coming and going. And ask them to be especially vigilant at all gates—we are very concerned that another heist could take place imminently. In fact, that the arms merchants may be using Julia to bring the stuff out…"

"Sure thing Greg. I will let you know if I come up with anything."

"Call anytime. We are now in Vienna and up. Bye for now."

છએઉ

Greg had showered, made some coffee in the hotel's

Nespresso machine, delivering one to a thankful Anne, who was just getting out of bed—still groggy from a night with lots of interruptions and love making on top of the jet lag—and was looking at his emails when his phone buzzed at a little before seven. He picked up immediately. "Yes? Charles?"

"Greg? Hi." Levinson's excited voice seemed very far away, and the connection was poor.

"Charles, so what do you have?"

"Well, security here tells me that Julia passed into Mayak through the Ozersk gate at just after eight a.m. in a black limo. So even before we talked earlier. Unusual, they say, because she normally comes with the little commuter van from town a little later. Right around nine, always—"

"So she went to the office?"

"No. As I said, her secretary never saw her. She had printed out the final version of Julia's presentation, but she never came to pick it up. But wait, there's more. The guards at the East Gate say they are sure they saw Julia leave just after eight-thirty in a black limo registered to the FSB with a man dressed in the ceremonial uniform of a major-general of the intelligence services."

"That's deputy director level. But it couldn't be...Boris Polyakov..." Greg was incredulous. "We saw him last night. Here, at the opera in Vienna."

"Is that the arms merchant, who was involved with Kallay?"

"No, that was the twin brother."

"Maybe it was another deputy director. There may be more than one, after all."

"In any case, an FSB officer. With Julia, in a black car. Hmm...a Black Maria? Could the FSB have arrested Julia? What for?" Greg wondered.

"She is an employee of an international organization, but also a Russian citizen. Possible, but not likely."

"Or maybe it could be Sergei Polyakov masquerading as his brother," Greg continued, voicing his thoughts. "That would fit well with the notion of another heist."

"Well, it's all very interesting, isn't it?"

"That's more than two hours ago." The timing had just dawned on Greg. "They could be well away from there by now. Did the guards find anything in the car?"

"They said no. Sorry, I can't help you anymore, Greg."

"Thanks, Charles. This is very useful. I'll let you know if I find out anything on my end."

જ્જ

While Greg was on the phone with Levinson, Anne called her former contact with the Austrian police, Lieutenant Haffner.

"Anne! What a surprise. Are you back in Vienna? But I thought you had left the service."

"Yes, Rudolf. I am here visiting with my husband. And yes, I left Interpol when I got married."

"So, can we still meet up for a drink?"

"Rudolf, this is not a social call. Remember our Russian physicist friend, who worked as an exotic dancer? Julia Saparova. Well, she has disappeared, and I would like to go by her apartment building to see what we can find out. Could you meet Greg, my husband and me there? Just before nine, say. It's not much notice, but it could be good to have you with us. And it would be fun to work together again."

"Of course, Anne. I will be there. I remember, it is the apartment we searched, when we almost deported her.

Until you stepped in to save her. Momsengasse, wasn't it?"

"Yes. She was a great help then, and we have become good friends since. Thanks, Rudolf, and see you there."

Chapter 9

Greg and Anne decided to skip breakfast and walk to Julia's from the Sacher since Anne wanted to pick up some *viennoiseries* from the Aida *Confiserie* right opposite her office building. That had been her regular practice when she worked there. She particularly loved their marzipan croissants.

Greg thought it would only take twenty minutes or so to get to Julia's, if he remembered correctly. He had walked her back home a number of times from the Revuebar Rasputin where she had worked performing as an exotic dancer when he was visiting Vienna some years back, trying to track down his erstwhile friend, Adam Kallay. Julia lived on Mommsengasse, just a few minutes away from the beautiful Schloss Belvedere in the Fourth District, and he knew the way well: through the underground Opernpassage, then across Resselpark, by the beautiful baroque Karlskirche, and up Argentinierstrasse. She had been just an illegal immigrant then from Russia trying to make ends meet, while Adam, her boyfriend, was trying to get her a job at the IAEA.

After all, she had a Ph.D. in nuclear physics, so she had no doubt been the best-educated performer at the Rasputin.

Greg shuddered involuntarily as he remembered that at least twice, on his way back to the Sacher on those late snowy nights, trying to be the gallant protector of his best friend's girl, he had the eerie feeling of being followed. Had it been the disappeared Kallay or the crooks he had gotten mixed up with who had been stalking him then? The same criminals who may now very well have kidnapped Julia again?

He would never know the answer, but the thought made him wonder whether those same gangsters might be shadowing them. Especially since Sergei Polyakov's twin brother Boris had seen them and even talked to Anne at the opera last night, threatening them again…the effrontery of it all!

But no, no one was there behind them this time, Greg was quite sure, as he and his wife made their way along Argentinierstrasse, then left onto Belvederegasse and next into Mommsengasse. Nevertheless, he was rather relieved to see the familiar, smiling face of Lieutenant Haffner, Anne's old contact at the Austrian police whom he had met on a number of occasions, standing in front of Julia's building, scrolling through email on his iPhone. Anne strode ahead and gave her former work friend a hug. After the greetings, Haffner went over to the door and pressed the bell marked discreetly "J. Saparova." They waited, then he pushed the bell again.

There was no answer.

The lieutenant pressed the doorbell once more, with the same result.

With a shrug of his shoulders and the comment, "Ms. Saparova seems to be not here. But let's just make sure," Haffner pushed the bottom bell for the concierge. It was not long before Greg heard a sort of shuffling sound and eventually, an aging, disheveled man in a tattered olive-green cardigan and soiled pants, wearing his worn

Hausschuhe, opened the huge wooden door a crack.

"*Ja, meine Herren. Darf ich Sie helfen?*" the concierge asked in a deep voice. To Greg, it seemed that the man flashed him a sign of recognition.

Greg explained that they were looking for an old friend, Julia Saparova, and were concerned that they had not been able to get in touch. Could they possibly go up to her apartment to see whether she was there and that she was all right? Perhaps she just had a late night.

After much discussion, the old man—with a glance at Haffner's police uniform—finally gave in and said, "*Ja, denn. Bitte, folgen Sie mich.*" But he reiterated a number of times that he would not be able to open M. Saparova's door for them—unless, of course, the lieutenant would force his hand with a warrant.

Greg, Anne, and Haffner followed the concierge to the elevator. They all piled in, as the caretaker pressed the button for the third floor. Once there, Anne stepped out first, and went straight to the entrance to Julia's apartment, giving the bell several long pushes. When there was no answer, Greg and she put their ears to the door and kept listening for a while. Eventually though, hearing nothing from the other side, they both stepped away, as Greg shook his head, "She's not there, I am sure. There is no one in there."

"*Ja, mein Herr,*" the concierge said, arms folded as if he had known all along. "*Das stimmt.*"

"I will come back with a warrant," Haffner said. "It may take some time, though."

"Have you seen her in the last week?" Greg asked the caretaker.

"Not since last Thursday, *mein Herr.* A week ago."

"Thank you. That is very helpful." Anne said. "Rudolf, will you get on the warrant right away? Let us—or the Interpol office—know when it comes through."

"Actually, Julia's mother may be in the apartment later in the evening." This from Greg. "She is coming today and said she would be staying there. So it would be good if you could get the warrant before then."

⌀⌀⌀

"Can I give you a ride somewhere?" Haffner asked after reiterating to the concierge that he would be back later in the day with a warrant.

"Thank you, yes, that would be kind," Greg answered, glancing at his watch. "We're going over to the Interpol office for a brief meeting, and then I have to get back to the Sacher."

"Sure, that's not a problem."

"I still have to prepare a bit of a speech," Greg added with a little laugh as he followed Haffner to the police vehicle parked across the street. "I heard Anne tell you over the phone that we are really here at the invitation of the Austrian Literary Society. I am their featured speaker this afternoon."

"Yes, thank you for reminding me. I was planning to come along, Greg, if you don't mind."

"I am not sure what you will learn, if anything, but I'll try to make it entertaining. You may be the only one in the audience."

"I wouldn't be so sure. I have had the pleasure of reading all your books, and I have enjoyed them. So I'll definitely be there. I may even be able to dream up a work reason."

Chapter 10

As Anne and Greg got out of the police car at the Interpol address, Anne bee-lined straight for the Aida *Confiserie*—by then they were both quite hungry, and Greg insisted on picking up a large assortment of pastries to share with Anne's former colleagues over coffee. No doubt, it would be appreciated.

They were met at the discreet entrance to Interpol's offices by Frau Huth, Anne's former secretary, whom she had shared with Nicholas Labrecque when she had worked there. The kindly woman Anne had been so fond of greeted them, saying, "Fräulein Rossiter…ah, Frau und Herr Martens, so nice to see you. Messrs. Demeter and Labrecque are just assembling in the Conference Room and have ordered coffees. What may I bring for you?"

Anne handed her the box of pastries, asking Frau Huth to serve them with the hot drinks, and requested a *mélange*—her favorite of the many coffee choices available in Vienna—for both of them as the secretary showed them into the Conference Room. The others were already there. They quickly exchanged greetings and briefly caught up.

"So, your beautiful Russian physicist friend has disappeared again?" Demeter asked as they all took seats around the table. "This seems to be becoming a habit for some of your friends. Or maybe it's just that the disappearing act comes with the job."

"Yes." Greg went straight to the heart of the matter. "Her mother tried to reach us last night—we were at the Staatsoper—so it was not until early this morning that we finally talked—"

"Oh," Labrecque interrupted. "We were there too. Marie Christine and I went to the opera yesterday, then dinner. A late night for me. But a terrific performance of *Siegfried.* Weren't Kauffman and Kokova fabulous? She particularly. Too bad, though, we could have met up afterward. But I hope you enjoyed it."

"Indeed, we tried to catch you, Nicholas, but you were out of there so quickly," Anne retorted.

"Yes, *Siegfried* was great. But to get back to the matter at hand—" Greg remained focused. "—Gospodja Saparova thinks Julia was kidnapped yesterday evening. I had several lengthy talks with her since then, including most recently, twelve hours after her daughter was supposed to have come home. I then called Julia's office in Russia, and her secretary reported last seeing her at five p.m. yesterday Mayak time. She was supposed to go in early this morning and fly here to make a presentation to the IAEA bosses on safeguards and security at Mayak and the other nuclear sites in Russia. The guards at Mayak reported seeing her enter the facility in a black limousine just before eight and leaving with—get this— supposedly the Deputy Director of the FSB in the same car. The vehicle happened to be registered to the intelligence services. Given that Anne and I also saw Boris Polyakov at the opera—we'll need to talk about that too—and the history of these disappearances, we think the kidnapper and the man in the vehicle may, in fact, have been Sergei Polyakov, the arms merchant, masquerading in this instance as his twin brother, the FSB executive."

"Yes, and we are quite convinced that this is all to do with the heist of some more nuclear material. They have done it before, stealing and selling fifty pounds of highly enriched uranium to some terrorists. Now they seem to be after another fifty pounds which would give those same terrorists enough for a bomb."

"You guys are scaring me." This from Demeter.

"You know that Boris Polyakov is a regular at the Staatsoper?" Labrecque asked. "That is partly why I was there, to keep an eye on him. I actually saw him come up to you, Anne, but stayed out of the way. He loves opera, particularly when his mistress Svetlana Kokova is singing. He's gaga over her and tries not to miss any of her performances. We encourage his visits to Vienna because here we can watch him and at least he is not causing any trouble that we don't know."

"Yeah, we were wondering whether you guys were on to him," Greg commented.

"We're actually looking at a lot of his activities. And we may soon have enough stuff on him to cause him some serious grief," Demeter said. "He is not a good guy, but the worst is his insatiable appetite for young girls…Disgusting."

"Yeah. Not nice. Just like his father, Lavrenti Beria. Well, he scared me with his threat. So you better keep a close trail on him. And please don't let him come anywhere near us." This from Anne.

"Sure thing, Anne. We'll do our best."

"Just so you both know, Greg and I came here by way of Julia's apartment." Anne looked at her husband. "On our way over."

"And?" Labrecque's curiosity was piqued, as he reached across the table for a second croissant.

"No sign of her there. I asked Lieutenant Haffner to join us—we rang and rang the bell."

"In fact, the concierge seemed to remember me, but he hasn't seen her the last few days. He let us in the main entrance, and then we rang the bell at her door too, but nothing. We couldn't hear any sounds through the door. Haffner said he would go back later with a warrant, but getting one could take some time. In any case, Julia's mother said she would be staying there starting this evening. She is on her way to Vienna, we think."

"But we have no idea of where Julia might be. Just to sum up: as Greg said, she seems to have left Mayak this morning in a car, probably with Polyakov, the arms and sex merchant brother. We fear for her safety but have no clue where they were taking her. Perhaps one of the airports near Chelyabinsk…and then where? That is the sixty-four thousand dollar question."

"I see. We've got a real problem," Demeter said. "So what do we do now?"

"Well, for one, I would like to go and talk to some of Julia's colleagues here in Vienna at the IAEA. They might know something we don't."

"I'll come with you when we are done here this morning," Labrecque said.

"Good," Anne said, "because Greg needs to go and prepare his speech for tomorrow afternoon. He is the keynote speaker at the Austrian Literary Society's annual meeting at the Sacher."

"Sorry, but that is what brought us to Vienna," Greg apologized. "And I think my added value here at this point is marginal."

"Well, backtracking a bit…" Anne was thinking out loud. "…the Hungarians have supposedly closed down their complex—the one these gangsters were using for human trafficking. As have the Montenegrins, the one in

Porto Montenegro. And Polyakov no longer has his penthouse suite at the Regent there. But bugger it—" Anne hardly ever used coarse language. "—we have no inkling of where this gang of criminals could be taking our friend. And as we said, more than likely, some stolen nuclear material with her."

"Terrible."

"John, it is imperative that you get Interpol in Russia to monitor any private jet flights out of all airports in and around Chelyabinsk. That's our best bet to track them. But that would only close one avenue."

"We could try to alert passport control to look out for her—and Polyakov—on any commercial flights," Nicholas suggested, "but I doubt that we would get their cooperation, with Polyakov's brother being a Deputy Director of the FSB.

"I believe the Border Service in Russia actually forms part of the FSB," Anne added. "At least it did in my active days—"

"It still does," Demeter confirmed. "And you are active again, Anne. Fortunately for us."

"And we do have suspicions that the intelligence services and the Russian military might tacitly be in support of the sale of some of the stored nuclear material," Greg said. "One way of monetizing an otherwise illiquid resource on hand would be to sell it to terrorists."

"Yes, and the connection there is very strong: as you just said, the arms merchant is the brother of a highly placed official of the FSB. It's a crazy, crazy world we are living," Demeter agreed.

"Just a thought: Nicholas, is there a way we could have your colleague Radomir…I forget his last name…in Montenegro check what type of plane Polyakov and that Brother Peter terrorist escaped in the last time we were closing in on them?" Anne asked her former colleague.

"There is at least a chance that Sergei Polyakov would still be traveling around with that very same private jet."

"Good idea, Anne," Demeter agreed, supportive. "Yes, Nicholas, you should definitely get on it."

"Sure, John."

"I have another suggestion that we might want to follow up on as well." Anne was pumping adrenalin now. "Nicholas, remember Polyakov's laptop that we captured in Porto Montenegro? Why don't we have Jakob—he's still with Interpol here, isn't he?—go through everything on it to see what other properties that Polyakov might have used or owned—directly or through any company—might come up on it? You know, the files, the correspondence—there have got to be references. There is a chance that they would be going to one of those—"

"You are one clever woman. I'll get our computer man to look into it," Demeter said, "while you and Nicholas go over to the IAEA."

"Great. It seems like we all have our work cut out for the rest of the day. Should we meet back here first thing? And we have each other's cell numbers, so if anybody comes up with anything, please pass it on. Greg and I would just like a quiet evening after his presentation if possible—we didn't get much sleep last night with all the interruptions. But of course, we can always meet sooner if need be. This is too important."

Chapter II

It is terrible that Julia has disappeared again," Labrecque said, as he and Anne got out of his car in the parking lot of the Vienna International Center.

"*Déjá vu,* as you say in French," she commented on their way to Building A, where the IAEA offices were located. "Not just with her, but Adam Kallay. And it seems that it's the same 'merchants of evil'—traffickers of arms, women, drugs, and God only knows what else."

"Of course. With the positions they had, they were both clearly targets."

"Yes. They could be tremendously useful to arms merchants wanting to get their hands on nuclear material. We know that. I am sure, Nicholas, that it is the same group this time as the one that attempted the previous two heists. Plus, Julia is a gorgeous woman, as we both know, no doubt prized by these sexual predators. We are very worried, because this may also all be leading up to another heist. And of course, Julia's safety is at risk…"

"Hmm. I see the concern."

"The problem, Nicholas, is that if these same criminals get their hands on another fifty pounds of highly enriched uranium and sell it to that fringe group—the Sons of Jesus—those terrorists would have enough nuclear stuff for an atom bomb. They already managed to get away with that much in the first heist, you may remember. Then there is also ISIS and al Qaeda, among other terrorists, who would love to get their hands on that much uranium."

"*Merde*, you're right."

"So we need to find out what Julia's secretary and colleagues know. If anything…"

❧❧❧

Señora Gomez, Julia's Peruvian secretary, could only tell them that she expected Julia to come in the next day—her flight got in at 17:05, and she would more than likely just go straight to her apartment, since she had a big day ahead of her on Friday. She was giving a major presentation to the Executive Board on the status of security and safeguards for the nuclear material housed at Mayak and elsewhere in Russia. She had last talked to her around noon Vienna time yesterday, which must have been four p.m. more or less at Mayak.

❧❧❧

Frustrated, Anne and Nicholas went by the office of the Head of Security for the IAEA. He was in a meeting, but the secretary recognized Labrecque, as well as Anne from when she was still with Interpol, so she knew this was likely to be important. She got up from her desk and knocked on the door behind her.

"Herr Timmermans, thank you for seeing us on such short notice," Anne greeted the Belgian who came out a couple of minutes later after some whispering by his secretary through the slightly ajar door. "We just wanted you to know that Julia Saparova may have gone missing again.

"Oh no! That is terrible. She is due to make a very important presentation tomorrow to our Executive Committee. Very sensitive material."

"Yes, we are aware."

"Could it be that? Did…whoever took her…get a hold of the presentation?"

"We think it may be another heist attempt—"

"No! Please, my friends, we must find her. And any missing nuclear material. Whatever it takes."

"We will do everything we can, of course."

"Please, let me know if you have any news. I will inform my colleagues immediately. And we will call as soon as we have anything."

"Thank you, sir," Anne said, as the very distressed Head of Security went back into his meeting.

Chapter 12

Julia woke from a deep sleep as the sleek jet lurched to start its descent. She looked out the window and saw turquoise waters below. Glancing back into the cabin, Hetzel's face leered at her from the seat to her left.

"Isn't it gorgeous?" The monster who claimed he had wanted to marry her, leaned across, pointing. "That is the Aegean below. And there, just ahead, you can see the island of Spetsos. It figured as Phraxos in my favorite novel, *The Magus*. John Fowles. And the smaller island there, Julia—called Spetsopoula—is owned by the Niarchos family. You know, the Greek ship owners."

What am I doing here? Julia asked herself. *Am I dreaming?* She had never been to Greece. And now, to be here as a prisoner of these criminals…

The plane flew even lower as it passed over the larger island, and Hetzel pointed excitedly out the window. "There, there! That is Sergei's place, down there. He has that whole peninsula. And that's where we will land, on his own private landing strip."

Julia saw an asphalt airstrip stretching from one side of the headland to the other, with a hangar and several helipads dotted around.

"And that town back there, that's Porto Heli."

As the jet circled around, she glimpsed the luxurious villa with the wrap-around terrace, swimming pool, tennis courts and other amenities, and the numerous inviting beaches that stretched along the entire coast of the peninsula. Julia noted to her dismay, though, that where it was not bounded by water the estate was protected by a high stonewall, making any hopes of getting away difficult.

So this was Sergei Polyakov's very own private playground, where he was now taking her.

To what purpose? Julia asked herself. *What will become of me? What horrors will these perverts have dreamt up for me now?*

As the plane taxied to a stop, she tried to ignore the men and focused on how she might be able to escape from her predicament, even though she was feeling nauseous and sick with all the trauma she was suffering. She simply had to.

For her sake, for the sake of the world. Try as she might, she could not come up with a plan, though, other than the vague notion that if ever she was not watched, she might be able to slip away, climb a wall and make it over to a neighboring villa. But all the other houses were so far away, she noted despondently.

છછ

Polyakov stood at the bottom of the stairs as Julia descended, blinking to adjust her eyes to the blinding sun. He had his arms open to receive the hug of a much younger man with a broad smile on his face, dressed in shorts, T-shirt, and sandals, who was just then walking over to him from the first of three open jeeps that had come out to meet them.

"Hello, son. So good to see you," the arms merchant said, greeting the handsome, sleeker version of himself.

"Hello, Papa. How was your trip?" the young man countered with a question, even as he could not help staring at Julia at the top of the steps.

"Very good. I'll tell you all about it. But now, let's get going. We've got some work to do." And as Polyakov beckoned toward the jeep, he rolled his shirtsleeves up to his elbows and started barking orders: "Andreas, you come with Anton and me. The three of us have got to discuss tomorrow. The Syrians. I hope you have both been formulating your thoughts. We will have to finalize the sale—"

"Of course, Sergei," Hetzel answered.

"Meanwhile, Ivan, you and Igor take the girl to the Aphrodite room. Stay with her as she cleans up and changes—and have her put on a bikini, for God's sake. She will have no problem finding one there. Oh yes, and give her another injection. I can see that the one we gave in Ozersk is wearing off." He glanced back at Julia, who was standing at the bottom of the steps with a frightened and lost look on her face before he continued. "Then take the bitch to the kitchen for something to eat—the poor girl slept through lunch on the plane—and bring her down to the pool after. And Ivan, give the bloody uranium to Petr for safekeeping."

The big guard grabbed Julia by the elbow and led her to the second jeep, as Polyakov's son—whom he had called Anton—kept turning around to see the beautiful blonde who had arrived with his father. Ivan shoved her into the back seat and, plunking the huge metallic briefcase beside her, climbed in on the other side. The other two thugs sat in the front, with the one she hadn't seen before driving.

So Polyakov has a son! Hmm. He is much better looking than the father. Was it he that Polyakov said she would meet?

And that was definitely uranium—probably the highly enriched variety—in the case beside her! Polyakov had just corroborated it. Julia's worst fears were confirmed. She had thought so all along: after all, it had been pretty obvious from the conversations the night Polyakov and Hetzel assaulted her that her main purpose was to help them steal some nuclear material from Mayak.

It seemed that their mission was a success, unlike the last time.

෨෬

It was no more than a five-minute drive to the front entrance of the villa, which was just down the hill and close to the beach. Igor and Ivan got out, and leaving the briefcase in the jeep with Petr, the driver, led Julia through the front door. Inside, she was greeted by the glorious view of the Aegean, the sun streaming in through the wall of picture windows on the seaside of a large entertainment area, tastefully appointed with modern furniture.

"Igor, you go get the injection ready," Ivan addressed his colleague. "I will show this slut where she is to get dressed. Or undressed, to be more precise." With his lewd laugh, he pushed her along a corridor that led off one end of the living room, and into an opulent bedroom with a king-size bed and floor to ceiling windows giving onto a deserted beach. "Here, this is one of the rooms that the boss usually likes his women to use. You'll find clothes in the closet and the drawers. Shower up if you want and put on a bikini for now—that's what the boss said. It will come off soon enough, though, I am sure." The big man chuckled, before continuing. "I will wait here till you are ready."

So that's it. I'm now one of his—Polyakov's—women? Or does he have me in mind for Anton? After last night having abused and raped me himself, the pig.

Either way, Julia knew disobedience was not an option at this point, so she looked through the drawers and found a red bikini that suited her. Then she went into the luxurious bathroom. Again, though, when she tried to close the door, the order came: "Leave it open." Igor entered the bedroom just then, so she had to endure being watched by both guards as she showered and put on the scanty swimming suit. Coming out, she wrapped a large bath towel around herself, but Ivan immediately grabbed it and uncovered her, saying, "None of that. Come, you bitch," as he seized her by the arm, twisting it in the process, and shoved her face down on the bed. "Okay, boss say we give you injection."

The next thing Julia knew was that he was on top of her, pinning her down, and he and Igor were tugging her bikini bottoms down to her knees, and then she felt a stab of pain, as with a loud groan Igor shoved the needle into her right buttock.

Involuntarily, she screamed and then started crying, whereupon the big guard whacked her across the rear end, saying "Stop that, or we'll shove something else into you, you stupid cunt."

Julia lay there with tears in her eyes, feeling ill and very sorry for herself as the two guards took turns going to the bathroom to urinate and wash their hands. Finally, Ivan pulled her to her feet and then tugged her along to the kitchen. "Come, you eat something now, boss say. You must be hungry."

There was a maid in the kitchen, and the guard ordered her to bring out some food. In no time at all, the woman whipped up a Greek salad and put out bread and fruit, a jug of red wine. Julia wolfed the food down, as Ivan poured two glasses of the wine—one for her and one for himself. She realized she had not eaten anything since the meager lunch in her office in Ozersk more than twenty-fours earlier. No wonder she was starving.

When she had finished, Ivan said, "Okay, we go down to pool. Everybody out there now. Waiting for you." The creep laughed, before continuing, "You see, morning, it is beach; after lunch, nap; maybe a little fuckie suckie; then, pool."

He obviously knew the routine at Polyakov's villa.

∽∾∽

The thug led Julia out on the terrace, and, despite how sick and frightened she felt, she reveled in the late afternoon sunshine and the glorious view out to the water as she followed. At the end, and a few steps down, the Olympic size pool greeted her, with lounge chairs all around and a small bar manned by a fit-looking barman in shorts and a T-shirt. She saw that some of the recliners were occupied by men: Hetzel was there, his hairless white body under an umbrella next to a large, red-haired, freckled man whom she had not seen before, and of course, Polyakov. And Anton, his muscular, tanned body looking good in a white Speedo. The two hostesses from the airplane were sunbathing topless: one, the brunette Polyakov called Nika stretched out on a mattress poolside, the other, raven-haired one, she had heard called Sofia, in a reclining chair next to the arms merchant. A couple of other nubile acolytes were lazing at the bar with drinks in front of them.

"Well, well, look who's here," Polyakov said, getting up from his recliner and coming over. He took her by the waist and tried to give her a Russian bear hug and a kiss, but Julia recoiled at his touch. Pulling back a bit but still holding her by the hips, he continued: "Now, now my dear, we're going to have to have a little talk, you and I. While you are my guest here, I expect you to do my bidding. If you don't do what I ask—what I want—then things will get a little rough, and you will be free game for everyone and anything here, including the guards. Is that a deal?"

Julia did not answer, so he continued. "But Julia, come, let me introduce you to a few people here. First, my son, Anton. I am sure you and he will get on just fine while you are staying here." And taking her by the hand, the arms merchant pulled her toward where the handsome young man was reclining, reading a book.

Twisted Reasons, Greg Martens's book Julia noted, in which she—or someone based on her—was an important character.

"Anton, come and meet Julia, Julia Saparova. She is the most beautiful nuclear physicist in the world, Anton, just as I told you." The young man got up and, looking her in the eyes, reached out to shake her hand, saying, "Yes, Father. She is gorgeous, just as you said." Then Anton addressed Julia. "And what an interesting life you've had so far, judging from this book." "Welcome, Julia. I hope you'll give me a chance to get to know you."

"Oh, forget that idiocy. I just gave it to you to read so you would have a little background on our beautiful and talented guest," Polyakov said to his son. "She has great genes…" Then leading her toward the redhead, who was still lying in the recliner, eyes fixed on Julia, he continued, "And this is my friend, Brother Peter. Peter, Julia Saparova, the IAEA physicist who helped us at Mayak. Just like I told you she would."

The large man got up and started to move toward her as if to hug her, but Polyakov interjected, wagging his finger and making sure that Hetzel also heard. "No, no. No touchee, Peter. This one is not for you. At least not till I say so."

So this Brother Peter was the terrorist Greg and Anne had talked about, the one who got away with half the uranium in Poti, and then escaped again with Polyakov when Interpol was hot on their trail in Porto Montenegro.

Did he have the uranium with him now? If so, there would be enough nuclear material here to devastate London or New York.

Julia recoiled, as Polyakov, with one hand on her left buttock, said, "You just make yourself comfortable on one of these recliners, my dear. And I will get Pavel to bring you a drink. We are having vodka tonics, so how about one?"

And when Julia didn't answer—trying to fathom the sudden change in the approach to her by the brute who had raped her the night before, and afraid to say no—he yelled over to the barman, "Pavel, a vodka tonic for my lovely friend here." And turning to Julia, he continued: "Now, Julia, let's take this darn bikini top off. Just like the other girls here. So you tan nicely all over." His hand deftly untied the string that held Julia's top, and he crushed the small piece of red fabric in his palm, throwing it on his lounge chair with a laugh.

Julia lay down on her stomach on one of the recliners in the sun, trying to shield her breasts from the leering male eyes. But just a few moments later, she recoiled as she felt the touch of a man's hand on her shoulder: it was Anton—not Pavel—bringing her drink from the bar, along with a pair of sunglasses. "Here, Julia, you can probably use these," he said, as he handed the shades to her, ogling her all over as she turned around. Julia put the shades on, had a sip of the drink, and closed her eyes to try to blot out the terrible world she had found her way into, praying that her monster companions would leave her alone.

Sometime later, she heard Polyakov's voice from far away, "Sofia, my dear, why don't you massage some of this sun cream on Julia's back. We don't want her to burn to a crisp now, do we?"

Julia half opened her eyes and in her drowsy state, glimpsed the dark-haired beauty come over and straddle her and felt her gentle but strong hands rub the silken lotion on her shoulders and back and buttocks. Sofia then nudged her gently to have her turn over, and Julia did so, against her better judgment, but thoroughly enjoying the experience. It all felt too wonderful on her abused and bruised body. The woman's hands rubbed the cream on her breasts, stomach, into the pubic area and all over her legs. Finishing, Sofia said aloud, "There, that should do it." She then leaned down to Julia's ear whispering, "You are one beautiful lady."

Eventually, the soporific effects of the massage, the drug, the drink, the sun, and the prone position had their effect, and Julia drifted off to sleep.

Chapter 13

Greg left the room early to go down to the Sacher's Marble Hall where the Austrian Literary Society's annual function was held. He thought that on this occasion since he would be truly there in his own right, he had better be on time. Frau von Hitzinger, the President, was already present in the salle, delighted to see him, and Crabbe, the previous head—a little weasel of a man—who had originally made the mistake of inviting Greg, also materialized from the other side of the room to welcome him sheepishly.

Now that his books were bestsellers, and Greg was somewhat known in literary circles, his earlier embarrassing appearance in front of the Society's members could be forgotten. He had then been invited purely as a result of a mistake by Crabbe, in the place of a more famous New York author of literary fiction with a similar name, Gareth Martens, and had been "exposed" during the question period by none other than Billy Crawford, an old acquaintance of his. Who then metamorphosed into Brother Peter, a key member of the Sons of Jesus terrorist group which had been implicated in several bombings in the USA, including a terrible one at Grand Central Station in New York that killed several hundred.

The seats in the large meeting room were filling up quickly, and Greg was pleased to see Lieutenant Haffner arrive and take an aisle seat. He was liking this competent and modest Austrian police officer more and more and resolved to speak to him after his talk, to get his views on his presentation—and not just to ask him whether he had any success in getting a warrant for Julia's flat. He knew Anne would not be there at the start, but hoped that she would arrive at least for the drinks part. After that, he would be ready to spend a quiet evening with her—maybe a nice romantic dinner at Appiano's, one of his favorite upscale *Wiener Stuben*—followed by love-making and a good night's rest.

Punctually at three p.m., the distinguished Frau von Hitzinger went up to the podium and opened the proceedings. She gave a glowing introduction of Greg and his writings, making light of his unfortunate previous experience with the Society. Greg followed by giving the desired thirty-minute presentation, peppering it with many examples from his own works as well as those of other authors, including his almost namesake, Gareth Martens. He finished by opening the floor to questions, hoping this time there would be no embarrassing ones thrown his way.

Frau von Hitzinger led off. "My dear Mr. Martens, would you care to tell our members which genre you prefer to work with: biography and memoir—that is, the truth—or fiction. You are obviously very capable in authoring both kinds of works."

"Thank you, Frau von Hitzinger, for that excellent question. While I like both genres, my passion is the latter. Fiction, I mean. I love to create a new world in my mind, a story that shapes itself, a plot and characters that take on lives of their own. Clearly, I do a lot of research for both types of book, and I must say, there is a lot of learning for me in the process of writing…and I would hope too, for my readers, in the reading. My novels are all based on reality—at least the realm of the possible—but then take off from there. My memoirs and biographies stay mainly with fact, although in these genres, too, everything is subjective and there is inevitably a little embellishment for dramatic effect. Memoirs particularly are eighty percent truth, twenty percent…well, embroidery."

"Thank you, Mr. Martens, for your excellent answer."

Greg fielded a few more questions, mainly about his books, work habits, and writing plans going forward.

Then a thin, sallow-looking man with shoulder length hair and lots of beads—a true hippie, all the way in the back of the room, raised his hand, and Frau von Hitzinger beckoned to him, saying, "Yes, the gentleman in the rear, please."

"Johnny Apostle here, ma'am. Hey, Greg, why is it that you are such a creep? You've been disparaging decent, devout Christians all your life. A fucking atheist, you are. Disgusting. Then you married that slut of an Interpol agent, and ever since have been writing these filthy thrillers and lying memoirs no one in their right mind would condescend to read—"

"Now, now, Mr.…Apostle, is it? There is no need to get personal," Frau von Hitzinger chided. "We need to keep things civil here—"

"Why don't you shut up, you phony stupid bitch—"

"Could security please escort this man out?" Frau von Hitzinger held her ground, ringing the bell on the podium with some urgency. "Now, please."

Greg saw Lieutenant Haffner jump up from his seat and grab the man by the collar, just as one of the hotel's security agents reached the interloper. It was no trouble whatsoever for the two strong law enforcement types literally to pick the man up and whisk him out through the etched double glass doors.

Frau von Hitzinger regained her composure and standing with back erect behind the podium said, "My deepest apologies, Mr. Martens, for this unpleasant intrusion. Perhaps, in any case, we are all ready to move on to a drink. If anyone still has questions, I am sure Mr. Martens will be available to answer them during cocktails. Our sincerest thanks go to you, sir, for this very enlightening talk, and again, please accept our apologies. The meeting is adjourned."

Just then, Anne appeared through the double doors, and Greg was distracted for a moment by her captivating smile, but quickly collected himself. "Thank you, Frau von Hitzinger, for giving me the opportunity to address this august literary group, and please, as you are aware, I am quite used to interruptions of this nature. Of course, I will be very happy to continue discussions over a glass of wine." With that, Greg picked up his notes, and descended from the podium, glad for the flûte of bubbly that was being proffered by a waiter. Also pleased to see that Haffner—who no doubt was taking his police duties more seriously after the recent unpleasant incursion—had followed his wife back into the salle.

Greg went over to the two, giving his wife a kiss, and they were soon joined by Frau von Hitzinger, as well as by a rather robust man in Tyrolean garb, with Crabbe lurking a few feet behind. The Society's President surprised Greg by asking him about *Cello's Tears,* an often-ignored collection of his poems that Greg had published early on, right after *Wintertime,* and which he personally thought was his *chef d'oeuvre.* Greg turned toward her, pleased with the question, and was about to answer, when all of a sudden, a deafening bang echoed through the room, even as Haffner tackled him to the floor. Greg reached out to grab Anne and pulled her under him as he went down. Glancing sideways, he saw a man a few meters behind the Tyrolean running toward the doors, with Haffner raising himself to go after him. As Greg, totally stunned, pulled himself up, his first instinct was to see that Anne was okay. It was only then that he saw Crabbe on the floor a few meters away, bleeding from a shoulder wound, yelling and screaming like a banshee. Frau von Hitzinger was already on her phone, probably calling the Austrian equivalent of nine-one-one—it strangely came into Greg's head that here the emergency number was one-one-twelve—to get help for her ailing predecessor.

A few moments later, Haffner, gun in hand, came back into the salle looking dejected. "The assailant got away. There was a black SUV with its engine running waiting for the shooter out front. He jumped in, and they were on the Ring in no time. I put out an all points alert radio call, but I am not sure my colleagues will respond quickly enough to catch the assailant and his co-conspirators."

"Thank you, Lieutenant," Greg said, still shaken. "Do you think whoever it was, was coming for me? And Anne?"

"Of course. The gun was pointing straight at you when I knocked you over. One or both of you could very well be dead right now."

"Again, we are very grateful, Lieutenant. But, Crabbe over there—"

"It is only a shoulder wound. I think he will be all right. A lot of hysterics. The ambulance is just pulling up outside."

"Phew," Anne said, brushing herself off. "That was close. And thank you, Rudolf."

"Who do you think it was, Anne?" Haffner asked as

he looked around the room to see if there were any more injuries.

"It must have been one of Polyakov's men," Greg answered since Anne was still too shaken. "The arms merchant. Or possibly an assassin organized at his request by his brother the Deputy Director of the FSB. Boris…he actually threatened my wife and me at the opera last night. Also, once several years ago. They must have known I would be here. There were placards all over town about my talk, and the event was widely publicized over the Internet."

"Yes, the two Polyakovs seem to be very closely connected. Not just as brothers, but also in their illicit trading venture—"

"Mr. Martens, I would advise you to be careful," Haffner said. "And you too, Anne. You are not safe here. You should consider leaving the country as soon as possible. For your own sake."

"Don't worry, Lieutenant. We'll be all right. But thank you."

"I will arrange some added security. But stay in your hotel or close by and be alert at all times, please."

"Of course, Rudolf. And thank you."

Chapter 14

Julia woke to the light touch of Sofia's hand. As she came to from her groggy, drug-induced sleep, she saw that her bare-breasted masseuse had put on her bikini top by now.

"Come, it's time to get dressed for dinner. You must look your most beautiful, Julia. For Anton. I have never seen him so taken with anyone before. No wonder. You are a gorgeous woman."

Julia was not quite sure what this all meant, but as she had drifted off to sleep, she had thought that the best avenue for her to survive this ordeal would be to cooperate with Polyakov and his crew, even though he no doubt had some nefarious plans for her. Was he intending her for his son? Or did he himself want to have sex with her again, the creep? Either way, the thought repulsed her. She was still traumatized from the terrible experience in Ozersk the previous night with Hetzel and the arms merchant.

The alternative to not cooperating that he had hinted at seemed even more terrible, though—and if what Sofia said was indeed right, and if she—she went with Anton— she might at least not have to suffer the advances of any of these despicable, debauched older men. Polyakov, or the pervert Hetzel. Or, for that matter, that awful Brother Peter. Ugh. Or all three, plus the guards, which is what Polyakov had implied. She shuddered at the hellish thought. And, hopefully, Anton would at least not hurt or torture her, if he was as taken with her as Sofia had suggested. But still, being forced to submit to her rapist's son, who was also the grandson of Beria and her aunt, was a very grim prospect indeed.

⌘⌘⌘

Sofia led her back to the Aphrodite room, and as soon as the dark-haired beauty closed the door, she turned to Julia, and pressing her body against her, kissed her fully on the mouth. When she came up for air, still holding Julia's hands, she said, "Julia, I want to help you before these awful men hurt you more and carry out their vile plans. We have to do something."

Shocked by the deep kiss, but pleased that she might have found a friend in Sofia, Julia wiped her mouth, and asked, "Why, what are they planning, Sofia? What do you know? Please tell me."

"Well—" Sofia started, but just then, they heard footsteps outside the door. "Shh! We'll have to talk later."

Ivan came into the room. "The boss told me to come and make sure no funny stuff goes on here. You, you get ready quickly." The thug grabbed Julia by the elbow and shoved her toward the bathroom. "I put out dress for you. You, Sofia, you go to Hera room. Get dressed there."

What could Sofia have meant? What were the vile plans of these men, as she had put it? Julia wondered as she rinsed off in the shower.

She focused her efforts on fighting against the terror from the trauma of the previous night and the effects of the drug, to collect her thoughts. *What is it exactly that I know? Well, they have the uranium. And if that creep Brother Peter has the other fifty pounds with him, it is enough for a bomb to kill hundreds of thousands of people if deployed in a busy city.*

And, God help me, I was instrumental in helping them get their hands on the nuclear material, and bring it into Europe!

I have to stop these criminals somehow.

And what's next for me? Will they just kill me? Torture me? Use me as their plaything? Sell me to one of the clients of their sex trade, like they did with Anne and Nadia?

Anne—That's what I need to do. Somehow get word to Anne and Greg of where I am, and what has happened.

Maybe...maybe Sofia can help me that way.

But wasn't that what Polyakov and Hetzel said, back in the villa in Ozersk? That they wanted me to be...bait...so Anne and Greg, who foiled both their previous plans, would fall into their hands?

What choice do I have?

Do I dare trust Sofia?

At least some kind of a vague plan was starting to emerge in her panic-stricken mind.

Julia mused thus until she heard Ivan's stern words again: "Come on, hurry up in there, or I will come and show you how." And he pushed the slightly ajar door completely open, staring as Julia tried to grab a towel to wrap around her. "Here, here is what you wear tonight." Ivan handed Julia a low-cut, navy blue tank wrap dress.

"What about undergarments?"

"You ask boss when you see him. This all he tell me to give you," the thug answered, cackling.

⌘

Ivan led Julia down the corridor to the entertainment area, and then out to the terrace where the others were assembled for drinks and the breathtaking sunset.

"You look absolutely stunning, my dear." The Russian arms merchant came over to her, gushing, with glass of champagne in hand. "Here, this is to celebrate your performance at the Mayak gates this morning. Roederer Crystal 2006. You were the ticket to our success. You deserve every sip. Julia, we drink to your skills and your beauty!"

God, am I hallucinating? This guy drugged me, brutally molested and raped me while his perverse buddy watched, then forced me to participate in smuggling nuclear material from Mayak, and now he is toasting me with one of the best champagnes in the world! What next?

Julia sought out Sofia's eyes. The dark-haired beauty blushed and looked down as she sipped her drink.

Polyakov took her over to Anton, who, dressed in navy slacks, loafers and white shirt with sleeves rolled up, was standing over at the railing, and looking out over the water toward the island of Spetsos, behind which the sun was sinking in a fiery cacophony of color. "Anton, we drink to Julia. This is her night to celebrate." The two men clicked Julia's glass, and then Polyakov discreetly walked away, seeing Brother Peter come out on the terrace. "Ah, Brother Peter, we need to talk, you and I—"

Anton brushed Julia's arm as he turned around to look at the twilight view out to sea, and then, putting his hand on her hip and burying his face in her hair, said, "You know, Julia, I know a lot about you from my father. And from the book I read. I could make you a very happy woman—" And then after a pause, sensing her resistance, he continued, "—or else, I fear that my father and these other men will give you a lot of pain and suffering. I could make your life so nice and easy and beautiful." A long pause, and then, "But if you do not wish to get closer to me, I would have to—to release you to those who could turn it all into something worse than hell. The decision is yours." Anton had a tormented look, as he looked deep into Julia's eyes before taking another sip of the vintage champagne.

What is this all about? This man hardly even knows me. He must be a tortured soul, with the father—and the grandfather—he was dealt by fate. He certainly doesn't know that he is my cousin's son.

Julia's heart and soul were in turmoil, but relief came as she heard Polyakov senior, from over by the open glass doors, say, "Come, everyone. Dinner is served."

Was this her only chance, really, to escape the fate she sensed these sex merchants had in store for her? And how could she trust the offspring of her rapist, the illegitimate grandson of her aunt by the Soviet monster, Lavrenti Beria? How could she submit to him, even if it was to escape a more terrible ordeal?

And there would be no way out then. Marriage—but it would really mean slavery. It was not a way out.

ecec

The candle-lit dining table was lavishly set for everyone, with five cut crystal glasses in descending size, Limoges porcelain plates, several iterations of monogrammed silver cutlery and large linen napkins. The table was positioned just inside the completely open sliding glass doors, such that, as Polyakov ushered Julia to the seat on the side facing out to sea next to his chair at the head of the table, she had the sensation that the room was an extension of the terrace and the outside world. The languorous warm evening breeze gently stroking her face only heightened this feeling. Anton approached on her other side, and it was he who pulled the chair out for her, as Polyakov did the same for Sofia on his right, and facing Julia, Brother Peter performed the courtesy for Nika. She sat diagonally opposite Hetzel, who just plunked himself down beside the Sons of Jesus terrorist.

As Julia glanced along at the sexual cripple, she tried to fathom the transformation in these men: the night before they had brutally used and abused her, and now they seemed mostly pleasant and courteous. Although Hetzel's lascivious leer at her cleavage told her that matters certainly had not changed: was this all just an illusion? Premeditated trickery?

Or is this just a prelude for more horrors? she asked herself again.

Dinner was sumptuous: the starter was pan-fried *Halloumi* with a fennel, olive, and mint compôte, the main course, *Barbounia,* or red mullet in a caper sauce, all accompanied by a choice of the Domain Skouras Grande Cuvée Nemea 2008 red, or the Gaia Wild Fermented Assyrtiko Santorini 2017 white. Julia thoroughly relished every bite, although she did try to sip her wine slowly, knowing that she needed to stay sharp. This was not easy though, as both Anton and Polyakov were making sure that her glass was always filled, with the arms merchant once even telling her, "Drink up, my dear! You deserve it. I want you to have a good time. We all want to enjoy ourselves tonight." This, of course, made Julia that much more suspicious of what might come afterward.

The conversation over most of the dinner was mainly between Brother Peter and Polyakov, with Anton and Hetzel occasionally chiming in, and revolved around Russia's interests in Greece. Julia learned that the party in power in Athens was, in fact, very close to Putin and his former FSB cohort, and, like most of the leaders of Syriza, Prime Minister Alexis Tsipras and Foreign Minister

Nikos Kotzias descended politically from the pro-Russian Greek Communist Party. Russia had essentially moved in to prop up the troubled Greek economy with loans and investments when Greece's European Union partners played hardball and refused to help except under very strict conditions. Several Greek ministers were frequent visitors to the Kremlin, and both the Foreign Minister and the Defense Minister, Panos Kammenos, had formally opposed the European Union sanctions against Russia. In fact, as Polyakov gloated, to Julia's surprise and dismay, "We have sufficient influence in this country now, that we can get our way on almost anything. It has been sort of a bloodless takeover. The best kind." Anton added the comment that "certainly this has all played really well for our interests."

It was as they were finishing the dessert of *Bougatsa,* the delicious lemon orange pie the chef served up with a lovely Malvasia di Candia Aromatica 2012 from the Douloufakis winery that Brother Peter changed the subject. "So, Sergei, where do we go from here? Now that you—we—have all the nuclear stuff necessary, we can finally carry out the deal we struck in Porto Montenegro. Remember? After things went so sour in Poti…"

"Yes," Polyakov answered. "The remaining fifty pounds for twenty-five million, delivery of both fifties in the Northeast USA for another ten. And I think you now have the money—at least that's what my brother tells me."

"That's right. One of my colleagues met with Boris just yesterday," the freckled red-haired terrorist agreed. "And he was kind enough to provide us with some funding. But there was something else," he continued as he emitted a playful chortle, pushing his chair back and taking a sip of the Malvasia. "You threw in two of the beautiful women you always seem to have around you, Sergei.

Although I must say, the ones here are quite a bit older than the teenagers we contracted for in Porto Montenegro." He moved closer to Nika and put his hand possessively on her thigh, kissing her ear. "But I don't mind. They will do."

"Don't worry, when we deliver the stuff, you will have your women, too. And for tonight—" Polyakov pointed at Nika. "—that one can certainly entertain you."

"Okay with me," Brother Peter answered, enchanted by his assigned companion for the night.

"What about me?" Hetzel piped up.

"You, Andreas, should take the opportunity to catch up on your sleep tonight. We have a very busy day tomorrow with the Syrians as you know. But, if you really insist—if you really are desperate for female companionship, and you must have a playmate or two, you can go down and get one or several of the girls we have in the lower huts. Igor and Ivan will help you select them. They are quite gorgeous, too." And looking at the dark-haired girl beside him, he continued, "The lovely Sofia, of course, will have the honor of entertaining me." Then smirking at his son, he said, "I trust Anton, that you and Julia have made some arrangements as well?" He added, almost as an afterthought, with a little laugh, "Because if not, we could trade. Or I might take both. I shall, of course, do everything required to facilitate the interests of all my guests. "

Julia was horrified with what she was hearing, but she almost choked on her wine when, Polyakov, putting his hand on hers, continued, "But, first, I will ask you, my dear Julia, to perform the famous dance for us that you used to do in Vienna to my favorite piece of music, Rimsky-Korsakov's *Scheherazade.* That will help get us all in the mood for the rest of the evening."

Julia knew that what Polyakov wanted was for her to

do the striptease act she used to dance at the Revuebar Rasputin from the time that she was trying to make a living as an illegal alien in Vienna.

She loathed the thought, mostly because it would be to these debauched sex traffickers she would have to expose herself yet again.

But if she were to refuse, what then? The consequences would no doubt be a lot worse.

"One more thing though, Sergei," Brother Peter interjected, "before we start the fun: tell me, how the fuck are you going to get the nuclear stuff from here to the USA? You can't just fly into JFK with your private jet without major customs formalities. The authorities will be all over us."

"Don't you worry, my friend. It's all in hand. Tomorrow, Anton and I have some business to attend to in Damascus—it's only a two-hour flight, and it involves a dinner, so we'll be back only the following morning. But we will have a quick turnaround, you'll see, and we'll take it from there."

"Sergei, what I need to know is where in the US, because I need to make arrangements, you understand."

"Well, the deal is the Northeast. We will meet my yacht in St. Pierre and take it from there. You and your buddies can pick a harbor or cove in northern Maine where we can land the stuff."

God Almighty! They intend to smuggle the nuclear material into the northeastern USA using Polyakov's yacht! Julia realized, panic-stricken. *But St. Pierre—is that French? Or perhaps Canada?*

Then turning to Igor, who was standing discreetly by the wall several steps behind, Polyakov continued, "Now, Igor, let the music play. *Scheherazade.*" And when the music came on, loud and clear, he said, "Okay, Julia, the floor's all yours—get out there and dance, honey."

ৎৎৎ

Knowing she had no choice, Julia got up, hesitantly at first, and then, looking over at the leering men and the two beautiful acolytes at the table, and the two huge guards standing arms folded in the background, she decided it would be in her best interests to obey the Russian gangster. She slowly started to move in time to the music with her back to the table. Then she swiftly turned around and with several moves untied the front of her wrap around dress. Now Julia suddenly understood why she had not been given any underwear: these sex fiends wanted more of the "strip" and less of the "tease."

Well, fuck it. I will tease these perverts to death!

Julia did a few pirouettes, and there was clapping all around and several exclamations of 'Wow!' as she faced the audience again and slid the dress down, so it just covered her nipples and lower body, tormenting the bastards by pulling it back and forth, exposing a bit more flesh here and a bit more there. She went on like this, rolling and scrunching the cloth up more and more until it just covered her midriff. And, as the music rose to the crescendo before the peaceful finale, she whirled around, twisting the dress off her body and waving it over her head before rapidly disappearing down the corridor that led to the Aphrodite room.

She was sure that no one in the audience saw the tears that flowed liberally down her cheeks as she made her exit.

ৎৎৎ

Some time later, in the darkness of the room, Julia felt someone slide in under the covers beside her. This was the moment she had been dreading, had hoped would not come, no matter who it was. She steeled herself, however, because she knew that the alternative to whatever came next would be a lot more horrendous.

"Julia." She heard Anton's voice, even as she felt his hands grope first her breasts and then her pubic area. "You were fabulous out there." And then, when her only response was to recoil instinctively, her unwitting first cousin once removed, added, "I am in love with you, Julia. I cannot live without you. Will you—will you marry me?" Although she had been somewhat expecting this moment with dread, Julia was too shocked to answer. Anton continued, not waiting for a reply. "Tomorrow I have to fly to Damascus with my father—we have a big deal we are doing there with the Syrian government—but we'll be back the next morning. He was planning to pick you up and take you with him to St. Pierre et Miquelon—you know those islands off the coast of Newfoundland. And after that, I don't know what, but I am sure that if I tell him about us, he will be pleased to leave you here with me. What do you say? The choice is yours." Anton's hand reached under her chin and forced her lips to his. Against all her fears, all her emotions, she willed herself to respond—at least mechanically, if not verbally or emotionally—knowing this was the only way to save herself from even greater horrors. She turned toward her rapist's son, and opening her legs, allowed him to enter her.

At least, it is clear now, the immediate alternative is to go with Polyakov to those islands off the coast of Newfoundland. Along with the nuclear material which will be smuggled from there into the northeastern USA.

Chapter 15

The maître d' at Appiano's recognized them, even though it was several years since they had been there. But Greg had always enjoyed the place for its distinct Austrian charm and, of course, the food had never let him down. They served a dessert he particularly loved—*Powidltascherl in Waldviertler bio Graumohnbutter,* little ravioli filled with prunes, topped with a sumptuous poppy seed sauce—but he also looked forward to the rest of the menu and the chance to peruse their very extensive list of Austrian wines and select one to relish with the meal. This was an experience he did not want to miss on any visit to the Imperial Capital, assailant or no assailant.

But as they walked the short distance along Argentinierstrasse from the Sacher, he was glad when Anne's remark, "Greg, have you noticed the two men behind us? They must be good old Rudolf's men," confirmed that what he thought he had observed was indeed a fact. And, although the security tail could not have had reservations at Appiano's, he was further heartened when after a heated discussion, with lots of glances in their direction, the friendly maître d' managed to find the two large police officers in *Mufti* a very small table by the entrance. The two men looked a bit ridiculous sitting there, but it meant that Greg and Anne would be as safe here as they could be anywhere in Vienna.

ळॐळ

As they settled in over an aperitif of two glasses of the Szigeti *1998 Cuvée Sekt,* Anne went straight to the subject at the back of both their minds.

"Boy, that was close at the Sacher. Thank God for Rudi and his quick thinking."

"Yes, we owe him our lives."

"But they never got the guy. At least I don't think so. I will call him in the morning to find out if his colleagues have made any progress."

"It seems to have been a well-organized operation. With the car out front and the speedy getaway."

"You're thinking the Polyakov clan again?"

"I have no idea, but they are the most likely. Who else would be our enemy here, Anne?"

"The FSB? Courtesy of Boris…"

"Also, that guy Johnny Apostle earlier—boy that was weird. It reminds me of—do you remember, Anne— the last time I was in front of the Austrian Literary Socie- ty, it was Billy Crawford—that guy Adam and I knew when we were young—who outed me. In a similar, ob- noxious manner during question period."

"Yes, and then he turned out to be the terrorist Brother Peter. The one who got away with half the HEU in Poti. A member of that Sons of Jesus group that blew up Grand Central Station in New York."

"Anne, I was just thinking—could the similarity of the occasion—and the name Johnny Apostle—could it be that maybe this guy, too, is linked to the Sons of Jesus? Could this hippie's alias be Brother John? Remember that video they showed on TV after the Grand Central bombing with twelve hooded men dressed like friars, sitting around 'The Voice of God', mimicking The Last Supper? The apostles? Do you get it?"

"Greg. That—that is a pretty scary notion. That would mean that they, too, are stalking us. Not just the Polyakov brothers."

"At least this Johnny Apostle creep didn't have a gun, like the other guy."

"Well, maybe he was there to distract us. And the police. And the assailant was supposed to finish us off."

"I don't know what to think anymore," Greg said. "Could the Polyakovs and the Sons of Jesus creeps be working together? Wow, do you think?"

"Whatever—I guess we had better be grateful for the extra security Rudolf has offered us. But he may be right, we need to be very careful."

"I think we should also consider cutting our trip short. I am scared."

"Okay, but let's sleep on it. Now let's talk about something else."

♥♥♥

They came out of the restaurant, arm-in-arm, happily sated and further fortified after a bottle of the red *Cuvée "Gabarinza" 2011* from the Weingut Heinrich on the Neusiedlersee with Appiano's delicious *Wienerschnitzel vom Milchkalbsschale mit Vogerlsalat und Kernöl* and a half bottle of the *Trockenbeeerenauslese "Or Liquide" 2008* by the Weingut Christ-Jedlersdorf with the Powidltascherl. As they made their way slowly along Schottengasse in the balmy summer Viennese night, then took a slight deviation through the beautiful square, Freyung, back to the hotel, Greg remarked, "Gee, Anne, despite everything, I still think it's great to back here again. This is always going to be my favorite city."

"Yes, but too bad our nice romantic getaway has turned into another mission in search of a lost friend and missing nuclear material," Anne answered with a little laugh, even as she turned toward her husband for a kiss. "And a good chance of getting killed."

"Well, yes," Greg acquiesced, "but I still want to enjoy my beautiful wife in this fabulous setting, while I still can—"

She tugged on his hand. "Let's get going."

And they found the shortest way back to the hotel.

Chapter 16

Dawn came, and Julia felt strong arms around her, fingers kneading her nipples. In her drowsy state, she realized it was Anton, wanting sex again before he had to go. Damascus, she knew, with his father. *May they perish there, these gangsters*, she willed, *and not come back in twenty-four hours' time.* She felt used and disgusted, but allowed him to touch and kiss her, however, she did not kiss back.

Anton asked again, "So Julia, what should I tell my father?" And when feigning sleep, she did not respond, he said definitively, "Well, I guess you're going to St. Pierre with my father and that awful Brother Peter. Lucky guy."

Even though she did not know what awaited her, Julia was momentarily pleased when, a few minutes later, she heard the door to the room close.

Pleased that Anton was gone, and that, in the end, there had been no big drama, despite the alternative that now faced her.

But the tears came again until she fell into a light sleep filled with terror and disgust.

⁂

Some time later, she woke to a softer touch, a tenderer embrace: instinctively, she knew it was that of a woman. Sofia. This was Sofia's touch.

Then her voice, "Julia, come you must wake. It is late. We must talk."

And she remembered. Sofia had promised to help. "Sofia, thank you. Quickly, yes, we have to act fast."

"What, Julia? What do you mean?" Sofia's hands were gently caressing her breasts, then her stomach, then down farther—

"We must make a call." Julia sat bolt upright. "Polyakov is planning to take me to some islands off the coast of Newfoundland with the nuclear material. His speedy yacht is to meet us there. Probably that is a staging point to get the stuff into the northeastern US. Which is where the terrorist group that Brother Peter belongs to wants to set a bomb off."

"Wow! That is scary."

"Is there any way you can get me a phone? Calling my office in Vienna would be the easiest."

"Here, I have my cell with me," she heard Sofia say as she reached for her iPhone, left on the night table.

"Thanks. Can I use it?"

"Sure, Julia. Make your call. But be quick."

Julia took the phone and dialed her office, at the same time noting that it was already nine fifty. Eight fifty Vienna time. So Señora Lopez had to be there.

Indeed, her Peruvian secretary answered, "International Atomic Energy Agency. Julia Saparova's office. Can I help you?"

"Señora Lopez? It's Julia. You must call Nicholas Labrecque at Interpol immediately. Tell him I am at a luxury villa with an airstrip on the coast near Porto Heli in Greece. Tomorrow, I think I will be taken to St. Pierre et Miquelon, with some stolen nuclear material…Polyakov's…yes, that's Polyakov's…yacht will be there—"

Sofia grabbed the phone, saying "That is enough, Julia. You will get me in trouble." She pressed the red hang up button, then asked, punching a few other icons, "How exactly do I get rid of evidence of the call? Yes, here—this will do it, I think." The dark-haired hostess put the phone back on the night table, and snuggled up against Julia, saying, "Well, my darling, we've saved the world, so now we must have a little fun—"

But Julia moved away, saying, "No, Sofia. Not yet. We first need to find where the nuclear material is. And we must hide it somewhere else, somewhere where these crooks will not discover it any time soon. Will you help me?" she implored her new friend as much with her eyes as with her words.

Footsteps outside the door interrupted them. "Come on, get up, you lazy slut." It was Ivan. "Last chance for some breakfast and then it's beach time. Put on the bikini again. Unless you want to come naked."

So much for looking for the stolen nuclear material. But maybe later we will have a chance, Julia hoped.

Chapter 17

Anne gave Greg a kiss as she stood up from their corner table at the Café Sacher, where she had accompanied him to grab a mélange before going off to the Interpol offices to meet with her former colleagues. Since Greg felt that he was not needed at the meeting, he decided to stay behind and do some work on his next writing project after reading the papers over a more leisurely breakfast.

Nevertheless, as Anne approached the nineteenth century building where Interpol's offices were situated behind the Börse, she could not resist stopping off again at the Aida Confiserie for her *de rigueur* marzipan croissant: after all, this had been her routine every morning on the way to work when officially employed by Interpol, so why not now that she was helping them out on this increasingly important project.

As she waited in line, she hoped that some of the leads her colleagues were following up brought results to help them find Julia, because otherwise, they would not have much to go on. Also, she hoped that Haffner or they—since she had called Labrecque to tell him about the affair when they had returned to their room after the drinks—had made some progress on finding the man who had tried to kill them yesterday after Greg's talk. She wondered again whether there was any link to that man whom Greg had told her about—Johnny Apostle, the one who had been so rude during question time. And was he in any way connected with these Sons of Jesus terrorists, as Greg had surmised? At least Haffner and the security guard had been able to grab that guy and hold him until Rudolf's colleagues arrived. No doubt the Austrian police would have questioned him. Yes, best call the lieutenant.

Anne scrolled down for Haffner's number and pressed the call button when it came up on the screen.

"Good morning, Anne." She was glad to hear the officer's reassuring voice.

"Hello, Rudolf. I am just calling to see if you were able to find out anything from that man yesterday?"

"You mean the one I was handing over to my colleagues at the Sacher just as you arrived? That…Johnny Apostle?"

"Yes. The one who was so rude during the question period after Greg's talk."

"Sorry, Anne, but unfortunately we had no grounds to keep him for questioning. He had not committed any crime. My colleagues felt they had to let him go after admonishing him to behave more politely in the future. Especially since he was a foreigner—in fact, he had an American passport—and they were reluctant to engage in a diplomatic incident."

"Too bad. Any leads on the assailant who then tried to kill Greg and me?"

"No. He and his team got away."

"Could the two incidents have been linked, do you think?" She wanted to probe what the police were thinking.

"No reason to believe so. We have no evidence pointing in that direction."

"We are rather concerned, you understand," Anne continued. "Also Boris Polyakov, the Deputy Director of the FSB and Sergei's twin brother, threatened Greg and me. At the opera. The evening we arrived. For the second time."

"So could he be linked somehow as well, you mean?" Haffner finished Anne's thought. "No idea…"

"In any case, Rudolf thanks for the extra security. Greg and I truly do appreciate it." Anne decided to bring an end to the conversation.

"The least I can do for old friends."

єᴈєᴈ

It was on the way up in the elevator that Anne came to the conclusion that Greg must be right: this Johnny Apostle just had to be connected. The Sons of Jesus. Must be their man in Europe, now that the hunt was on for Brother Peter. They had been, up until then, a home-grown American terrorist group. Out of the limelight for quite a while now. But what were they up to here, in Europe?

And the Polyakovs, too—what were they up to?

Lots of questions but no answers.

Frau Huth greeted Anne with a big smile at the door. "The usual?" she asked. Then said, "Come, the others are in the Conference Room. Command Central."

Anne followed her into the familiar room, there to be greeted by John Demeter, Nicholas Labrecque, and Jakob Dorfmeister, the office computer geek.

"Anne, we were wondering when you would get here," Demeter said, glancing at his watch. "It's well past eight."

"I've never known you to keep civilized hours, John. I'm not even on your payroll, and I am here before eight-thirty. So what's so urgent?" Anne asked, hoping that they would surprise her with some positive results.

"Well, Anne—" Labrecque seemed eager to impart what he had found out on his phone calls. "—I just got off the phone with our colleague Radomir in Porto Montenegro. I had asked him to track down the airplane Polyakov and that Brother Peter escaped in the last time, just as you suggested. To Chechnya, it was, I believe they flew. Our Montenegrin colleague found out for me that, in fact, there were a number of private flights in the direction of Russia out of Tivat that day, but the only one that fits the time slot was a Gulfstream 550."

"That would have been them. Polyakov and the friar creep. Good work, Nicholas," Anne complimented the Frenchman.

"Yes, but I am still waiting to hear what if any private jets took off from one of the Chelyabinsk area airports yesterday late morning. Annoyingly, I can't get Russian air traffic control to cooperate."

"Could be orders from the FSB. Boris, the Deputy Director, Sergei's twin at it again."

"Yeah, you're right, Anne," Demeter interjected. "In fact, the FSB and members of the Russian armed forces may well be in on the heist for all we know. We are aware that typically, they rake off thirty percent of the proceeds of any sale of arms through backdoor channels. In the name of the state. But really for themselves, the crooked individuals. A nice little business."

"Anyway, Nicholas, we'll need to keep at it—trying to see if we can get anything from them," Anne continued.

"Sure thing, Anne."

"The research with Jakob on the Polyakov Empire, though, was quite productive actually," Demeter reported, seemingly pleased with the results. "Jakob, why don't you take us through what you came up with."

"Well," the young man, thin and wearing black horn-rimmed glasses, a T-shirt and skinny jeans started speaking nervously. "We looked through all the stuff on the arms merchant's laptop—the one you had picked up in Porto Montenegro. There were several locales or pieces of real estate that came up, in addition to the compounds in Hungary and Montenegro." He pulled up some images from the laptop on the screen in front of them. "Here, a ski chalet in Switzerland for one." Jakob clicked on the mouse pad. "A Georgian mansion near Regent's Park in London. A beautiful beach property in Brazil. Another one in Angola." The computer expert paused a moment before going further, "And most intriguingly, one in Greece as well. Situated south of Athens, on the Peloponnese."

"Wow. That's quite a lot of property." This from Labrecque.

"I believe that the Greek estate is going to be our most likely candidate," Anne said, excitedly. "Greece is in Schengen, and if Polyakov and crew manage to get in there with the nuclear material and—and any trafficked women—those crooks can go anywhere in Europe. No problem."

"The property is near the town of Porto Heli," Jakob added. "And has its very own private air strip."

"Yes. I think you're right, Anne. That's where they must have gone to hole up, the bastards." Demeter said. "I will get our local Interpol guys to check it out."

"No, John, not just yet. I don't think we should run the risk of telegraphing anything to these gangsters. I don't trust the network—our network, I am sorry to say. Plus, if the Amis get wind of it, they may bomb the place to smithereens. Perhaps even in spite of the nuclear material, we don't know. And then we would never see Julia again."

"Hmm. You're right again, Anne."

"John, do you know any of your Interpol colleagues in the Athens office? Personally, I mean."

"No, not really. Although I did meet the station head there once…Archimedes Papagos was his name I think." Demeter paused before continuing, "But then, if we don't get in touch, how can we get confirmation that that is where they are?"

"John, I have worked with one agent in Greece before—Alexandros Stavros—whom I would trust. Let me contact him first. We've got to be totally in charge here if we ever want to see Julia alive again and get the nuclear stuff back. These crooks seem to have their contacts everywhere. Even inside Interpol, I would wager. Without knowing everyone in the Greek office, I wouldn't necessarily trust them."

"Yeah, I guess you're right."

"And John, I think I should get myself out there as soon as possible. To Greece, I mean."

'I agree. If you're so sure they have gone there."

"Ninety percent sure. Should we ask Frau Huth to come in here to make the arrangements?"

"Good idea," Demeter said, getting up to go instruct the secretary.

Nicholas, who was tinkering on his laptop all the while, beckoned to Anne. "Here, you are. I found the property on Google Maps."

Anne went over to look. "Hmm. It does have an airstrip, I see. In fact, there is a plane parked there, outside the hangar. That must be it. But the place seems pretty isolated and well defended. Walls—probably guarded—all around, except maybe on the seaside. We'll have to see how to penetrate it. Maybe we'll have to enter from the water."

"It will be tough however we cut it. No doubt they will have guard dogs all over the place. And it will be difficult to find Julia quickly and extract her. Let alone the nuclear stuff—that will be like looking for a needle in a haystack."

"Unless Julia has a clue and can help when we get to her."

"Anyway, let me call Alexandros. Will you come with me, Nicholas?"

"I will follow first thing tomorrow. I am meeting the IAEA senior staff this afternoon to brief them on the gravity of the situation. Plus I have something else to finish off, but I know, this is important."

ଔଔଔ

Anne was just in the throes of finalizing the earliest flight arrangements to Athens with Frau Huth when Nicholas stormed into the Conference room.

"Anne, I just had a call," he said excitedly, "Oh, sorry, am I interrupting something?"

"From whom, Nicholas?"

"Julia's secretary. At the IAEA. You know, the Peruvian—"

"Señora Gomez? What did she say?" Nicholas had Anne's attention.

"Apparently, Julia had called and left a message saying that she was being held captive at Polyakov's estate in Porto Heli. Greece. So we were right. Your instincts pinpointed it correctly."

"Good. What else?"

"Well, with the stolen nuclear material. That is all there, too. And she thinks that they will be moved tomorrow to St. Pierre et Miquelon. You know, those French islands off the coast of Newfoundland, in Canada. And Polyakov's yacht will be there. It seems strange, that—"

"So we have confirmation. That they are now in Greece. Good."

"Yes."

"I will proceed with the plans to get myself there ASAP." Anne had immediately made up her mind. "Meet up with Alexandros and try to get Julia and the uranium back. But I think, on reflection, you, Nicholas, should make your way to those islands off Newfoundland. I will also get Greg to go with you. He is done with his speech, and you two can fly out tomorrow. No doubt, they are using St. Pierre as some kind of a staging point to get the nuclear stuff into the northeastern US."

"I am sure you're right."

"This will give us two tries to catch these crooks. We have to stop them, no matter what."

ღჳღჳ

Anne glanced at her phone, hoping that the call to Alexandros would not take too long. They had not seen each other for quite a few years and had a lot of catching up to do, but all that could wait. She still needed to go back to the hotel and pack, and she wanted to say a proper goodbye to Greg if she was going to go off to Greece, since who could tell what the outcome of this crazy operation would be? He would surely want to come along, but she did not want him there: besides, Nicholas would be able to use his help. And at least he would be out of Vienna, which seemed to be getting dangerous for them. Not that doing a mission to stop these criminals in St. Pierre et Miquelon was safe, but all the more reason for her to be successful in Greece.

Anne had last seen Alexandros when she was a rook-ie agent, in fact. It all came flooding back. A six-months posting to Athens, which had been more fun than serious work. Alexandros had been a strapping young Greek god then, and he had tried to make amorous advances on her, but she knew the type, and never let him get past a few innocent kisses. Just as well, she thought, it would have ended in tears when she moved on to Vienna. They had remained friends after he got married, and stayed in touch on Facebook. It would be good to see him again, and she knew that she would be able to rely on him in a mission.

"Hello, Alexandros? This is Anne. Anne Rossiter."

"Anne, how nice to hear from you. It's been too long."

"Yes, it has, Alexandros. But I am on my way to Greece now."

"Ah, when will you arrive? I will take you to my place by the sea—"

"No, this is for work."

"What? You left the service, I heard."

"Yes. But I am back. I have been recalled as it were, to help rescue a kidnapped official of the International Atomic Energy Agency. A good friend of mine. Also, to help recover some stolen nuclear material."

"Wow. That is big."

"Yes, and I need your help. We need to get to Porto Heli as soon as possible and penetrate a coastal site near there where we think my friend is being held. Along with the highly enriched uranium."

"Porto Heli? Very well. I will make some prepara-tions."

"Thank you, Alexandros. I knew I could count on you." Anne was sure that whatever the "preparations" were, they would be worthwhile and thorough.

"When are you coming, Anne?"

"I am arriving in Athens at two thirty-five this afternoon on Aegean flight eight-eighty-one. Can you come and get me?"

"Of course. See you then. We will drive straight to Porto Heli. I am really looking forward to it. It will be wonderful to see you. And do a mission together."

Chapter 18

Anne made her way back to the Sacher, hoping Greg would be in the room. She needed to tell him what they had found out. Yes, she would try to get him to agree to go to St. Pierre et Miquelon with Nicholas. That would be the best. Probably safer than this operation in Greece. Though still fraught with danger. It was all mad, she knew. She would not tell him how crazy it was. Just she and a Greek operative she had done a mission with way back when, plunging into a den of hardened rogues and sex merchants to try and rescue another beautiful woman. And find some stolen nuclear material—like a needle in a haystack. The gangsters would relish the opportunity to capture her, she had to admit, but as a friend of Julia, she just had to do everything she could to get her out of their clutches.

Yes, it would be good if Greg were in the room. She wanted to make love before they parted. If he went off to St. Pierre et Miquelon, they might not see each other for a few days. Or—a dreaded thought—perhaps ever, if something happened to one of them. But no need to dwell on that.

On the other hand, if he was not there, a short lie-down just to rest would be nice too, time permitting, since with the jet lag she still didn't feel a hundred per cent, Anne told herself, as she pressed the elevator button in the Sacher's lobby

"Hi," Greg had a smile on his face as he opened the door and reached forward to kiss her. "So what's up, dear?"

"Well, my love, just so you know, I am on my way to Greece this very afternoon."

"What?"

"And tomorrow, Greg, I would like you to fly to St. Pierre. As in St. Pierre et Miquelon, the French islands just south of Newfoundland."

"God, that sounds pretty drastic. Don't you love me anymore?" Greg knew his wife intimately but thought a little irony might not be out of place given the circumstances. "Why am I being sent off in exile? To some rocks in the remote North Atlantic. While you go off to frolic with a Greek Adonis in holiday land?"

"Nothing of the sort. You and Nicholas will be doing a mission to try to rescue Julia. And save the world."

"Wow."

"And maybe rescue me too, if my mission to do the same in Greece fails. That's where Julia is being held now, along with the HEU, we think. And there are plans to move them to St. Pierre."

"You are one incredible woman, Anne. The secret services of the world could not cope without you. And to think that you allowed a schmuck writer like me to whisk you away."

"Greg, you are an amazing man, and I love you. And you are the only Adonis I want. Greek or not." Anne put her arms around her husband and kissed him on the mouth. And then, starting to peel her T-shirt off, she added, "If we hurry, we might be able to have a quickie before I have to catch my flight to Athens."

So much for the short little nap. But this would be better, she knew: she could always sleep on the flight, but she might never hold Greg in her arms again. Such was the life of an Interpol operative.

Even an ex one.

ℭℴℭℴ

It was as she was dressing and packing for her trip, that Anne filled Greg in.

"Nicholas had a call from Julia's secretary at the IAEA a few hours ago. Julia had called her and recounted where she is being held in Greece, but, more importantly, that she thought that she—and the nuclear material would be moved. Polyakov apparently announced that they were all going to St. Pierre et Miquelon."

"God…why?"

"Well, if you think about it, those islands off the coast of Newfoundland are a part of France, and France is in Schengen. So there will be at most a cursory customs check—one that these criminals would certainly know how to circumvent. This is all guesswork, but there, they would be very close to the coast of the Northeast USA. An easy trip for Polyakov's boat, which from what Julia told the secretary, will be meeting them in St. Pierre. And if it's anything like the yacht he had in Porto Montenegro, it will be a super-fast one. That's what Nicholas and you have to check out, and if Julia and the nuclear material show up there, you have to try and get them away."

"Okay, boss. I am on—"

"As I said, I am on my way to Greece, which is where they are now. A former Greek colleague of mine and I will see what we can do to rescue Julia from Polyakov's place there. And, of course, try to retrieve the nuclear material. At least if we can get Julia free, then I think we should bring the Americans in, although we'll have to consider that going through the official channels runs the risk of a leak."

"I see. If you don't succeed, then Nicholas and I would still have a chance."

"Yes, and if all else fails, we notify the Americans. But then I am afraid that probably means sacrificing Julia if these gangsters are still holding her."

"God, Anne, what a mess. I will try to do my part. But above all, you be careful. Take care of yourself. I love you." He kissed his wife and added, "I could not stand losing you."

She kissed him back passionately. "I love you too, dear."

Chapter 19

It was just after eleven-thirty that Sophia, sunbathing topless on the beach below the house, raised herself on her elbows and, nudging Julia beside her, announced to the others, "Gee, I think I'm getting too much sun. I'm a bit dizzy. I have got to go in now. I'll see you all at lunch, if that's okay."

Julia responded to what she thought was a hint. "Me too. God, look at me, I'm starting to look like a lobster!" It was not true, but she stood up, as did the dark-haired girl, whom she followed along the path to the house. On the way, Sophia, first looking back to make sure no one was following, whispered to her, "Let's get dressed quickly. Then we can look around for that nuclear material."

"Just what I was thinking, Sophia. And thank you."

Julia quickly showered and put on a sundress from the collection in the closet, and then made her way over to where Sophia was staying in the Hermes Room, which was the first bedroom in the other wing, just beyond the entertainment area. She knocked and heard her new found friend say, "Enter."

"Good, Julia. Here's what I think we should do. We need to look in all the rooms in the house first, and then case out the other buildings after," Sophia said. "Actually, we may only get to some of them later in the afternoon."

"We do have to be careful, though. I don't think Ivan and Igor followed us up from the beach, but there are the other guards too. And the local staff as well. We don't know what they would do."

"Maybe it's best if we split up, Julia. That way, if anybody asks, we can say that we just got lost. If it's the two of us walking around together in the house, it would seem much more like we're up to something."

"Good idea. Why don't you check the rooms along the rest of this corridor, while I do the other wing, Sophia? That way at least we can claim we just got lost looking for our own rooms."

"Makes sense. But be sure you turn up for lunch by one. Otherwise, they will be suspicious and come looking for you."

❧❧❧

Julia wandered back into the hall, and feigning innocence, walked through the main entertainment area into the east wing of the building, then past the entrance to her room. The next door along, she saw was the Artemis Room, and she gingerly tried the doorknob, even as she looked around furtively. Fortunately, the door opened easily, and she slipped inside without being noticed. A quick glance told her that this was a woman's room, probably the one Nika used when she was not entertaining that horrid Brother Peter.

The thought of that awful terrorist brought her to the realization that it was actually in his room where she might have the best chance of finding some of the uranium. That is, if indeed—as she surmised from some of the conversation—he had brought the half he had managed to get away with in Poti with him, for delivery into the Northeast USA along with the fifty pounds that she had been forced to help smuggle out of Mayak this time. She knew that the two lots could not be kept together. There had to be at least ten feet separating them at all times. Otherwise, the nuclear material could reach critical mass for a major explosion. And he might just want to keep the one lot the Sons of Jesus already owned near him.

Julia quickly checked the obvious places where a case containing the uranium might have been hidden, and based on her cursory assessment that there was nothing suspicious anywhere, concluded that it would be a better use of her time to try and find where Brother Peter was staying.

The next entrance off the corridor on this wing of the villa was to the Athena suite. Julia hesitated, because, she was sure it was getting close to lunch, and its occupant, whoever it was, might be in there changing. But, looking over her shoulder, she decided to brave it, and turned the knob, pushing the door open. The lodger here was obviously male, and it took her less than a minute to conclude that it must be the creep, Hetzel. The open case containing various sex toys that he must have used with his unfortunate victim or victims of the night before, coupled with the blood on the sheets and the rug, were all too distressing for Julia to stay and take a thorough look through the rest of the room. In any case, she told herself, it was unlikely that Hetzel would be asked to guard any of the nuclear material.

And that reminded her: hadn't Polyakov told Ivan to give the stuff they had brought over to Petr, the driver? So he was the obvious link for the fifty pounds she had helped smuggle out. As for the other fifty, she was sure she was right that Brother Peter would want to keep it close to him. She absolutely had to find where he was lodging.

But now it was lunchtime, Julia noted, hearing the bustle from the entertainment area, so she would have to check the last room at the end of the corridor out later. She had better join the other guests. Otherwise, she might be missed. Just in time, she told herself as Brother Peter and Nika were serving themselves from the copious buffet tables.

Any further ferreting around would have to wait until later, she told herself. Maybe she would see where the two retired to after lunch, hoping it would be Brother Peter's lodgings where they would take their little "nap," as Ivan had said, so she could case it out after. And her task would be the easiest, if it were the room at the end of the hall her room opened off.

ↄ◌ↄↄ

Late afternoon was pool time at the Polyakov villa, and even though the host and his son were not there, it was here where everyone assembled. Julia, tanned and splendid in her red bikini, was one of the first at the inviting pool, and she waited eagerly for Brother Peter and Nika to show up. Lunch had taken a while, but she had noted with satisfaction that after finishing, the two had made their way along the east corridor, past her room, and judging from the noises, past the door of Nika's room as well. So they must have ended up in the Hera Room, at the end of the hall. And this must, therefore, be where Brother Peter was lodged, Julia surmised.

A little while after the terrorist and his tart had settled on their lounge chairs with their drinks, Julia knew it was the time to act. But she had to find an excuse to go back into the house, making sure she was not being followed, and then quickly search the last room in the wing.

She had just the thought. "I'm going to run inside to get one of the books in my room," she said aloud, standing up suddenly from the recliner she had stretched out in her bikini. "It is so seldom that I get a chance to read."

Julia quickly made her way inside, past the entrance to her room, right down to the end of the hall, opened the door, and entered the main guest suite. Clearly, the terrorist leader—the paying customer—had been assigned the most luxurious quarters in this wing.

Where to start? Julia asked herself, panicking. She did not have much time, she knew, before someone down by the pool would get suspicious. Be methodical, though, she told herself.

First, the closets. Some hanging clothes, but nothing that resembled a case that might contain fifty pounds of highly enriched uranium.

Then the larger drawers, behind all the furniture, under the king-size bed, still with Nika's undergarments strewn all around it. The smell of sex pervaded everything, she noted, disgusted.

The bathroom: yes, maybe the bathroom.

But no. Nothing suspicious there, either.

There was only the terrace left. She opened the sliding glass door, looked around outside, and down some steps in the little tropical garden. Nothing.

It was when she went to open the sliding doors to go back inside that she noticed the large, leering man with his fat belly spilling over his flower-patterned bathing suit, just on the other side. Brother Peter.

"Well, well, well. What are you doing here, Julia? Did you come here to seduce me, you little slut? Are you going to give me a private little striptease? You want to suck my cock, do you? Let me guess. But really, I think I know why you are here."

"I was just looking for a book," she said lamely. "I couldn't find one I wanted to read in my room."

"Tell me another one, sweetheart. But don't you worry, right now, you are going to come with me to see our friends, Ivan and Igor." The creep grabbed her by the arm with one hand and slid the other one inside the back of her bikini bottom. "They will know what to do with you until Sergei comes back and feeds you to the wolves. Unless of course—" And he tried to turn her around and kiss her on the mouth.

"Fuck you, you creep," she said bringing her knee up hard into his groin at the same time as she bit him on the lips.

"Ow, goddammit, you bitch!" Brother Peter slapped her across the face then shoved her against the wall, before tugging her toward the door and down the corridor. "Okay, if that's what you want, I'll just have Ivan and Igor deal with you."

Chapter 20

As soon as Anne left the hotel room, Greg took a quick shower and got dressed before calling Nicholas Labrecque as he prepared another coffee on the Nespresso machine. He knew he would have to act fast.

"Nicholas, hello. I understand we're both going to St. Pierre et Miquelon. A bit crazy, I know, but Anne—"

"Hi, Greg. I was about to call you. Yes, Anne is now on her way to Greece, and you and I will need to backstop the operation in those islands off Newfoundland since that's where it seems the merchants of evil will be heading from Greece."

"Let's hope she is successful, and if not, then that we're able to stop these gangsters there. Although she will only have one of your colleagues with her and have no more manpower than we. Wouldn't it be better to concentrate all our resources in one attempt?" Greg was concerned since he would rather be going to Greece with Anne.

"She will be working with an excellent Greek agent. One of our men there she has done some operations with before."

"Well…"

"Greg, I've had Frau Huth look into flights for us to St. Pierre. The best she could do is for us to arrive there tomorrow at two-fifteen p.m. That's if we can leave here at two-o-five p.m. today and we overnight in Halifax."

"That works for me," Greg said, glancing at the time on the TV. "At least we will have some fresh Nova Scotia lobster for dinner."

"Good. I'll have her reserve the flights, and ask her to book rooms at the Hotel Robert. Also known as the Hotel du Vieux Port. I believe it is right across from where all the yachts would be docking, so we should be within easy reach of Polyakov's boat."

"Thanks, Nicholas. I'll see you at the airport, my friend."

❧❦❧

Greg had the hotel order a car to take him to the airport, and packed everything up quickly, including the clothes, make-up and other feminine paraphernalia Anne had not taken to Greece. He then went to check out. As he did so, he was happy to see that one of the tails Haffner had put on to protect them was there in the lobby. He hoped the other one had followed Anne at least as far as the airport.

In any case, he thought to himself, it was a good time to be leaving Vienna, given all the danger signals over the past couple of days or so. Although he was sure that what Anne was up to, and the mission he was about to embark on, were going to be, if anything, much more dangerous.

Oh well, such was the life of one married to an Interpol agent. A former Interpol agent, Greg corrected himself. *At the very least, it will provide good material for my writing.*

☙❧

Waiting at the airport, Greg took his laptop out and just for fun, looked up *Götterdämmerung* at the Wiener Staatsoper on Google. Indeed, there were three performances scheduled, starting two weeks or so hence, all with Svetlana Kokova and Jonas Kauffman. These will no doubt be fantastic, he told himself: the fourth opera in the Ring cycle was his absolute favorite. He made a mental note of the dates, although there was very little chance that he and Anne would be back in Vienna then. Oh, well, he thought to himself, at least I saw a great *Siegfried.*

And then the question came into his mind: would Boris Polyakov be there? To see his mistress perform, to hear her sing?

Chapter 21

Anne recognized Alexandros Stavros right away as she came off the ramp and into the terminal. The broad grin on his handsome, tanned face and the twinkle in the blue eyes framed by bushy, dark eyebrows were dead giveaways.

"Wonderful to see you, Anne," her former Greek colleague said, wrapping his muscular arms around her in a bear hug. "It's been too long."

"Yes, it has, Alexandros. But I am back now, as I told you. And we have work to do. Important work."

She had said very little on the call from Vienna. It was only as she sat beside Alexandros, who drove his red Porsche 718 Boxster with the roof down the entire two and a half hours along E94 and then onto EO10, that she went into the details of the mission: that they were going to attempt to rescue a female official of the IAEA, and retrieve enough stolen nuclear material for a bomb that could devastate Athens, London, or New York.

"No problem, Anne," Alexandros said. "We try to do our best. We are in luck. My cousin's brother-in-law is from Porto Heli. I already talked to him. Yorgos will be happy to help—he says people in the village don't like strangers who live in big, walled villa on the peninsula.

They're Russian, or something. Gossip tells us they may be trafficking women and children. Disgusting. Ugh."

"Well, they may just be right on that, Alexandros. These same merchants of evil sold me to a Chinese oligarch when we were investigating them the last time, before I managed to get away…But they are also the most dangerous arms dealers, trafficking in stolen nuclear material. They just smuggled some out from one of the Russian nuclear sites, and they are planning to sell it to terrorists. We must get it back."

"Sure. But, Anne, what happened?"

Anne told her former Greek colleague all about how she and her husband had been called back to Vienna a few years back to help find a kidnapped Julia Saparova, the same IAEA official who had disappeared this time and who was a good friend of theirs, and that in the process she herself had been taken by these sex and arms merchants, who had then attempted to auction her off, finally selling her to a Chinese politician. But she and Julia had managed to get away because she had shot one of these perverts and insisted on going with the ambulance to the hospital where he was being taken.

Alexandros found the story fascinating, and at the end said, "Well, we will get these bastards. But it seems to me that maybe they are not just after the nuclear material and this Julia Saparova, but you too, Anne. It would appear they want you to come rescue Ms. Saparova again. So they can get you."

"You may have a point. I have had similar thoughts, Alexandros."

"Then we have to be extra careful."

"So, Alexandros, how do you think we should get into that compound?" Anne was ready to change the subject, and get on with the mission.

"Well, as I say we are in luck, you will be pleased to

hear, Anne. The best friend of Yorgos makes food and wine deliveries in his van from Porto Heli to the estate before sunrise each morning. Yorgos says his friend has agreed to—to smuggle us in there tomorrow in the back of his van."

Anne was not so sure that this was just luck—it seemed to be the Greek way.

"Hmm. I hope that is enough because the arms merchants are supposed to be leaving tomorrow with the IAEA official and the nuclear material."

"Well, we talk to Yorgos when we get there. He has his buddies watching the place very close ever since I get in touch with him. Nothing will happen there that we do not know, you can be sure, Anne."

೧೩೩

Anne took a liking to Yorgos right from the start. He was knowledgeable, understood immediately what needed to be done and was ready to take charge. With a figure like a wrestler, he also seemed to be very fit, someone you would not want to mess with in an altercation. He likely had the respect of most locals.

"Anne, an airplane took off from the private airstrip very early this morning, with three passengers. All male. No women went on board as far as my contact could determine."

"Excellent, Yorgos. That means Julia must still be on the premises."

"Where do you think they were going?" Alexandros was curious.

"The plane took off, and adopted an east-south-east course," Yorgos answered. Anne remarked to herself that this man's English was excellent. "Somewhere in the Middle East, I would say."

"Hmm. We'll find out, but for now, that is irrelevant Alexandros. It seems from what you say, Yorgos, that Julia was not on board, and I would think it unlikely too that they would be flying this nuclear material in that direction."

"Unless they want to blow Damascus sky high." This from Alexandros.

"Well, you may have a point," Anne conceded. "But the Russians would not want that. My hunch says no. In any case, if Damascus is the target, there is nothing we can do about it now. Yorgos, what do you have on the situation on the ground? At the villa, I mean?"

"We know there have been three women and four men staying in the main house. If three of the men plus the pilots went off in the plane today, that makes the odds better for us, but we know there are probably at least ten male guards or staff, who we should assume will be loyal to the owner. Although we do know that most of the local help might be ready to switch sides…"

"Good," Anne said. "When will your friend take us into the compound?"

"We will come for you at five a.m. sharp. Where you stay tonight?"

"We will try the Hotel Rozos," the Greek Interpol agent answered for her. "I will let you know if we don't get in there. In any case, we will be ready at five."

co&co

It was still dark when Yorgos and his friend Nikos pulled up at the front entrance of the Hotel Rozos promptly at five a.m. Anne was feeling the adrenalin pumping inside her. It was surely the combination of the excitement of the first mission she was undertaking since she left the service and the strong Greek coffee she had gulped down at the front desk. She was glad though for the Glock 19 pistol Alexandros had handed to her as they had said good night in front of the doors to their respective rooms.

"Anne and Alexandros, you climb all the way in as far as you can go," Yorgos pointed into the dark back of the van. "Right up behind those crates there. And cover yourselves with that tarpaulin."

Anne did as she was told, and Alexandros scampered in after her, throwing the heavy cloth over them, while Yorgos and Nikos got in the van up front.

"You leave it to us, we get you inside that compound no problem."

"Good. Thank you," Anne was pleased so far with how everything was going.

"Don't thank us. You're not in yet, and coming out may be the bigger problem. We will try to take our time as long as possible with the unloading, but cannot give you much more than half an hour with the van. And it is not sure that we can keep the staff from noticing you even if you do come back. But here, Alexandros," he continued, reaching something under the tarpaulin to his brother-in-law, "one of my cousins who works inside the compound gave me the keys for a boat down at the docks. It is the smaller wooden speedboat—a beautiful Van Dam mahogany one, which he says, is the pride and joy of the villa owner. That is your backup to get away. Good luck!"

With Nikos driving, the van took off through the town of Porto Heli. Anne had to hold on, as the ride was bumpy, with many twists and turns, and several times she was thrown against her former colleague.

"Just one thing," Yorgos said after a lengthy conversation with his best friend, "Nikos tells me that his sources informed him that one of the women staying at the house was taken down to the beach house late yesterday afternoon. Handcuffed. She is beautiful blonde, still in her bikini, and did not come back from the beach house to the villa."

"Oh God! I am sure that is Julia. I hope she is okay. Hmm. The fact that she is separated from the rest and in handcuffs—terrible—does not bode well. Do you know anything more, Nikos? Did they do anything to her? Is she under guard?"

"Nothing. But do you remember the location of the beach house?"

Anne did remember, as Alexandros and she had studied and memorized the layout of the compound. So she knew exactly how to get to the little hut from the dropping off point. But she did not like this development, not at all. Why would Julia be kept in the beach house overnight—and still in her bikini—while Polyakov and probably Hetzel had flown off somewhere? At least they weren't there to abuse her, but what about the other men? And the guards, they were all thugs.

Finally, the van came to a stop, and, hiding under the tarp, she heard the faint sound of a buzzer—presumably Nikos ringing it at the entrance to the villa. It seemed that an outside gate was maneuvered sideways, and Anne then heard someone address the driver. She loved the casual, joking manner in which Alexandros' brother-in-law's best friend talked to the guard at the gate—this seemed to be an older man, so probably an uncle or something, judging from the gaiety of the banter—and they were let through without so much as a cursory inspection.

The van roared along the internal dirt roads for another few minutes, and then finally pulled up. Nikos and Yorgos climbed out, and Anne heard lots of "Yassous" and "Kalimeras," accompanied by much loud chatter that seemed to be joking or teasing. Alexandros peeked out from under the tarpaulin as Nikos opened the back door of the van and started pulling out one of the crates. He signaled for them to wait, while Yorgos and the two Kalashnikov-toting men who had come out to greet them from the kitchen engaged in a deep conversation punctuated with loud laughter. After lifting out several of the boxes and putting them on the ground so as to maximally shield their exit, Nikos signaled to Alexandros to clamber out and run into the nearby bushes, then for Anne to follow. As she did so, she saw that less than ten meters away, Yorgos was lighting up morning cigarettes for the two guards, who were facing away from them as they inhaled the smoke. She did note a tiny flicker of anxiety in the face of the brother-in-law as she disappeared into the undergrowth behind Alexandros.

ℰↃℰↄ

The sun was just starting to rise above the horizon as they skirted the sleeping main house through the wooded park to approach the hut down on the beach. The entrance on the side away from the water and toward where they were hiding in the underbrush had a small portico flanked by two fake white Doric columns, and Anne immediately saw that her friend, wearing only a red bikini, was tied to one of these. Julia was barely able to stand up after a sleepless night and the exhaustion caused by her experiences. She surmised that she had been there since yesterday probably without any food or drink.

"Oh God, we must get her away," Anne whispered more to herself than to Alexandros.

"Sure, but remember, we also need to retrieve the uranium."

"She may be our best chance to find it."

And then the thought came back to Anne: *Has Ale-*

xandros been right? Is Julia the bait—so obviously teth-ered there, ripe for rescue—to capture me? No doubt, Polyakov was still extremely miffed at her and Greg for foiling the previous attempts to heist nuclear material. He had certainly lost a lot of men as a result, and no doubt each failed attempt had financial as well as reputational costs for the arms merchant. In fact, that time at the in-termission in the opera in Vienna, his brother, Boris, the Deputy Director of the FSB had so much as warned her that they would be coming after them. And the Polyakovs knew very well that the last time they had kidnapped Julia, her friends had come to rescue her, so why wouldn't they come again?

"We've got to check to see if there is anyone inside the beach house. Or on the other side," Alexandros said. "I will go around and approach it from the water. You stay here." With that, the Greek agent moved off silently through the bushes.

Anne's heart went out to Julia as she saw her stir and moan, shift her head from one shoulder to the other, ob-viously suffering from discomfort, hunger, and the cold. And then, much to her dismay, she saw the door of the hut open, and she thought she recognized one of the burly thugs who served as Polyakov's trusted guards come out and approach the tied-up girl with a lascivious grin on his face.

Anne was close enough to hear him say, "Okay, hon-ey," as she saw him reach down behind her, taking pleas-ure from pressing his body full frontally against hers. "Enough of this for now. Boss wants you to clean up, get ready to go with him. He back here in a couple of hours, and then we take you somewhere else. No more vacation for you. From now on you earn your keep again." He un-shackled the handcuffs that had been attached to a ring on the column and started leading Julia up the path toward the main house.

Anne knew it was now or never. She had to act fast if she was going to rescue Julia. Once they were back at the house, it would be much more difficult. There would be other guards and less of a chance to get away. Now, if she managed to free her friend, with any luck, they could get to Alexandros and that Van Dam speedboat.

It was going to be one on one—she certainly couldn't count on the still handcuffed Julia—although her opponent was much bigger than she, but she was nimble and would have the element of surprise. Anne pulled the Glock out from where she had stuck it in the back of her jeans, wishing she had a silencer for it, even as she moved silently to head them off as they made their way along the path up to the main villa. It would have to be one fatal bullet: no wild shootout or loud scream-ing—even one shot would attract attention. But she knew she had to risk that. There was no other way.

Anne moved farther along to hide behind a large cy-press tree just five meters from the path. The thug was pushing Julia along up the slope at the same time holding her up from keeling over. Now, now, she had a clean shot. She pulled the trigger, and with a boom that tore into the silence of the early morning, the bullet shattered the thug's skull—blood and brains spewing all over Julia, and onto the path and the surrounding vegetation.

Anne ran forward to hug her friend, clasping her hand on the mouth of the exhausted prisoner to squelch the involuntary scream just in time. "Come, we must get down to the water quickly," she whispered, knowing that the speedboat was their only chance, hoping that, hearing the shot, Alexandros was running toward it with the key in his hand, ever on the lookout for them. She hurried Julia gently back down the path, around the beach house, and—and straight into the menacing gun barrels of Kal- ashnikovs in the hands of two guards, standing beside the still twitching body of Alexandros, whose throat had been sliced with a huge bloody hunting knife discarded beside him, and whose blood was turning the sand all around a dark crimson.

Chapter 22

Drop your gun, bitch, or we both pull our triggers, and you two die," the bigger of the thugs screamed.

Anne saw that she was out-gunned and had no choice but to obey. In her heart, she was still weeping for Alexandros, for his wife and young children, and knew she would never forgive herself for bringing him in on this crazy mission. But that was the nature of the work they did at Interpol, she knew. It often ended with the ultimate sacrifice. She let the pistol fall to the ground and slowly put her hands up.

The guard in charge grabbed her by the wrist and took pleasure in twisting it as high as possible behind her back while the other thug took hold of Julia around the waist—she was nearing a breakdown, tottering unsteadily when Anne let go of her. "We go now to the main house. Boss will be here soon," he spat in Anne's ear, as he shoved her back up the path. "He will be very angry. You see."

When they got to the body of the guard lying in the middle of the track leading to the villa—head blown away, blood and brains spewed everywhere—the bigger thug asked Anne, incredulously, "You did this? You kill

my friend, Petr?" And when she did not answer, he continued, giving her a whack with his gun and a big shove
forward, making her stumble over the corpse, "Wait till
boss hears of this. You will regret it very much."

The two Kalashnikov-wielding guards led Anne and
Julia out to the terrace and secured them to the iron railing with handcuffs. "You whores stay here until boss
come and decide what to do with you." Julia collapsed on
her knees, as Anne asked, "Could you at least give us
some water, please? This poor woman has been through a
lot." The terrace was south facing, and the strong Aegean
sun was starting to shine directly at them. Soon, Anne
knew, it could get unbearably hot.

"No water. No, we give you nothing. Until boss
arrive. You bitches suffer till then."

⹁

They were there out on the terrace in the sun perhaps
for a little over forty minutes, while Anne wondered
whether Yorgos would get concerned at some point during the day that Alexandros did not get in touch with
him—the plan they had vaguely formulated was that if
they succeeded, Alexandros would drive Julia and one lot
of HEU in his Boxster to Interpol in Athens, while Anne
would accompany Yorgos in his van with the other bit of
nuclear material. This was all since they knew they had to
keep the two lots of fifty pounds well separated to prevent a possible nuclear explosion. Of course, this took it
for granted that Yorgos would be their first call after getting away. Anne now hoped that the brother-in-law
would mount some kind of a rescue when no such approach came, but she knew deep in her heart that this was
unrealistic.

Her hopes were indeed dashed when she first heard and then saw a jet coming in low over Spetsos and landing smoothly on the airstrip just behind the house. That must be Polyakov and his retinue returning from wherever, she thought, and he would no doubt be immediately briefed on what had taken place on his estate in the last few hours. Anne feared the worst, and her apprehension turned to panic as the memories of being raped by the monster in Poti flooded back.

"Well, if it isn't the lovely Anne Rossiter? What a pleasant surprise," Polyakov said with a smile as a few minutes later he pulled aside the sliding glass door to the terrace. "I see you could not stay away. How nice, you have come back for more of what I gave you in Poti. Don't worry, my dear, I will indulge you, in due course, you can be sure of that, but first, there are a few things I have to attend to." The arms merchant came right up to Anne, and with his right hand grabbed her behind, with his left, her neck under the chin, squeezing tight and lifting as he continued, "Bitch, what the fuck are you doing on my estate? Who told you this cunt is our prisoner—" A vicious kick to Julia's back. "—no doubt you are here to try and cause problems for us again." Then releasing his hold, he let his hands slide down Anne's body. "And where the hell is that wimp you have for a husband? You usually travel together, don't you? Has he run away?" Then to Igor, "Any sign of the bastard? Have we done a thorough search of the premises for other trespassing idiots?"

"We shot one guy, but that is all. We think the two were brought in with the food delivery."

"Get those fuckers."

"Already on it, boss."

Then he turned to Anne again. "So you are hoping your hubby will come and save you in time? You are one naïve bitch. Now I have you for myself again, you little cunt." He punched her in the stomach, hard, so Anne doubled over. "Anyway, we are all going on a nice little trip now, my dear, and then I will give you what you have come for." The gangster walked away with a raucous laugh, and it was only then that Anne noticed the creep Hetzel had been standing behind him, alongside a rather perturbed looking younger version of Polyakov, who could not take his eyes off Julia.

At the sliding door to the terrace, the arms merchant turned around and yelled to his men, "I want these two sluts washed and dressed up nicely. Just in case." And seeing his son's glum look, he added, "Sorry, Anton, you can't have a quickie with the lovely Julia now. You and she had your chance. It's all over." Then he addressed the guards again. "Igor, Ivan, give them both injections, so they behave on the flight. We depart in half an hour." As an afterthought, he added, "One of you go get Brother Peter out of the sack. It's time for him to stop fucking the lovely Nika, and getting on with business."

Good God! So that terrorist is here too, was the thought that jumped into Anne's mind.

ⱷⱺⱷⱺ

The guards untethered the two women from the terrace railing, and still handcuffed, took them to the Aphrodite room. "Okay, you both get in there and shower up or whatever and when you are ready, come out, and we will give you clothes to wear," Ivan commanded. "Don't even think of closing the door."

Anne and Julia went into the bathroom, and Anne let Julia take the first shower since she was still covered with the drying blood and brains of the guard she had shot. However, she desperately wanted to ask her friend some questions, so she quickly undressed behind the door, and opened the steamed over glass entrance to the spacious stall, hoping that the guards would not notice—or take issue, since no doubt, they would find the sight of two women taking a shower together titillating—and that in any case, the water would drown out the sound of their conversation.

"Julia, we need to talk. First of all, how are you? We are very worried." And she hugged her friend, relishing the warm water stroking both their bodies.

"So, so…very exhausted. Used…But glad you came." Julia's tears melded on Anne's shoulders with the water streaming from the showerhead. "I am so sorry."

"Never mind. We'll get away. It was good you called Nicholas. He is on his way to St. Pierre et Miquelon, as is Greg." She soaped her friend's neck, back, and hips. "How do you know that is where they are off to next? And probably taking us—"

"Polyakov said so over dinner."

"What else can you tell me?" Anne asked, washing her friend's thighs and calves.

"They forced me to bring out some HEU from Mayak—after Polyakov raped me. While that pervert Hetzel watched."

"Oh God, not you too. Their depravity is limitless." Again Anne hugged her friend. She, too, was close to dissolving, but her professional side forced her to focus. "And Julia, do you know where the uranium is now?"

"No. But I think the idea is to get the nuclear material to those islands. And also the stuff that Brother Peter got away with earlier. By the way, he is here, too, that terrorist creep."

"Yes, I gathered that."

"Polyakov's yacht is meeting them all there—in St. Pierre, that is—and then they plan to smuggle the uranium into the US."

"These guys are not stupid—" Anne's comment was cut short by rapping on the glass door, as a leering guard standing on the other side said, "Hurry up in there. We don't have much time. No more talking and hugging." The thug opened the door and grabbed Anne by the arm, pulling her out. "Here, dry yourself, you lesbian slut." He then reached back in and did the same to Julia, tugging both girls into the bedroom. "Igor, give me a hand. First, we'll do this one." The other guard, a syringe in the right hand, grabbed Anne with his left, while the first one tore the towel away from her and shoved her down on the bed, naked and face first. With one swift motion, Igor stuck the syringe in Anne's buttock, then slapped it hard, saying, "You're done, bitch. Now put that dress over there on, real quick." Then to the first guard as he got another injection ready, "Ready for the other slut." They manhandled a sobbing Julia to the bed and performed the same act with her. Afterward, they picked up the mess as they forced the two women to dress in front of them then led them out of the room and up the path leading to the airstrip.

Chapter 23

Handcuffed again, the two women were led by Igor and Ivan to the sleek Falcon jet sitting on the tarmac and up the foldaway stairs. Anne followed Julia out of the blazing sun and into the air-conditioned cabin. Entering, she was struck by the lavishness of the fittings as a striking-looking woman dressed in a sky blue uniform greeted them.

"Nika, where is Sofia?" Anne heard Julia, obviously disturbed, ask the lone hostess.

"You will find her in the rear of the plane, my dear," Polyakov, already sitting in one of the plush leather seats just beyond the galley, glass of champagne in hand, laptop in front of him, answered for Nika. "Back where you will be sitting. But the whore Sofia will be with us only for part of the trip. We have a special treat in store for her."

"You're goddam right—some special punishment, you mean." This from Hetzel, sitting beside him, also sipping bubbly. And then muttering to himself, he added, "Stupid cunt."

"We will feed that one to the sharks, you might say, won't we, Andreas?" And with a raucous cackle, Polyakov slapped his perverse buddy on the knee. "Or a shark, rather. That's what happens to people who disobey me or who are in any way disloyal to the cause. My dear Julia, it was just too obvious that it was that fucking bitch who helped you get a message to your Interpol friend here, so you'll see. She will now have to make herself useful by lubricating a big deal for me." He slapped Hetzel on the other knee as he added, "That's a good one, too, no? Lubricate—ha, ha, ha."

The other creep grunted a "Yeah," before Polyakov continued. "But Ivan, Igor, hurry up now and take these tarts to their seats. We are already running late." Then, as the guards hustled Anne and Julia down the aisle, "You guys, after you put them in their places, bring the two briefcases on board. And don't forget the separation."

As she was shoved along, Anne heard the big redhead sitting across from Polyakov, also with champagne glass in hand—she had recognized him immediately as the terrorist, Brother Peter—say to the arms merchant, "Sergei, I would like this one to be part of our deal. The lovely Julia, I mean." Then he, too, recognized Anne who was right behind Julia, and added, "Well, well, if it isn't the beautiful Mrs. Martens. Remember, we met in Vienna, at the Sacher, some years ago with your dick-finger of a husband, Greg? You need to include her in the transaction as well, Sergei. I have some unfinished business with her shithead of a mate, and I can think of no better way than to fuck his wife. In fact, better these two then Sofia and Nika or any of those teenagers."

The deal—that must be the deal Polyakov and this terrorist have contracted in Porto Montenegro for the second fifty pounds of highly enriched uranium, plus its delivery somewhere in the Northeast USA. Anne remembered seeing the videotaping of their conversation on Polyakov's yacht in Porto Montenegro. *And yes, the merchant of evil has agreed to the terrorist 'friar's' insist-*

ence that two trafficked women be part of the deal. So maybe now it will be Julia and me. The depravity of it all. And the briefcases, those must be the containers with the highly enriched uranium inside!

"We'll see, my friend. We'll see. You may have to pay a little extra, my friend, since these cunts are exceptional. They would fetch a great price on the market. Plus, I have some important business with these two as well. I will decide, all in its time," came the answer from the Russian. "But in any case, for Sofia, we have another deal in mind as I was saying."

As Igor and Ivan pushed Julia and Anne into seats on either side of the jet and secured their safety belts, Anne saw Julia give a look of recognition to the beautiful raven haired girl with a terrified look on her bruised face, all trussed into the very back seat. The two guards clambered back off the plane, and she heard Julia ask in a whisper, "Sofia, are you all right? What have they done to you?" It was only when she did not hear any answer that Anne looked again and saw that the poor woman had bruises and burns and her mouth was taped tightly with see-through packing tape.

It did not take long for Igor to reappear with one of the large metal cases, and as he passed Brother Peter, Anne heard the terrorist say, "Is that mine? I would like that put right over there." And he pointed at the seat across the aisle.

"Doesn't matter, my friend," Polyakov said somewhat testily. "That one goes in the back because otherwise, we won't be able to get the second case past here. You know what I mean? Ten feet of separation?"

"But—"

"Don't be a jerk. Each of the cases contains fifty pounds, and we know you have already paid for one of them. And you will pay for the other one because you want to have enough HEU for a bomb. So it makes absolutely no difference which half is closer to you right now."

"Well, okay."

⊘⊘⊘

The plane took off, and headed west-northwest, Anne determined, as she tried to think what the options ahead of her were.

Will there be any opportunity to disrupt the plans of these evil men? she asked herself. And what of her husband, and Nicholas? Were they on their way to St. Pierre et Miquelon? Would they be able to mount a rescue? Had it been a wise strategy on her part to dissuade John Demeter from calling in the troops?

At least, for now, they were alive, Julia and she. Her former colleague, Alexandros, though, was dead, and these arms merchants were about to conclude a deal with some terrorists that will put them in possession of enough nuclear material to devastate a major city. Yes, she would have to do something.

But what?

These thoughts were churning around in Anne's mind, and eventually, the early start, the stressful events of the past few hours and the drugs she had been injected with, caught up with her, and she dozed off.

⊘⊘⊘

It was as the plane started its descent that Anne slowly started to regain consciousness. The sound of Polyakov's voice penetrating the void finally brought her back to reality: "...we shouldn't be longer than a couple of hours here at Le Bourget."

"So that's where we are. Finally. Outside Paris?" Brother Peter asked, looking out the window. "Good. This is where we have arranged to meet my bro, Friar John."

"Yes. We need to refuel and take on supplies for the flight across the Atlantic. I have also arranged a meeting with the Minister of Defense for Saudi Arabia, His Royal Highness Prince ibn Mohamed Hussein. The head of foreign sales for Brassault Aviation will be here too, to try to finalize a sale of *Tempête* fighters."

"Wow, impressive company you keep."

Polyakov ignored the redhead's comments. "Andreas, I want you in the meeting with me. And Peter, I am afraid I think you had better go in the back with the girls and try to make yourself invisible when we land. In fact, I want you to take Sofia's place right at the back. We will move her up closer so His Royal Highness can see the bitch from where he will be sitting. And Igor, clean her up a bit, will you? Make her look real good…She will…ahem…lubricate this Saudi deal for us, as I said. But you, Brother Peter, you run a small risk that you might be recognized, so it's best if you are not seen until your friend comes, which we should schedule for the end of our layover." And glancing at his phone, the boss added: "Say, how about two p.m.?" And don't worry, Igor and Ivan will keep you company back there. They will also make sure all the HEU stays where it is."

Will there be no customs check, no security, nothing? Anne wondered. *Of course, this was still within Schengen. And weren't those islands, St. Pierre et Miquelon, parts of France too? So there would be at most some kind of very cursory passport and customs check there, but probably not even that—and lo and behold, the nuclear material would be right on the shores of North America.*

So Polyakov had outsmarted them all. For a cool thirty-five million dollars.

And the likely devastation of a large part of New York, Boston or Washington.

⌘

Once the plane had come to a stop in a remote corner of the tarmac, and its doors opened and staircase down, within moments a black Peugeot pulled up alongside. The Brassault executive arrived first, and it seemed to Anne that although he and Polyakov were on a first name basis—they had obviously done business together—the man the arms merchant called Alain was a bit nervous. It was clear from their conversation that it was Polyakov who was trying to force the deal to come together, and that the Frenchman was not at all convinced that the sale of the twenty fighters would go through.

"No need to worry, Alain," the Russian said. "If all else fails, we have a special enticement to make his royal highness sign on the dotted line. He will not be able to refuse. You'll see."

Before Lemaître could answer, a youngish man, thin, with handsome dark features, impeccably dressed in a well-tailored dark suit and skinny black tie, stuck his head through the open doorway.

"Ah, Your Honor," Polyakov said, addressing the newcomer. "Welcome to my humble flying office." It was only he who laughed at his joke.

"Sergei, so good to see you again," the royal visitor countered. "But let's get this over quickly. I have to go into town to see the President."

"Your Highness, I think, knows Alain Lemaître, the Head of International Sales for Brassault."

"Yes, yes, of course. Greetings, Monsieur Lemaître."

"Your Highness…"

"Monsieur Lemaître, let me get straight to the point. As I indicated in our previous correspondence, unless your price has changed, we will not be signing a deal with you today. I have come here to give you one last chance, really out of respect for my good friend, Sergei. We have better offers from the British and the Americans, directly," the prince said, giving Polyakov a look.

"Your Highness, let me interject here." Polyakov took over. "The *Tempête* is the best fighter on the market today. We all know that. Much better than anything we can offer from Russia. Or indeed the Americans. I am delighted to broker this deal between friends. The original transaction we were proposing comprised twenty planes at a deeply discounted price for the best fighters in the world. Today, we will sweeten the offer even more for you by throwing in a twenty-first item that I am sure Your Royal Highness will be absolutely delighted with. If you would just care to look behind me…"

Anne saw the prince's eyes follow Sergei's gesture, and stop suddenly when they lighted on Sofia, cleaned up and sitting in a flimsy little dress in a seat behind Polyakov. Anne could see that he was completely mesmerized by Sofia's beauty, even as Polyakov continued in a soft voice, "Of course, Your Highness, this part of the transaction will remain…shall we say?…off the books. Undocumented. You can take her with you now, straight to your plane, right after you sign the papers. Her name is Sofia, and she is—without a doubt—fantastic."

Anne cringed as the prince hesitated a moment, glanced at Sofia again, then sat back down, picked up the special Mont Blanc pen that happened to be in front of him and put his royal signature on the documents proffered by Polyakov. After initialing each page, the three men shook hands. The Russian beckoned to his thugs, who followed the prince out the doorway, tugging a very frightened-looking Sofia between them.

When they left, Polyakov smiled at his French guest. "See, Alain, it wasn't hard after all. Know your client is what it takes. But you, my friend, definitely owe me one."

"Yes, of course, Sergei." The Brassault executive was visibly elated, no doubt thinking about his bonus. "We will top up the payment for your consulting services by a million. Plus, the next time you are in Paris, you can be sure we will look after you. And thank you, I never thought this deal would happen."

☙❧

Monsieur Lemaître left, and, after making a few notes on his laptop, Polyakov turned to Brother Peter. "Okay, you can tell your colleague that we are ready for him."

The red-haired friar did a few things with his fingers on his iPhone, then putting it to his ear, said, "Hi, John. We're ready for you. Anytime."

A few minutes later, Anne saw a tall, skinny figure with long hair, dressed like a hippy in a soiled yellow Indian *kurta*, beads and sandals and all, appear at the front of the cabin.

Brother Peter greeted him. "Johnny, so good to see you. Let me introduce my friend Sergei. Sergei is Boris's brother—remember, you met Boris in Vienna. And this is Andreas Hetzel." Then turning to the others, he continued, "My colleague and friend, Johnny Apostle. Also known as Brother John. One of our stalwarts."

So this sallow looking hippy, Johnny Apostle, met with Boris Polyakov in Vienna. No wonder we came across both of them there. But what could the two have been up to? Anne wondered, overhearing the conversation in the front of the plane.

"Peace and ecology, my friends," Johnny said, making the V sign with his fingers. Straight out of the seventies, Anne thought to herself. A real throwback. But what was he doing with these religious fanatics? These crazy terrorists?

"Please sit down," Sergei pointed the newcomer to the leather seat vacated by Lemaître. "What can I offer you to drink?"

"Ya got some prune juice, man?" Brother John asked. "And, hey, yo, ya got any weed?"

"Sorry," Sergei answered rather icily. "The closest thing to prune juice we might have is Slivovitz. No dope here, we are crossing international borders."

Never mind the uranium, enough for a bomb to devastate any major city in the world. Anne could not get over the hypocrisy.

"What the fuck is that you are offering me? Shit-and-wizz? Sounds pretty disgusting, man. Yo—"

"It's plum brandy."

"Shit, man. Fucking brandy? That will knock yer socks off, I'm sure. Okay, I'll have some. I'm not wearing any socks as you see, so it doesn't matter." Johnny Apostle laughed at his own stupid joke, but no one else did.

His colleague managed a forced smile. "All right, John," Brother Peter interrupted. "So what are the instructions? Tell us."

"Well, anyway," Johnny Apostle answered, "we think the best place to land the stuff would be Cutler Harbor. A sleepy little village, with a great harbor. Deep water. Easy for your boat to get in and out of. Right up to the land." And then sniffing the shot glassful of Slivovitz Nika handed him, he continued. "Jesus fucking H Christ, this stuff smells potent. Ya, the best is that I have a good friend there, and man, he has the meanest dope. Sergei, I'm gonna getcha some if this deal goes through, you just wait and see. It's the best, man. You will just love the stuff."

"Your men will be there, ready to collect it? The highly enriched uranium, I mean."

"You can be sure of that, Sergei." This from Brother Peter, seeing that Johnny Apostle was having trouble focusing.

"And if there is any trouble? You'll be prepared?"

"We'll shoot the shit out of any motherfuckers who try to toy with us," Johnny Apostle said, even as he took a big slug of the Slivovitz. This resulted in a major bout of coughing as the aging hippy clutched his throat, after which he continued in a very gravelly voice, "Holy shit, man! What the fuck did you give me here? Turpentine?"

"Slivovitz." Sergei downed his, no problem. "A real man's drink, man. And so your men will be armed?"

"Is a frog's ass watertight? Is the pope Catholic? What the fuck do you take us for, man? We'll have your Kalashnikovs up the wazoo, maybe even some heavy artillery. We don't fuck around when it comes to a big deal like this, man." Johnny Apostle took out some cigarette papers and a zip lock bag full of marijuana.

"Fabulous. Cutler Harbor it is then," Sergei said, trying to end the conversation. "I take it from Brother Peter that you are hitching a ride with us?"

"Yeah, man. If that's okay." John started rolling a joint. "My job here is done, in Europe. You'll see on the news. Big stuff. I gotta get out of here. Sure ya don't want one?"

Anne, who had been listening to all this intently was dismayed. *What did this freak mean by that comment?* She dreaded the answer.

"Sure. We'll take you. But you need to find a seat farther back." It was quite clear that Polyakov did not like Johnny Apostle. "You can go back there, with those girls, and smoke your dope. Maybe give them some too, if you will, to loosen them up a bit. Tight-assed cunts. Anyways, we've got some work to do up front here."

Chapter 24

The flight from Halifax landed in the thickest fog imaginable. Greg had hoped to catch sight of the islands, and the town, maybe the harbor and even the yacht itself, but no such luck. *It is really good at least that modern aircraft can be landed with instruments only, without any visibility*, he nevertheless thought to himself.

He was surprised at how lax formalities at the airport were. There were a few customs and immigration officials standing around, but apart from a cursory passport check, they were not questioned at all.

"This is France, after all," was Labrecque's explanation. "And if terrorists do get in, what damage could they do here anyway?"

The taxi queue moved quickly. Even though the flight from Halifax had been full, there were enough vehicles at the stand to accommodate everyone. No Uber or Lyft here, for sure, Greg thought to himself.

In the thick fog, it seemed to Greg that the car quickly took a swing onto a major thoroughfare, probably the main road into town. Visibility must have been no more than fifteen feet at the most, but the driver sped along, unconcerned. Eventually, they came to a more built up area, and then a bit farther along on his right, Greg could make out the ghost-like shapes of boats in the harbor and deserted pretty little houses across the street on his left.

The taxi pulled up in front of a white clapboard structure right on the road, just opposite the entrance to the port. Labrecque paid the driver, and they pulled their roller bags inside, Greg preening his eyes to try to make out the lifeless shapes in the water through the thick mist.

Having missed lunch, they were ravenous, so at the reception desk Labrecque asked the rather chunky young woman whether they could still get something light to eat in the restaurant, and since the answer was yes, they agreed to just dump their bags in their rooms and meet up for a quick meal.

Coming back down after washing his hands, Greg remembered that on the flight over, he had read that during Prohibition, the islands had played a significant role as a smuggling transshipment center for illegal alcohol from France and neighboring Canada, and that, in fact, Al Capone, Bill McCoy and other notorious gangsters had visited St. Pierre numerous times. He found it ironic then, that if Polyakov had his way, this little outpost would now be the focal point for one of the most significant criminal operations ever: the smuggling of highly enriched uranium into the USA, with the intent of exploding a nuclear bomb in a major population center. Much more serious than alcohol.

We simply have to stop that from happening, Greg told himself, as he entered the restaurant.

❧❧❧

His French friend was already sitting at a window table sipping some red wine, two glasses and a carafe on the table, so he bee-lined over to join him.

"Too bad, we can't see anything in that pea soup out there," Labrecque observed, pouring Greg some of the wine. "Here, have some of the house plonk to drink your troubles away. At least it's French—the wine, I mean."

"Yeah. After we have a bite though, we better go out there and reconnoiter."

"I agree. They could get here any time."

The waitress came over. Greg ordered a *croque monsieur,* Labrecque an *omelette aux fines herbes.* After some discussion, they decided to a share a *salade verte.*

"So what do you make of this place?" Nicholas asked, sipping his wine. "The island, I mean."

"Boy, a real backwater. But a bit of France, I guess, in the New World. All that is left, really."

"Well, that's probably why our friends chose it as a staging point, you can be sure. It feels more like home to me than Vienna, though."

"I can't believe how foggy it is out there," Greg said, glancing out the window again.

"Just like in Bretagne. Good for smuggling," the Frenchman said with a smile.

Their conversation was interrupted by loud laughing and shouting from the only other occupied table across the room. Greg looked in the direction of the noise and saw four big men, all in black overalls, several tables over finishing their lunch of *steak frites* and salad, with bottles of red wine from which they were amply filling their glasses.

They were definitely speaking Russian, he determined, but he couldn't quite make out what they were saying. He studied their faces as one of the men picked his teeth with a toothpick, but he was quite certain he had never seen any of these Russian-speakers before.

"We could be lucky," he said to his companion, just as the waitress brought their order. "My hunch is that those are Polyakov's men. We need to keep an eye on them."

"Yeah. We could use their help to lead us to his yacht in this fog."

They ate quietly, exchanging just a few words about the history of the islands, trying to piece together the little they knew, but not really working at it. Then, seeing that the men ordered coffee and dessert, they too asked for espressos.

"Nicholas, I am very worried about Anne," Greg said, downing his quickly, and standing up as he put his cup down. "If you will excuse me, I would like to go and call her, see if she sent an email maybe. There was a computer in the lobby—in a little alcove just off the front desk, I noticed—I'll do it from there, so I can keep a look out if these guys bolt."

"Sure. I'll keep an eye on them in here. Just in case…"

At the computer, Greg opened up his Gmail. There was nothing from Anne. But just as he was about to close his account to try his phone, he noticed several messages of *Breaking News.* The title on the one from the Huffington Post read *Terrorist bombing in Brussels…*

"Jesus, what now?" he muttered to himself, even as he clicked on the message. Glancing through the article, he quickly read that the European Parliament Building in Brussels as well as some of the other buildings in the European Quarter, including the largest, the Berlaymont, had been targeted with explosives. It was thought that three bombs had gone off within several minutes of each other—it must have happened just over half an hour earlier, he determined, looking at the time in the upper right corner of the computer. The explosions gutted the Parliament and destroyed most of one wing of the Berlaymont, and, it was surmised, killed countless officials and innocent bystanders. Too early to know how many. Although there would have been many more casualties, had the bombings occurred a couple of hours earlier—as it was, the buildings were closed to visitors, and most of the office workers and officials had gone home for the day. Authorities were cordoning the whole area off, even as rescue teams were entering the devastated buildings. More would be learned later.

The article quoted one eyewitness report from a person who had been cycling along the *Rue de Trèves* when a powerful blast blew him off his bicycle: Fortunately, he only suffered a few minor cuts from the flying shards of glass, but through the rubble and broken glass, he could see the fires that had broken out. As he called one-one-twelve, he could already hear the sirens from the city's emergency response services.

There was no indication yet as to who might have carried out this vile act, but the Belgian and European authorities vowed to do everything to catch the perpetrators. There was a lockdown on the city of Brussels, and checkpoints had been set up on roads, waterways, at train stations and airports in the region. The article went on to say that the implications of this bombing were immense, and the terrorist act could be at the heart of an attempt to destroy Europe. Could it have been jihadists, disgusted at the latest measures mooted in the European Parliament to increase the return of refugees to Middle Eastern and North African countries? Or Brexiteer-type nuts? Other right-wing nationalist groups, intent on destroying the European Union? The Russians? There were no answers, yet. It was all guesswork at this point.

Greg glanced at his watch, unsettled by this terrible turn of events. He closed his Gmail account, signed out from the computer, and took out his cell from his pocket to call Anne.

There was no response. He saw that it was already three thirty-seven p.m., and figuring back, determined that it would be eight thirty-seven p.m. in Athens, seven thirty-seven p.m. in Vienna.

So she should be picking up. Surely the operation in Greece was over by now. Could they be on their way to Athens already? But she would answer. Unless—unless it has all gone awry and she has been captured. Or—don't go there—she has turned her cell phone off for some reason, he told himself, recovering. *I'll try again.*

Greg was breathing heavily, trying to calm himself down as he dialed Anne's number again a minute or two later when he heard the Russian voices get louder. Looking up, he saw the four men come into the lobby from the dining room. Then, as they passed by, he glanced sideways to see them depart through the hotel's main door. He watched through the window as the noisy group turned right and disappeared into the mist just as Nicholas, too, rushed out from the restaurant.

The two did not hesitate before they exited through the same door to follow the Russians. This time, Greg was grateful for the fog, but all the same, he knew that they would have to keep back just far enough so that the men would not see them if they were to turn around. The four continued their loud conversation without looking back as they walked shoulder to shoulder along *Rue du 11 Novembre,* which skirted the harbor, so it was relatively easy for Greg and Labrecque to stay out of sight. Squinting sideways several times, Greg shivered at the sight of the vessels to his left and the houses on his right: they were otherworldly silhouettes in the gray murkiness that enveloped everything.

Visibility was still no more than fifteen feet at most. Nevertheless, the two sleuths pressed on, knowing that these men would surely lead them to Polyakov's yacht.

Greg desperately wanted to tell Labrecque of the news of the Brussels bombing but knew that it would have to wait.

The Russian thugs kept going past the first several jetties, continuing to skirt the basin, until Greg was starting to wonder whether they might have realized that they were being followed and were, in fact, leading them to a spot where they would take them on and overpower them, then dump their bodies in the sea. Labrecque's silent presence reassured him though, and they continued to follow the men.

Just as Greg was starting to think that they would have to abandon the chase, they approached an area where two black SUVs were parked close to the water, and just a few paces beyond, another pier with boats on either side seemed to jut out into the harbor through the fog. Two of the men broke off, taking a loud leave from the others, and climbed into the driver's seats of the SUVs. Greg and Nicholas scrambled to hide behind another seemingly abandoned car but just managed to catch sight of the other two thugs who turned up the protruding wharf and disappeared single file into the mist.

As the SUVs turned and sped away, Greg whispered to Nicholas, "You know what? I think they have been ordered to go pick up the boss and his entourage. At the airport. So they must have arrived."

"Yeah, we had better move quickly," Greg heard Labrecque say, as what Polyakov's arrival in the islands off Newfoundland implied about Anne's mission in Greece flooded into his mind.

Things did not look good. But he had to put these thoughts out of his mind and concentrate on the operation.

❡❡❡

Greg and Nicholas waited just a couple of minutes in the chilly grayness to allow Polyakov's men to get to their boat before they dared venture along the jetty. Even so, the two proceeded very slowly, not wanting to have a bad surprise. But luck was with them: out at the farthest end, they found the target, now seemingly deserted. The men must have gone aboard and disappeared inside.

On the bow of the sleek looking yacht, Greg deciphered the name, *Rasputin.* A dead giveaway, he remarked to himself with a silent chuckle. The boat was named after the rogue Russian monk in the court of Catherine the Great who was supposedly her lover and had also given his name to the strip club Polyakov had owned and used for his sex trafficking in Vienna. He noted also that this boat was very similar to the one the arms merchant had in Porto Montenegro, and which he thought had been confiscated by the Montenegrins and then sold.

Is this one also a specially designed super high-speed Millennium One-Forty?

In fact, could the yacht from Porto Montenegro have ended up back in the arms merchant's possession? And simply renamed? Perhaps via a third-party intermediary? Or is it a sister ship? Who knows? Greg thought. *Anything seems possible for these Russian crooks.*

That this was Polyakov's boat, he was absolutely sure.

But what to do? Get on now, before Polyakov and gang arrive? Or wait to make sure that they all come?

Or go for help?

The local police would be useless, and could, for all Greg knew, be in the pockets of the merchants of evil. And there simply was no time to call in reinforcements from Canada or the USA, and any such approach might simply telegraph their intentions. Then they would never be able to rescue Julia. And—the dreaded thought came into Greg's mind—Anne, as well, if indeed everything had gone wrong in Greece.

Clearly, he and Nicholas would somehow have to get on the boat. Without being seen. And then take control of it. A tall order, with just the two of them against Polyakov and his entire retinue. But it had to be done. This would be their last chance to foil the plans of these criminals.

∽∾∽

Greg looked back along the pier and thought that the fog might be lifting, if ever so slowly. Or was it just an illusion? That made it all that much more urgent: they had to make their move fast and get on the boat. Confronting Polyakov and his gang along the wharf was not an option. They would be totally exposed and grossly outnumbered.

"We may be in luck, and there will only be a skeleton staff manning the *Rasputin* now. In fact, maybe just those two men we saw," Greg observed quietly, wanting to cheer himself up.

"Great. Let's hope you're right, Greg."

The jetty had spurs on either side, where the boats were tied up, so it was easy to go right alongside each vessel. Seeing no one on the deck of the *Rasputin*, Labrecque, pistol now in hand, led the way across the small rope walkway that took them on board. They moved quickly to the rear of the yacht, which is where from experience with Polyakov's previous Millennium 140, they knew they could gain entry below deck. Still, they saw no one, and Greg was convinced that he was right, with at least two of the four-man crew having gone to the airport in the SUVs to fetch the boss and his entourage. Labrecque whispered that they should go below, to the guest or crew quarters, since that was the least likely place that they would be detected when the absent crew-members returned with the full team and the prisoner. Or prisoners, if they also had Anne. They hid in one of the rear staff rooms downstairs, leaving the door slightly ajar, and settled in for the wait.

Chapter 25

Looking out the window, Anne could see only the grayness of the dense pea soup fog as the Falcon started its descent. She was glad the long and tedious transatlantic trip was coming to an end, although she was apprehensive about what would come next. Her one hope was that Greg and Nicholas had arrived in St. Pierre and would be able to do something to help foil the plans of these merchants of evil. And come to her and Julia's rescue. Because she was pretty certain from all the comments that either Polyakov or the terrorist—rather terrorists, as now there were two of the Sons of Jesus clan tagging along—or for that matter, all of the above, would want to have their way with them. And that once these animals had had enough of playing with them and the boss took the view that they had served their purpose, the Russian would no doubt kill them. Or, as she had overheard them discuss earlier, make them part of the deal with the terrorists. She shuddered at the thought.

Anne could see not much more as she stepped down from the plane and onto the fog bedecked *terra firma* of the tarmac, arm gripped tightly by Ivan. A few steps farther and two black SUVs emerged out of the murkiness. She and Julia were shoved into the very back as Igor put the briefcase in the space behind for baggage, then Ivan climbed in and spread out in the seats just in front of them. Johnny Apostle got in the front passenger seat. The other vehicle must have been for Polyakov, Hetzel and Brother Peter, and of course, the rest of the nuclear material, she surmised.

So there are to be no customs and immigration formalities at all? No questions asked, nothing? Is this routine for flights coming from France—no, Polyakov certainly has made some special arrangements, Anne thought, although she knew that in the end, it was all irrelevant. The vehicles did not even stop at the terminal but drove straight out of the airport grounds, and within minutes, were on what she thought must have been the major thoroughfare leading into town.

The thug in the driver's seat had the radio on the local station, Radio St. Pierre et Miquelon, playing heavy metal and rock. Anne's interest perked up when the musical offering was interrupted by a breaking news radio announcement. Her French was good enough to understand that there had been a series of explosions in the European Quarter in Brussels. The excited reporter announced that much of the building that housed the European Parliament when it met in Brussels had been destroyed, as was apparently a wing of the huge Berlaymont Building, which was the headquarters of the European Commission.

Johnny Apostle interjected an excited, "What are they saying?" but Anne hushed him up with a loud "Shh!" as she listened further. There were casualties to be sure. So far, it was not known how many, the reporter went on to say. It was deemed fortunate though that the explosions had come after hours, so the offices were partially empty, and the buildings closed to visitors. The authorities had not yet identified who the perpetrators were, but the Belgian President, the President of the European Commission, and the President of the European Parliament had gone on record, vowing to find the bombers, whoever they were, and to bring the full force of justice down on their heads. The radio announcer went on to say that they would keep their listeners up to date with the news as further developments became known.

Then, as the program returned to more heavy metal, a cowed Brother John asked again "What did he say? What's going on? Did anybody understand—"

Against her better judgment, Anne answered the hippy terrorist. "There was a bombing—a series of bombings in Brussels. The European Parliament. Much of it was destroyed, as was a wing of the Berlaymont Building—the main seat of the European Commission. There were casualties, apparently, but they don't yet know exactly how many."

"Did they say who did it? Do they suspect anyone?"

"No. But they have vowed to hunt down the perpetrators—"

"If they ever find them. We'll see," Johnny said, a little too smugly for Anne's liking.

She was frustrated and wanted to know more herself. *Could it have been a jihadist bombing? Maybe. Or the far right, one of the many such movements in Europe? Or the Russians, Vladimir Putin wanting to cause more chaos and devastation to destroy the European Union? It could be any of these, or countless other groups. Or could the man in the front passenger seat have had something to do with it?*

Anne cringed in horror at the terrible thought that had suddenly come into her mind. *The Sons of Jesus? Could they have been involved?*

⌘

It was a short ride to the port of St. Pierre and then just a brief walk along the narrow jetty through the lifting fog before they reached the boat. As she was tugged along by Igor, Anne caught a glimpse of the name on the bow, *Rasputin*—which was not the same as the name of the vessel in Porto Montenegro, she remarked, although the sleek yacht certainly looked the same. The thug forced her along the spur, and she crossed over the swinging walkway onto the yacht between Hetzel and the guard. Shoved into the opulent staterooms through the glass door at the rear, she noted that even the two rather risqué bronze statues on pedestals on either side just inside the entrance seemed to be the same as the ones she remembered from the other vessel.

Maybe, then, it was the same boat, after all, just re-named. The arms merchant must have bought it back through a third party or repurchased it somehow after it was confiscated by the Montenegrin authorities. Or more likely, just had tremendous and very corrupt contacts at the auction.

On Polyakov's orders, Igor and Ivan took the two women straight through to the main lounge area, where there was a floor to ceiling pole in the middle of the room. They found two handcuffs somewhere and tethered the girls to the post, one on either side. "You bitches stay here, until boss come," Igor instructed them.

A few minutes later, Hetzel appeared. "So this is where they brought you, my beauties. Aha, the fun will begin soon, knowing my friend Sergei, we can be sure of that."

What could the pervert mean?

"Would either of you like a stiff drink while we wait?" he continued, with a chuckle. "It will help dull the pain when it comes. Haa."

"Let's rather talk about how these two hot babes can give us pleasure, Andreas," Brother Peter said, appearing at the top of the staircase that led below.

Seeing his colleague approach, Johnny Apostle, who had been lurking over at the bar, seemingly studying all the drinks possibilities—perhaps looking for more of that slivovitz, Anne thought to herself—said, with a smile on his face, "Hey, Bro, did you see? The gig in Brussels seems to have gone well."

So these bastards did have something to do with the bombing. They must have, with a comment like that.

"Why, Johnny, what did you hear?"

"Just that. But let's see if we can turn on that TV there." He nodded in the direction of the big screen on the wall, even as he came upon a remote on the far end of the bar, and started playing around with it. "It would be great to see what actually happened."

TV5, the French news channel, came on.

The picture showed smoke billowing from a building, flames leaping from the rubble and lighting up the night sky, broken glass and twisted metal everywhere, first responders scurrying around, sirens and screaming breaking the silence. The French reporter said in an excited voice, "…we still have no handle on the casualties, but the picture speaks for itself…"

"Holy shit!" This from the hippy. "What's he saying?"

"That is quite something, John." Even Brother Peter was shocked.

Tears were streaming down Anne's cheeks as the vivid scenes of destruction and death brought home the enormity of it what had happened in Brussels. She muttered to herself, "Oh, no! God, this is worse than I thought."

"Okay, my friends. We have some business to transact here. So turn that fucking thing off, Johnny," Polyakov interrupted, coming down the spiral stairs from the navigation deck. "Before anything else, we need to get serious about our deal, Brother Peter."

"Sure, Sergei. Whatever you say," Billy Crawford agreed, signaling to Johnny Apostle to follow the instructions.

"Before I give the order to start up the engines, you guys—the Sons of Jesus—need to pay the first installment for the HEU. As we agreed, one-half of the twenty-five million is due now, with the other half and the ten million, on successful delivery within the boundaries of the continental United States. I know from my brother that you have the money now and just need to make the transfer. This boat is not moving out from here until the first payment is made."

"But of course, Sergei. I will call our bank and put you on the phone so you can give them the transfer details. Is that good?"

"Okay by me."

"Do you have a burner phone that can't be traced?"

"Sure, we've got a supply of them. Igor, will you get Brother Peter one of those throwaways?"

"Of course, boss."

Anne's eyes were still glued to the screen. She was mesmerized as the pictures continued to change, showing the utter devastation in Brussels. The Berlaymont Building, too, was burning, or at least the wing that had been reduced to rubble. There was very little chance that anybody inside would have survived, Anne thought to herself.

While Igor went to get the phone, Polyakov popped open a magnum of Bollinger Grande Année Brut 2005 Champagne and poured glasses all around, including for the ladies. "Andreas can help you take a sip here and there, my dears. We have this big transaction to celebrate with our friends here, and after all, you two are…key aspects of it. And even more so, if I agree to Brother Peter's request to include you in the price. Cheers everyone."

"I thought that was a done deal." Brother Peter feigned surprise, as Hetzel got up and tried to force first Anne and then Julia to drink. A few drops of the delicious nectar indeed went down Anne's throat, despite her efforts to refuse. The rest streamed onto her T-shirt.

"Nothing is done until you make the first payment," Polyakov retorted.

"Well, let me make the call." Brother Peter started dialing a number on the burner phone Igor had handed him.

"Hello, Stacey?" the terrorist "friar" said into the cell. "This is William Crawford. Church Street Capital. I need to have you transfer the first USD twelve and a half million we talked about, value today. Let me put Sergei Polyakov from the recipient entity on to confirm the transfer details to you."

So he uses his real name, the bastard. But the Sons of Jesus has a corporate entity—Church Street Capital—where their money is collected. And invested.

And laundered?

"Hello, Stacey? Sergei Polyakov here. Please make the transfer to the account of Hellenicarms Corporation, account number six-nine-one-seven-six-nine-one-nine at the Bank of Cyprus in Nicosia. You have the IBAN and SWIFT details, Mr. Crawford tells me, from your recent meeting. I'll hold so you can confirm that the action has been taken."

Silence, and then, "Thank you…Stacey. I will verify receipt with my account manager. If there are any problems, we will be in touch, you can be sure." Polyakov hung up, glanced over at Anne and said, "More champagne for the girls, Andreas. We want them to feel good while they are our guests." And as Hetzel went over again with the two glasses to pour some champagne down their throats and all over their attire, the Russian made another call. "Ianni, Sergei here. Polyakov. Did a transfer come through just now? Twelve and a half million dollars. Account nine-one-seven-six-nine-one-nine. Yes, I will wait." He put the phone on speaker and then down on the bar, while he sipped his bubbly. A minute or so later, a voice from the other end came on the line saying, "Yes, Mr. Polyakov. The money came through. Just now."

"Good, put it in a money market account for now. I'll give instructions on what to do with it in the next few days. Have a good day."

"Thank you. You, too. Goodbye."

The arms merchant turned off the phone, then said, "Okay, Peter. The other thing we need to do is discuss details for the transfer of the merchandise." Then to Igor, as he went over to the bar to pour himself some more champagne, "Igor, tell Captain Petrov to come down here to get his marching orders."

"Yes, boss," the thug answered as he disappeared up the spiral staircase.

"What the fuck are you gawking at?" the Russian shouted at Anne, who could not take her eyes off the screen, which now showed a video of thirteen men dressed in the dark brown attire of monks, hoods covering their faces, sitting around a table, even as the subscript streaming at the bottom translated into French what the big man in the center was saying: "This is the Voice of God. Today my brother Sons of Jesus successfully attacked the very heart of the secular, atheistic, God-denying European Union, which is led by corrupt, money-grubbing criminal bureaucrats. We will continue our war against sin and godlessness here and across the entire world, until—"

"Look at that, Peter," Anne heard Johnny Apostle say. "Wow, eh?"

Oh God, so it was the Sons of Jesus! The same terrorists, who now have enough nuclear material to devastate a large metropolis in the northeastern US.

"Johnny, turn that fucking thing off, I said." Polyakov addressed the hippy with obvious disdain. "We don't need all the distraction."

As Brother John followed his orders, the boss continued: "You were saying on the way here that the delivery should be made in Cutler Harbor. Are you absolutely sure your people there will be ready to receive the HEU?"

"Yes, of course," Brother Peter interjected. "They are already in position even as we speak."

Just then the captain appeared on the spiral staircase. Polyakov addressed him: "Mikhail, how long will it take us to get to Cutler Harbor in Maine?"

"Well, boss, I need to look at the charts to give you an exact time. But it is just under one thousand kilometers, I believe. Our top speed is seventy knots per hour, but we wouldn't want to go at that speed all the way. Plus, it could be quite choppy out in the open water, which could slow us down considerably. I would say we need to give it a full twenty-four hours, maybe more to be safe."

"That would put us at our destination at around seven p.m. tomorrow evening here time. Let's allow a bit longer and dock just after dusk. Say nine-thirty p.m. their time?"

"Very good, sir. That is certainly doable. I will give the orders to rev up the engines and cast off immediately."

"I'll be up a little later," Polyakov said, turning back to the Sons of Jesus terrorists. "Peter, you heard that. We'll need your guys near the port area, close to where we can moor at nine-thirty p.m. tomorrow."

"Sure thing. I will get on it. Apparently, you can come right up alongside the wharf, or so they tell me."

"And you know, you'll need two separate vehicles to carry the stuff."

"Of course. Johnny will take one briefcase and walk it over to the parking lot where there will be two vehicles waiting. Then I will take the other lot."

"No, my friend. Here is how it will work. Igor will take the women over for you after Johnny takes the first lot. But you, Peter, before you leave with the other half of the stuff, you will need to pay the second installment."

So the bastard does intend to hand us over to these terrorists.

"But—"

"No argument. It only takes a minute or two, as you saw. Otherwise, the deal is off."

☙❧

With the transaction logistics out of the way and the engines starting to rev up, Polyakov went over to the pole where the girls were tethered, and grabbing Anne by the chin with one hand, the buttocks with the other, said, "Now it's time you two whores amused us a bit."

"Yeah. It's about time." Hetzel echoed his friend's command.

"First, we'll have you perform," the Russian continued. "You both showed so much skill as strippers in Vienna, remember, and Julia also put on such a terrific show in Greece for some of us. But our friend, Johnny here, has not had the pleasure of seeing you ladies dance."

"Yes, Julia's act was stunning," Brother Peter interjected. "A real turn on."

"Now I want the two of you to do a show together. And it had better be good," Polyakov continued, running his hands sensually down Anne's body. He turned to Ivan and ordered, "Take those cuffs off these bitches and start the music."

"Sure thing, boss." Ivan came up to Anne to undo her handcuff first, then Julia's.

"Here, before you start, have some more champagne. That may help you get in the mood," Polyakov added, handing Anne her glass. And then, "Come on, when I say drink, you drink, you whore."

Anne took a sip then put the glass down to rub her sore wrists where the handcuffs had made a red mark. She glanced at Julia who now had a frightened look on her face. So this was going to be the start of the debauchery they had known all along they were in for.

"No, the whole fucking glass, you stupid bitch. Come on! Down the drink, both of you. This is really expensive stuff. I should be making you drink turpentine, not this exquisite bubbly." Polyakov picked Anne's glass up again and moved it to her mouth, pinching her chin hard with his other hand to pry it open, then poured the golden liquid down her throat, with much of it going down the front of her T-shirt.

Oh well, maybe it is better if I do get drunk. As the creep Hetzel said earlier, to dull the pain.

The boat was starting to move, maneuver its way out of the port as the music came on, the strains of Rimsky-Korsakov's *Scheherazade* Anne remembered Julia dancing to at the Rasputin in Vienna. Knowing there was no point in resistance and that doing a dance would at least gain them more time—although for what, under the circumstances, she had no idea—she nodded to her friend to take the lead: she would just follow and try to copy her moves.

Greg and Labrecque have obviously not made it to St. Pierre in time, Anne told herself. *So I will have to figure something out myself. But what? We must not let them smuggle that nuclear material into the USA under any circumstances.*

Somehow, I have to get my hands on a phone. Maybe that burner cell Brother Peter left on the table. Anne frantically looked around, desperately trying to find a way out, some way to defeat these criminals.

Julia started to move hesitantly, and Anne followed. Although it was more difficult for her since she was still in the jeans and the now very wet T-shirt she had donned for the operation in Greece, while Julia had on a skimpy dress she was given after being brought in from the terrace in Porto Heli. But they managed somehow, and the six-man audience gawked at them with lascivious pleasure.

When the girls were down to just their panties as *Scheherazade* became expansive, Johnny moved out on the floor and started dancing with them, coming first very close to Anne, trying to paw and grind against her. Then, when she moved away, he grabbed for Julia, pulling her into his body. Polyakov shouted at him, "Get the fuck off the dance floor, you asshole, and let them do their act. Just wait your turn." The hippy did indeed move off, back to the table where he had left his pot smoking paraphernalia.

After a few more passes by the girls, Hetzel yelled out, in a frenzy, "Okay, to the pole now, you two. And get it on, for fuck's sake. With each other."

"Now, now, Andreas, let's not get ahead of our-selves," Polyakov cautioned. "Let's proceed gently. The girls are doing a great job with their act."

"They sure are," Brother Peter chimed in, as Anne and Julia kept dancing in their panties with the T-shirt and dress in their hands, pulled across their breasts.

After a few moments, the boat seemed to be speed-ing up, and Polyakov piped up, "Okay enough. I see you guys are getting too turned on—and a bit out of hand. So I think right now we should just have Igor and Ivan take the women below and…ahem…get them ready for us, while we go upstairs and watch this amazing machine takeoff. I can tell you, frankly it is a real macho thrill, and it will certainly get you in the mood for sex with these whores." He let out a raucous laugh.

"Good idea, Sergei," Hetzel, as always, agreed with his Russian friend.

"Okay, Igor, you can turn the music off now. And take these bitches downstairs."

"Sure thing, boss."

"On second thought, put the Interpol cunt in the mas-ter. I think she came back for a second round with me," Polyakov, said, grabbing Anne and ripping the T-shirt from her hands as he pulled her into his body and ca-ressed her ass. Then trying to kiss her, he mumbled, "Didn't you, you slut? You really liked what I gave you back there in Poti, I know. We will do it again before I hand you over to my friends here, rest assured, babe."

"Ugh…" Anne said, trying to turn her face away from the beast.

"Afterward, Brother Peter, you and your friend can have both these bitches, if you still want them. Well used of course, but still good value." The Russian twisted Anne's arm behind her and fondled her breasts. "And for

now, as I said, I want this one tied up in the master for me."

Anne was trembling as the big guard grabbed her and took her toward the double doors leading into the luxurious main bedroom. Before she was shoved through, she glanced back and saw that the other thug was tugging Julia downstairs, while the three men climbed the spiral staircase to the navigation deck.

What will become of Julia and me now? Please, God, not another rape, no, no! Greg where oh, where are you? Please, please help...

Chapter 26

Below deck, with the door to the downstairs hall slightly ajar, Greg and Labrecque had heard the arms smugglers and their prisoners board the boat very soon after they settled in for their wait. Right from that moment, Greg was itching to confront them and go to his wife's rescue, but Nicholas held him back. He knew from experience that their best chance lay in biding their time and trying to pick the thugs off one by one. They heard the shouting and shoving, the music and dancing, and Greg could scarcely control himself as he had visions of Anne and Julia being made to strip for, and abused by, those vicious perverts.

He was finally relieved when the music came to an abrupt halt—he had recognized the piece, *Scheherazade* from the Revuebar Rasputin, and could visualize his wife and Julia stripping to its strains—and they heard movement come in their direction. Suddenly, there were people at the top of the stairs. Nicholas gave Greg a silent nod but held him back as the scuffling came closer and closer. Peeking through the crack of the doorjamb, Greg saw one of Polyakov's thugs tug a frightened Julia—naked, all but for her panties—into the adjacent room. He heard him shove her on the bed and smack her as she cried out then the clanking of some handcuffs.

"Those lucky bastards upstairs," Greg heard the thug mutter to himself. "Boy, would I like to—"

It was then that Nicholas gave the signal, and they moved rapidly into the next room. The guard had his back to them, and before he could react, Greg jumped on him as Labrecque quickly closed the door. Then as the thug turned around trying to shake Greg from his back, the Frenchman punched the gangster with a hard left hook to the chin that knocked him cold. Greg rushed to Julia, hugging her, and asking, "Julia! Are you all right?"

The Russian girl broke out in tears as Labrecque frisked the unconscious man's pockets, and finding the key to the handcuffs, came over to release the prisoner. "All right, Julia. You'll be fine now. See if you can find some clothes in the drawers. Then it's best if you stay down here and keep an eye on this jerk." The Frenchman went over with the handcuffs to where the guard was lying on the floor as Julia tried to pull herself together. She managed to stop sobbing and listened intently to the orders of the French Interpol agent, who continued, "We will tie this criminal up and gag him somehow. Here, we'll leave you his pistol. Just shoot the bastard if he makes a move. But I think he is out for the count."

"Are you okay?" Greg asked again, still not sure if Julia should be left alone.

"Yes, yes, I can handle this," she answered, wiping the tears away, as she pulled an oversized T-shirt out from one of the drawers. "Go, go."

"Come, Greg, let's see if we can find where Anne is."

"She was taken into the master bedroom by the other guard. Just up one floor." Julia slipped the T-shirt over her head. "The double doors going to the front," she added, looking for other clothes in the closet. "Polyakov and the others went up to the navigation deck. They wanted to see and experience the boat speeding up. But after that, they were going to come down to us…" And she started crying again.

"Thanks, Julia. That's good information." Greg hugged her before following Labrecque into the hall and up the staircase.

৩৩৩

They moved silently but rapidly up the steps, treading on the side of the risers so they would not creak. Nicholas peeked over the top, and seeing no one in the lounge, beckoned to Greg to follow. The double oak doors at the far end were only partially closed, and they could hear muffled noises from inside. This time, the Frenchman went first, and as Greg followed, closing the door quickly behind him, he saw his beautiful wife wearing only her panties, tied to a pillar on the far side of the king-size bed.

Anne had a terrified look on her face but managed to nod toward the en suite bathroom, from where emanated the sound of a man grunting and groaning. Labrecque moved rapidly in the direction Anne was indicating, threw open the door, and surprised the thug sitting on the toilet, with his pants down to his ankles.

"Stand up, you creep, and put your hands on your head," Nicholas said. "And if you so much as let out a peep, you are a dead man." The thug hesitated, but, since he was naked from waist to feet, recognized that he was at a disadvantage. Seeing him frontally all naked, Labrecque took pity on him and with a snigger, said, "Okay, you shithead, pull your bloody boxers up. But your pants stay down. And put any weapons you have on the floor and throw me the keys to the handcuffs for the woman next door. No false moves, or I will splatter your balls and pecker all over the tiles of this stink hole."

Meanwhile, Greg had gone over to hug his wife. "My love, I'm so glad you are not hurt. I am going to kill these fucking monsters." He pulled the cover off the bed and covered her. Labrecque came to the bathroom door to throw him the key for the handcuffs, even as the Frenchman kept his pistol pointing at the thug. Greg undid the shackles and handed them to Nicholas, who used them to handcuff the guard to a hot water pipe in the bathroom.

"You fucker, just so you know, if you try to rip this pipe out, you will be scalded all over. Burnt to a crisp." And to prove the point, Labrecque shoved the guard down onto the duct. The man screamed in pain. The Frenchman gave him a kick in the groin. "No more of that, or I will shoot you, asshole."

Greg embraced his wife again, then went to the closet to look for some clothes for her. Within moments, he returned with some jeans and a T-shirt that more or less fit Anne.

Labrecque said, "Anne, you stay here. Guard the prick in the bathroom. Greg and I will go upstairs after the others."

"No way, Nicholas. I am coming with you. I want to get these bastards. The guy here is well secured and will not give us any problems."

ⒺⓈⒺⓈ

They moved quietly out into the lounge, and as they approached the stairs, they could hear the muffled voices and laughter from the bridge up top.

Labrecque signaled to Anne and Greg with a whisper that they should go back in the master to hide, but be ready to knock off anybody who comes down the staircase, while he went back down below to see if there were any other crewmembers there.

"Better to minimize the odds against us," the Frenchman whispered in explanation. "Take them out one by one."

Greg took Anne's hand and led her back into the master, leaving the door ajar. They sat down on the bed, first sharing a long kiss. In a whisper, Greg asked. "How are you, my dear? Really? Tell me what happened? Since you left."

Anne quickly recounted all that had befallen her since they parted ways in Vienna, and ended by telling Greg that Billy Crawford and another member of the Sons of Jesus gang were on the boat, as was Polyakov, who had agreed to sell the terrorists enough nuclear material to blow up New York or Boston. And this, after they had just devastated the heart of the European Union with three bombs in Brussels.

"Yes, I saw that news headline. But wow, I didn't know it was them. Hmm, now these jerks are active in Europe too! Not good."

"Yes. They are really dangerous. We must not let them get into the US with the stuff. Even if it means sinking this boat."

Through the crack in the door, they saw Labrecque, wide grin on his face, appear just then at the top of the stairs from below deck, Julia following, pistol in hand.

"That shithead is still out. I guess I coldcocked him really hard," he whispered as he ducked into the room. "Never mind. But we also got another bugger, who must have been sleeping in one of the other rooms, and woken by the noise, was just coming to check. Fortunately, he was still very groggy, so there was no resistance. He, too, is out for the count down below."

"Good job," Greg said, as they all heard some movement up top. Julia quickly tucked herself back inside the double doors.

Just as well, because one of the guards came down the stairs, walked across the lounge and proceeded to take out five mugs from the cupboard under the counter and fill them from the pot in the coffee machine. As he walked over to get a tray from a stack at the end of the bar closest to where they were hiding, Labrecque was upon him before the thug could so much as even blink. It was only when the Frenchman had the man on the ground that Greg realized that he had garroted him with a thin piece of wire.

"One less bastard to deal with," Labrecque whispered, as he pulled the dead man into the master bedroom with as little noise as possible. "But we must be very alert because if this guy does not go back up there soon with the coffees, they will get suspicious."

Indeed, not even fifteen minutes had gone by, before another one of Polyakov's men came out on the landing up top and not seeing his buddy down on the main floor, clambered down the steps, even as he looked around the lounge. With a, "Hmm," he went over to the staircase leading below deck and yelled, "Pavel! Pavel, are you down there?"

When there was no answer, the man started down the stairs, with Labrecque stealing after him.

A few minutes and some muffled sounds later, the Frenchman reappeared, saying smugly, "One more gone."

Then back in the master, in a whisper, he addressed the three friends, "Okay, I am going up to the bridge now. With hot coffees on a tray. You Greg, Anne, follow close behind. Julia, you bring up the rear."

Labrecque poured out the by now lukewarm liquid from the cups, and replaced it with piping hot coffee, then picked up the tray with the five mugs, his gun hidden but cocked underneath, and stealthily proceeded up the stairs. He kicked the door open and threw the tray with the coffees in a very surprised Hetzel's face, simultaneously opening fire and downing the captain at the helm. Greg, entering right behind him, took aim at a man he recognized as Billy Crawford, who was lunging for a pistol on the dashboard. The terrorist went down screaming with a bullet in his shoulder.

Anne came onto the bridge next and, seeing Polyakov reach inside his breast pocket for a gun, shot in his direction. Her aim, though, was spoiled by Hetzel, who was crawling toward her on the floor and just managed to grab her right leg. Polyakov succeeded in getting a shot off, and Anne went down with a cry and a thud. In turn, the Russian was felled by a wildly shooting Julia, who came through the entrance right behind Anne. Recovering from the recoil, Julia saw that Hetzel had managed to get by her and was already scurrying down the stairs, so she moved back onto the landing and felled him with a well-aimed shot. To her shock, his entire head just disintegrated from one moment to the next, spewing blood and brains all over the lounge below. The remainder of the now headless corpse stayed standing for a moment, then toppled down to the lounge below. Greg saw a skinny, hippy type without a weapon, try to open the door to the outside to escape, and went to grab him just in time. It was when he twisted him around and shoved him down onto the navigation deck that he recognized the man as Johnny Apostle, the weirdo who disrupted his presentation in Vienna and caused such a stir.

So he was involved with these criminals too!

With three guns pointing at him, and no weapon at hand, the wounded arms merchant, still lying on the floor, yelled, "Don't shoot! Don't shoot! I surrender."

Brother Peter just whimpered a silent "I do too," as he lay propped against the wall.

Greg, surveying the scene, noticed that Anne was not moving, still lying on the floor, a pool of blood starting to collect under her torso. "Oh, Anne!" He rushed over to her, and kneeling down, cradled her head in his arms. "Oh, Anne! Stay with us, my love. Don't leave me." Then in desperation, he yelled, "Please help! Anyone…"

"Greg." Anne's voice was very faint, and he leaned right down, putting his ear to her lips, the better to hear. "I love you—I—"

Anne exhaled one more time, and then nothing.

Nicholas, who had in the meantime managed to slow the vessel down to a crawl, and was now guarding the Russian, Brother Peter and the hippy—for which he now enlisted a trembling Julia—went over to where Greg was inconsolably trying to resuscitate his wife. He reached down and picked up one of Anne's limp arms, and felt for a pulse. Then he bent down, all the way to her lips, and looking very grim, put his hand on Greg's shoulder, saying, "I am really sorry, Greg. But I think it is—it is too late. She is gone. No pulse. No response. There is nothing anyone can do."

Greg buried his face in his hands, sobbing as he slumped over onto his wife's lifeless body. "These gangsters will not prevail, my dear. I vow to you. We will get them."

Chapter 27

Labrecque took control, and Greg was glad for this. He was too distraught at his wife's death. He watched as the Interpol agent took in the entire scene, visibly comforted that apart from poor Anne, neither Greg nor Julia nor he had sustained any major injuries. The Frenchman quickly assessed the situation at the navigation deck and seeing that the captain was dead, he pulled him over to the side, out of the way, even as he asked Julia to find something with which to secure at least two of the other three criminals.

She looked in the closets on the rear wall of the bridge on either side of the door leading to the deck below and found some rope at the bottom of one. Labrecque used this to tie first Polyakov and then Johnny Apostle to a bar that ran across the top of each closet.

Checking that these were solid and could not be easily ripped out, he muttered more to himself than the others, "That will have to do for now. This fake friar is losing too much blood to be any danger," he continued as he nudged Brother Peter—who was lying in the corner—with his foot. Once that was done, he asked Julia to see if she could find a first aid kit, so they could stem the blood loss from Billy Crawford and Polyakov since he wanted to make sure that they would be fit enough eventually to face up to their crimes and go to trial.

"There is one on the top shelf in the closet over on that side," the arms merchant piped up, nodding with his head in the direction of the storage space where Labrecque had just finished securing the hippy terrorist, knowing he would be one of the beneficiaries. Julia took it out and administered first to Brother Peter and then—somewhat reluctantly and somewhat cursorily—to the Russian.

Meanwhile, Labrecque went over to the navigation deck, and after quickly figuring out the controls, started the engine up again. Seeing that the sea was—at least for the time being—relatively calm, he gradually ratcheted the speed up to forty kilometers per hour.

"I think they were generally heading in a southerly direction," he mused. "Probably the idea was to come ashore somewhere in Maine. Hey, Polyakov, if you tell us where, maybe we can offer some leniency."

"Fuck you," was the answer that came back from the Russian.

Julia, who was over comforting a still distraught Greg, perked up. "Never mind, Nicholas. I overheard these criminals say earlier that the handover was supposed to be at a place called…I believe, Cutler Harbor. Yes, in Maine. And Polyakov was planning it for just after darkness falls tomorrow. Nine-thirty p.m., I think. He told Brother Peter and Johnny Apostle to arrange for their colleagues to be there to receive the HEU."

So this Johnny is indeed one of the Sons of Jesus creeps. Julia had confirmed for Greg what he already suspected.

"Stupid cunt." This from the Russian again. "I'll get you."

"Ignore the beast. Do you remember anything else, Julia?"

"Brothers Peter and John were supposed to carry the two lots of nuclear material to the terrorists waiting in their vehicles on shore. Oh, yes, and Brother Peter was to call his bank to transfer the last installment on the payment just before he left the boat."

"Good to know. Thanks, Julia. Let me see if I can put Cutler Harbor into the automatic pilot here." Labrecque started fiddling with the GPS and the controls.

"Why don't we just call in the US Coast Guard?" Greg piped up, starting to pull himself together. "After all, we have these crooks in custody, and we have the nuclear material. At least, I think we do, although I haven't actually seen it." He looked up at Labrecque with a face full of pain and suffering, as he added, "We've already lost Anne—" And here he started to choke up as he added, "—we don't need any more casualties."

"I've thought of that, Greg," Labrecque said. "Believe me. I've also considered going back to St. Pierre or turning west and putting in at Halifax. But actually, I think it would be a real boon if we could catch the terrorists on the receiving end as well. And for that, we have to go through with the operation, if possible." After a brief pause, the Frenchman quietly added, "We owe it to Anne, don't you think?" And then looking first at Greg, then at Julia, "Are you up to it?"

"Of course." Greg could not argue with Labrecque's logic but found himself tearing up again. Julia just nodded as she put her arms around her friend.

"I am going to call both the US and Canadian Coast Guards in a few minutes and tell them about all this. I want them both to track our progress. I also want to get the Americans to field a team to cover the handover and catch the terrorists on the ground. We need to put an end to this once and for all, don't you think?"

"Good."

After a minute or two, while he finished setting the autopilot, the Interpol agent said, "There, we're on track now." He turned to Greg to continue. "On reflection, Greg, we may need to use some subterfuge to carry this off. You Greg, and I, will have to pretend we are these Sons of Jesus friars—I take it from what you said Julia that this hippy freak is one of them too?"

"Yes. He goes by the alias Brother John."

"So anyway, Greg, you and I will have to impersonate Brothers Peter and John as we carry the nuclear material on shore. It is the very moment when their Sons of Jesus colleagues come to fetch us and the HEU that I will have the US Coast Guard move in."

"Good! You've got it all figured out," Julia remarked in admiration.

"It will, of course, be dangerous. But that is the only way we can catch the other terrorists and hopefully bring an end to this dangerous freakish organization."

"I see what you mean."

"Greg, are you with me? Are you prepared to be one of the fake couriers?"

"Of course, Nicholas. As we said, we owe it to Anne."

☙❦❧

They heard a sudden clanking, a loud swoosh and an unearthly scream from down below. Greg rushed to the door, "I am going downstairs to check. It must have been the guard you handcuffed to the pipe, Nicholas."

"Here, take a gun. Just in case." Labrecque threw him a pistol, and he was already on the stairs. On the way down, he kicked the headless body of Hetzel out of the way, and looking around, was disgusted by the sight and smell of his blood and brains everywhere.

He pushed through the double oak doors of the master and stepped inside. Suddenly, he found himself gasping for air, as he was being strangled from behind by a pair of handcuffs. He realized he had been unprofessionally careless, shaken by Anne's death.

"Drop your gun. I will kill you if you make noise," his assailant whispered in his ear, slamming the door shut with a kick. The thug Nicholas had handcuffed to the hot water pipe must have torn it right out of the wall to free himself.

Greg had barely enough air to mutter, "Okay."

"What happened upstairs?" the guard asked. "You tell me truth."

"The captain and the beautiful woman you tied up down here—who was my wife, you bastard—are dead. Your boss and one of the terrorists are badly wounded. They and the hippy are tied up, out of commission. Of your two other friends downstairs, one is dead and the other in a coma. My Interpol friends have taken control of the boat. The US and Canadian Coast Guards know about our situation and are tracking us." Greg took a flyer on this, but he was sure that even as he was speaking, Nicholas was onto at least one of those organizations.

"Umm…"

"Your only hope, my friend, is to give yourself up. If you help us, I can make sure you will be treated well." As he said this, his assailant started to release his stranglehold, and Greg, seeing that he was making headway, switched to a softer approach, asking, "What is your name, man?"

"I am Igor. Igor Petrenko."

"Igor, I promise I will help you if you help us. I promise." Greg turned around and saw the man's scalded face, twisted in pain. So Labrecque had been right—the pipe burst just as he had predicted. "The Interpol agent will kill you if you don't."

"How can I be sure you will help me?"

Greg had an idea. First, to test the man, he could get the guard to help find the containers with the HEU.

"You have to trust me. Igor, I need to find the two briefcases with the nuclear material. Do you know where they are on the yacht?"

"I know where one is."

"All right, Igor. Here is what we will do. To show that you will cooperate, you tell me where the one is, and I will go up and tell the man from Interpol that you will help us. Meanwhile, you stay down here and look for the other one." Greg realized that he was taking a bit of a chance: the guard Nicholas had coldcocked could have come to by now, and the two thugs might know where weapons were hidden on the boat and could mount an attack against them. But Greg trusted that, coupled with the thug's fear of Labrecque, his reference to the Canadian and US Coast Guards was threat enough, and his promise of amnesty outweighed any upside of loyalty to his captured boss at this point.

"Okay. I do as you say. But you get me off. No prison and new name and hide in USA."

"I will do my very best, I promise."

Igor hesitated a few seconds then said, "Briefcase is in closet over there. The boss he keeps it here in his room."

"Thank you, Igor. I will go up and talk to my colleagues while you find the other nuclear stuff. I think it is likely to be in the room where the big redhead friend of your boss was supposed to stay." Greg said, as he went over to the closet, and lifted the heavy container out. He took the sheet Anne had shed when she got dressed and a blanket from the bed to cover his wife and the captain—he found that he simply could not function upstairs with the corpse of his beloved staring at him—saying, "For my dead wife," and then carried the bundle and the case with him out of the bedroom and up the stairs, not looking back at the Russian guard, hoping that he had not made a grave mistake in trusting him.

Chapter 28

Labrecque was on the radiophone as Greg came back up to the bridge with the sheets and the briefcase.

"Excellent, Richard," Greg heard the Frenchman say. "You will have the coast guard captain call me as soon as possible. Thank you." Nicholas hung up and addressed Greg and Julia. "That was Richard Peters, a friend of mine from the CIA who has been seconded to serve as the deputy section chief of the FBI's relevant International Terrorism Operations Section. He will have Captain Brewster, the commander of the coast guard's operations for northern New England call me back as soon as possible, and is himself flying up from Washington with some colleagues to take part in the operation. I have asked for some serious backup, and he is absolutely sure the coast guard will provide it to us. Fortunately, he took on board the gravity and the urgency of the situation."

"Good, Nicholas."

"So Greg, what happened down below?"

"Well, the man you handcuffed to the pipe broke loose—although, just as you warned him, he scalded himself badly in the face and arms in the process. He put a stranglehold on me as I entered—a bit carelessly, I admit—but I managed to convince him that he had better surrender since we had his boss tied up as well as the terrorists, and his other colleagues were out of commission. After much convincing, he finally agreed to cooperate and told me where one batch of highly enriched uranium was—here, I will put it in the corner over here. He is now below deck looking for the other one."

"Fucking traitor." This from Polyakov. "I will have his balls."

Greg knelt down beside his wife's corpse—Labrecque had moved it discreetly to the side—and with tears in his eyes, closed her eyelids, gave her one last kiss, and covered the body with the sheet. Meanwhile, Julia threw the blanket over the captain.

Just then, the radiophone bleeped. Labrecque pushed the button. "Agent Nicholas Labrecque, Interpol here. On the yacht, *Rasputin*." Then a pause as he switched on the speaker.

"Captain Brewster. US Coast Guard. Portland Station. Agent Labrecque, your friend Richard Peters from the CIA tells me you have taken control of the yacht of some Russian arms traders who were smuggling nuclear material into the USA. Job well done."

"Thank you, sir. We are on the way to Cutler Harbor, where the arms merchants had planned to land the material, delivering it to a group of terrorists known as the Sons of Jesus—"

"The Sons of Jesus? They have been on our watch list for several years now. Very good indeed."

"We have two of the terrorists on board, one badly wounded, the other in custody. They were supposed to take the material in two separate batches to terrorist vehicles waiting in the parking lot at Cutler. My intent would be for us to go through with this plan—I will carry one of the batches and my friend, Greg Martens, the other. We would need your men to be there to catch the receiving terrorists red-handed, stopping the operation in mid-delivery. That is, if you agree, Captain Brewster."

"Excellent plan. What else do you need from us?"

"I would think a force of eight or ten well-armed men with fast, unmarked vehicles, if possible, hidden nearby, but with visibility of the port and the adjacent land area. Also, a high-speed vessel, in case the terrorists try to escape by boat. And a couple of ambulances with medics to take care of the wounded. Plus, we have three dead on board, possibly four."

"We will deploy twenty men, and as well, coordinate with police up there to help with the local aspects of the operation. When do you expect landfall, Agent Labrecque?"

"We are still targeting nine-thirty p.m. tonight."

"Very good. In the meantime, we will track your progress on radar and have one of our Fast Response Cutters keep a closer eye on you and block any escape routes for the terrorists."

"We need to be careful though, Captain. These Sons of Jesus freaks are very sophisticated. We do not want them to have any reason to suspect that we have them cornered."

"Roger. I hear you. Leave that to us, Agent Labrecque."

"Thank you, Captain."

"Until tonight, then. Good luck." The captain signed off, and Labrecque put the microphone back on the hook.

"Fucking assholes." This from Polyakov, still writhing on the floor over near the closet where he was tied up.

❧❦❧

Greg heard a noise from the landing. The next moment, the thug from below appeared with the second large briefcase.

"Oh, my God!" This from Julia, seeing his burnt face.

"Igor, you fucking traitor!" Polyakov tried to wriggle forward to kick and trip his former security man. "I will kill you when this is over."

"No chance of that, my friend," Labrecque weighed in.

"I found the rest of the nuclear material. It was downstairs in the main guest room, just as you thought."

"Take it back down to the lounge, will you. We don't want it close to the batch we have up here," Greg said, quickly eyeballing the distance between the Russian guard and the HEU he had placed in the corner a few minutes earlier. It was barely ten feet. They had to be careful, more careful than this. What they didn't need right now was any kind of nuclear accident in the middle of the ocean.

"On second thought, I will take it down myself and put it in the master bedroom. I will also see what I can rustle up for us to munch on." He was getting hungry. It was now a good fourteen or fifteen hours since he and Nicholas had eaten their late lunch at the Hotel Robert, and for poor Julia—who had been a handcuffed prisoner since leaving Greece—it had probably been a lot longer, he guessed.

Chapter 29

Dusk was setting in as the GPS reading told Labrecque and Greg, who were standing side by side on the navigation deck in the cockpit, peering out at the sporadic distant lights on shore, that they were approaching their destination. The Frenchman had gradually eased up on the controls, and the *Rasputin* was quietly zooming along at a comfortable pace as it approached Cutler Harbor.

"I sure hope Brewster and your friend Peters have their men in place," Greg said. He was eager to reach land, to be back in his home country, although he was not a hundred percent sure about this reckless plan Nicholas had concocted. But so much had happened since he and Anne left Vermont just a few days ago, and so much still could in the next few minutes, he knew. Glancing over at the shrouded corpse of his wife, he came close to tears as he realized that she would no longer be with him. Things would never be the same.

"Yeah. Otherwise, we'll be walking into the hands of these terrorists, with the very goods they want right now," came Labrecque's response.

"Yeah, the HEU, you mean…"

"And we'll be handing over half of it to them for free

if what Julia said is right. Since I won't be calling on their behalf to make a payment, that's for sure." Labrecque chuckled as he said this.

"I'll go wake her. I guess it's time to get ready to execute your plan." Greg was nervous as he turned around to go down below. But the sight of Anne's remains over in the corner brought back his resolve.

"Oh, and Greg, see if in the luggage these creeps brought on board, there is anything we could wear that would help us disguise ourselves to look like them." And then as an afterthought, the Frenchman added: "I guess I'll need to be Brother Peter since I am the bigger of the two of us."

"I can always just take the Indian kurta and sandals off our friend here." Greg looked over at the tied up Johnny Apostle. "Although…ugh…I'm sure it's not all that clean. I'll need some kind of a hat too, to hide the fact that I don't have the long hippy hair."

"Sure thing. I certainly don't want to put on that asshole's bloody clothes," Nicholas said, glancing over at Brother Peter, who was by now very weak from losing blood.

Greg went down the stairs to the lounge, stopping in the master bedroom where Julia was taking a much-needed rest. He poked his head in to wake her and then made his way down to the guest quarters below deck, where he presumed the two terrorists were to be lodged.

The first room he looked in was the one where they had rescued Julia earlier. He checked on the guard Nicholas had coldcocked, and he was still out, barely breathing, and presumably, in some kind of a coma, Greg thought. Urgently in need of medical attention. Like Brother Peter upstairs, whose life was rapidly ebbing away.

He looked around the room for a suitcase and then opened the closet. Here, he was pleasantly surprised to see the brown hooded monk's attire that the Sons of Jesus terrorists had worn for their videos, hanging neatly on a hanger. Bizarre, that the creep would have this along. Reflecting a bit more though, he asked himself, *Was this what Billy Crawford had intended to wear to carry the nuclear material to his terrorist brothers? This, so they would recognize from afar that the couriers were the right ones, fellow Sons of Jesus terrorists? And not some impostors…Well, they will be in for the shock of their lives. And so much the better, because then this is what we will wear—that is, if in Johnny Apostle's room, I find a similar hooded monk's robe. Yes, especially since the cowl will take away the problem of not having long hair.*

Greg quickly took the robe off the hanger, searched in the suitcase at the bottom of the closet for a pair of sandals—and yes, they were there in a plastic shopping bag. He grabbed the bag as well then quickly moved to the neighboring room. This, at first sight, he was sure, must have been Hetzel's room—judging from the order everything was in—but he checked the nametag on the suitcase just to confirm it. Of no interest now, he decided.

In the room opposite—from the pot paraphernalia, he immediately concluded this was Johnny Apostle's—as he rummaged through a duffel bag smelling of weed and dirty socks, he found stuffed in willy-nilly at the bottom, a slightly smaller but similar friar's mantle. "Perfect," he muttered to himself, folding it over his arm. He looked further, but there were no sandals either in the closet or the room.

I'll just have to borrow the ones from Johnny Apostle upstairs.

And happy with the success of his mission, Greg quickly climbed back up the two flights to the top deck carrying his loot.

⌗⌗

Back on the bridge, Greg handed Nicholas the robe he had retrieved from Billy's closet. "Here, look what I found. And sandals, too! They should fit you."

"Gee, I never thought I'd be preparing for a life of celibacy and prayer. But that's perfect. For now, anyway," the Frenchman said with a smile, holding the rough woven wool garment up to see. "I guess we had better put them on soon and get ready."

Greg slipped the cassock over his head as he said, "Yeah, I just have to borrow Johnny's sandals." He went over to where the hippy was dozing on the floor and started pulling one of his sandals off. "God, they stink! Oh, well…"

"Fuck you, you bastard. I hope my bros shoot you dead when you walk out there in my Jesus boots." So Brother John had been taking in their conversation all along and knew that they were going to impersonate him and his fellow fake monk. "Just don't get your sicko blood all over them as you bleed to death…"

They were getting close to shore, so Nicholas, looking otherworldly in the monk's robe, started giving instructions. "Okay, Igor. When we make land, I want you to be ready to tie the boat up. Then, first Greg will go ashore with some of the nuclear material, and I will follow with the rest. We are going to trust you to keep order here with Julia, Igor. She will have a gun in her hand at all time, and if anyone—including you—tries anything she doesn't like she will shoot to kill. But I am sure that you will not want to die or else rot in a US prison for the rest of your life, so you will work with us as you agreed."

"Yes, of course," Igor said quietly, glancing over at Polyakov.

"Greg, I think it's best if you get ready downstairs now with the load of uranium from down there, and move out first. That will give me time to make sure we moor properly before I go out and follow you. I will be twenty-five meters or so behind."

Labrecque was already maneuvering the yacht into the deep water harbor, as he peered through the tinted windshield to find the obvious place to make landfall.

"Here, this is good. We will dock here." The yacht's lights lit up a perfect place to moor—a concrete wall with metal rings on it—right along the shore. "But let's not give anything away. We are being observed. Okay, Greg, time to go down to the main deck. Get ready to move out. As soon as Igor jumps on shore to tie us up, you move out."

Chapter 30

Greg's heart was beating double time as he struggled to heave the heavy metal case over the side of the moored yacht and onto the shore. He quickly leaped after it. Getting back up in the monk's cassock was a bit of a chore. He picked the briefcase up, looked around hesitantly, and then started slowly making his way toward what, as he squinted, in the darkness he made out to be a parking lot with several vehicles hiding behind some trees. He was reassured somewhat when he finally heard Labrecque thump onto land, followed by a few words of French cursing, and then his measured footsteps behind him.

Shuffling closer to the parking lot in Johnny Apostle's too big sandals, Greg realized that there were two pick-up trucks sitting there side by side. He was almost to the line of trees when suddenly he was blinded by the vehicles' reflectors—all four turned on at the same time—shining straight at him.

Shielding his eyes with his arm and moving quickly sideways out of the glaring beam, he saw a window being rolled down, with two silhouettes sitting there. He heard one of them yell through the night, "Hey, Brother Peter, is that you? Have you got the stuff?"

He put his free hand to his mouth to muffle his answer as much as possible, "No, this is Johnny—Brother John—with one half of the HEU. Brother Peter is right behind—" It was at that moment that the engines of both pickups came to life with a roar and he saw a rifle poke through the window of the one closest to him. "—me."

Greg had just managed to finish his sentence when he realized that at least one of the vehicles was moving rapidly in his direction. Briefly wondering what might have given him away, he heard several loud bangs from somewhere behind him as darkness enveloped everything. The lights of the truck, which he suddenly grasped was almost upon him, had been shot out. Greg rolled toward the protection of the trees as the pickup veered and just missed him.

Then, all of a sudden, everything was bathed in the glare of floodlights, and the noise level became deafening as machine gun fire from the roof of the boathouse riddled the two trucks. When this stopped, with his ears still ringing, Greg could hear a voice yell through a loudspeaker from the direction of the rat-tat-tat, "Come out into the open with your hands well above your heads, if you want to stay alive."

Just then, Labrecque came up to him with a military type. The two helped Greg to his feet.

"Greg, are you okay?" the Frenchman asked.

"Yes…yes, thank you. I think so." He brushed his monk's robe off, then seeing Labrecque was no longer wearing his, decided he did not need the extra garment either, so pulled it off over his head. "Let me take this off."

"Hello…Mr. Martens? Good work. Captain Brewster, US Coast Guard," the officer said, smiling, as he stuck his hand out to shake Greg's. "Actually, we would be pleased to take that smock from you. As evidence."

"Sure thing. Glad to be rid of it."

"And this must be the other half of the nuclear material. In this briefcase?" Captain Brewster asked Greg, pointing to the container Greg had left under one of the trees.

"Yes, sir. And I'd be glad to be relieved of that, too, if you don't mind."

"But make sure you keep it at least ten feet from the other batch. Preferably even farther," Nicholas added the cautionary note.

"Of course. And Mr. Martens, thank you again."

"Call me Greg, please."

"Greg, your brave action tonight will have saved many American lives. But let's all go over to the boathouse. We need to take stock of the situation. See who from among these sick Sons of Jesus terrorists we were able to take alive. And we'll need to ask you some questions, if we may."

"Has anyone gone to the yacht yet?" Greg asked. "Two of the terrorists are there, with an evil arms merchant, all being guarded just by a young woman, helped by a turncoat from among the arms merchants men. The situation there could be quite precarious…"

"You may be right, Greg." This from Nicholas. "We had better go back to the *Rasputin* as quickly as possible. And we could probably use the help of a few of your men, Captain Brewster."

The captain looked around, and yelled over at a group of coast guard soldiers, "Lieutenant Casey, take your men and go with these gentlemen to the boat. They need some backup."

⋙⋘

Just as they approached the *Rasputin*, the loud bang

of a gunshot emanated from somewhere inside the yacht. Nicholas and Greg ran the last few meters, and vaulted over the side, scurrying up to the bridge. Inside the navigation deck, Julia was in tears and shaking, close to a nervous breakdown, Greg ascertained, and Igor was just about to take a still smoldering pistol away from her when Greg and Nicholas burst in with four of Brewster's machine-gun-toting men right behind.

She collapsed into Greg's arms, as Labrecque asked, "What's going on here?" deftly interposing himself to take the gun from Julia before the Russian guard could get to it.

It was only then that they saw the gaping hole in the torso of Polyakov, with blood streaming profusely across the room from where he had ended up in front of the closet. Nicholas went over for a closer examination but came away shaking his head. "There is no life left in that bastard, that's for sure."

"Julia. Igor. What happened here?" Greg reiterated Labrecque's question, even as he stroked the girl's hair. But seeing that Julia needed a moment or two to collect herself, he backed off. "Never mind. Tell us whenever you are ready."

In the meantime, the Frenchman asked Lieutenant Casey to send for an ambulance to rush the by now almost lifeless Billy Crawford to a hospital. "Also, can you send two of your men to fan out downstairs and check everything, including the engine room. There is at least one other guard down there who may still be alive and requires urgent medical care."

"Nicholas, speaking of medical care, I am very worried about Julia," Greg said, still stroking her hair, and holding her tight. "Let's get an ambulance to take her to the hospital as well. She has been through a lot, and she is much more important and deserving than any of these criminals. She needs to be thoroughly checked out. And she must have lots of rest."

"Of course. You are right," Labrecque answered. "Lieutenant, could you please see to that as soon as possible. This woman has been a tremendous asset in this operation, but needs medical attention and care immediately."

"Yes, sir." And he was on his walkie-talkie asking for another ambulance.

"So Julia, before you go can you tell us what happened here?" Labrecque repeated the question.

Julia's face was contorted in pain as she looked up. "He—he—Polyakov—" She glanced over at the still bleeding corpse of the arms merchant with fear and loathing. "—he was threatening that if we—that is Igor and I—don't release him and help him get away—his twin brother—my other cousin, and the bastard emphasized this—the Deputy Director of the FSB, would make sure that all our relatives in Russia are rounded up, tortured and exterminated. And we would both end up ourselves like—like poor Anne over there. He called her that Interpol bitch." As she said this, Julia broke out in sobs again, while Greg—who could hardly hold himself back from tearing up at the mention of his wife—tried to console her.

It was Igor who continued. "I was standing near him, and somehow he managed to kick out at me. It was then that Ms. Saparova fired the gun."

"I—I wanted to kill the beast. For what he did to Anne. And to me. And so many others. He was the devil. We needed to be rid of him."

"A clear case of self-defense," Labrecque said. "Don't you think?"

"Yes. A clear case," Greg agreed.

Within moments, the ambulance was there, and

Greg, giving Julia one last hug, passed her over to the medics, even as he said, "I will come to the hospital right after we wrap up here, Julia. And I will stay with you until you are healed and totally back to yourself. I promise."

"So I take it, this one was the head of the arms merchants," the lieutenant asked, pointing at Polyakov as the medics helped Julia off the yacht. "Captain Brewster instructed us to bring him and whoever else was either on his team or one of the terrorists over to the boathouse. But now that he is such a mess, we will leave him here with the other dead."

"Very good. But this creep, Johnny Apostle," Labrecque said, pointing at Brother John, "is one of the Sons of Jesus terrorists, we're quite sure. You should take him with you. Under guard."

"Suck my dick, you piece of shit." This from Johnny Apostle. "You don't know nothin' man—"

"This other individual—" Ignoring the comment, Labrecque pointed at the sullen, crestfallen Igor. "—was one of Polyakov's guards. But in the end, he cooperated with us, until as, Ms. Saparova was saying, Polyakov, his boss, started threatening both of them and their families. We promised him asylum and a new identity, but, of course, I am sure we will want to question him."

"All right, sir. We'll bring them all over to the boathouse. I think the captain is expecting you, so why don't we see you there in a few minutes."

℘℘℘

Greg and Nicholas walked over to the boathouse, through the now floodlit port area. The coast guard men glanced at them respectfully as they went about their business moving the prisoners from the yacht and combing the harbor and its surroundings.

Inside the building, they were greeted by a small group of men, among whom Greg immediately recognized Captain Brewster.

"Hi, I'm Richard. Peters. And this big guy is an old friend." The tall, well-built blond man standing beside the captain introduced himself even as he embraced Nicholas. "Long time, no see, you bloody frog! What's been keeping you from getting involved in some serious business?"

"Man, what do you call this, you sissy?" came Nicholas's answer. They obviously were old friends, glad to see each other again.

"This is my colleague from the FBI, Agent Bernie Stewart."

"And this is my good friend, Greg Martens, without whom we would never have captured these creeps."

"Welcome to both of you," the FBI operative said. "And thank you for your work," he added as an afterthought.

"Okay, now let's see who we have over here," Labrecque wanted to get back to business after the lighthearted banter and moved in the direction of a group of soldiers standing in a circle, guns pointing toward the middle where sat a number of surly looking men.

"Well, we captured four of these terrorists who must have been in the two pickups," Brewster said, following him. "These three, plus one was rushed to the hospital. Don't know if that one will make it because he was shot up pretty bad. And then, of course, there are the ones being brought over from the yacht, thanks to you."

"Only one for now. The other one has also been taken to the hospital, and may not make it either. But did you get anything out of these guys?" Greg asked, looking the three prisoners over. One of them was quite stocky, with penetrating eyes and longish oily black hair. Another, slightly smaller, with glasses and an intelligent look on his face, while the third was much younger and very nervous and fidgety.

"Not yet. We'll start questioning them when the other one is here."

"That'll be Johnny Apostle or Brother John, a real hippy looking dude," Labrecque explained, "who is one of the thirteen main guys, we think. The Jesus freak and his twelve apostles. It'll be interesting to see the reactions when you put him together with this lot."

"Yeah, that's what we're hoping," the FBI man said, as Casey and his men escorted the terrorist over.

"Another one of these Sons of Jesus bastards who has been key in this operation all along—Billy Crawford, alias Brother Peter—is the one taken to the hospital," Labrecque said. "But as Greg said, he lost a lot of blood after sustaining a bad wound."

"Well, we'll get to him later," Brewster said, "but let's just see what gives here."

Lieutenant Casey pushed Brother John into the circle and ordered him to sit down, as they saw him exchange a brief look with both the stocky black haired man and the one with glasses.

"Hmm. Those two could also be Sons of Jesus apostles," Greg muttered to himself. "So we may have as many as four of them in custody now."

"That would be pretty good. I wonder if that could be a death blow to the group," the FBI agent mused.

"Don't count on it. That's only four out of twelve—no thirteen—and they have a habit of replacing their lost apostles very quickly," Greg said. "And getting on to the next thing."

"Well you can be sure, these men will be put through the wringer, and then we'll lock them away for a good long time."

Lieutenant Casey came over to the group and said, "Gentlemen, we have sent all the wounded to the Down East Community Hospital in Macchias. About half an hour away. Also Ms. Saparova."

"Good work, Lieutenant." This from Brewster.

"But, Captain, what do we do with the bodies on board the yacht? There is a young lady on the bridge with a sheet over her, as well as two men now—we think the head of the arms merchants and another one who looks like he was the captain of the boat—as well as a couple of other men down below."

"Lieutenant, the lady on the bridge was my wife," Greg said with some difficulty. "I don't know, I am still too shocked and overwhelmed. Could she be taken to a mortuary nearby and kept until I can attend to her? As you can no doubt understand, there is a lot I have to deal with right now."

"If it is all right with you, Greg," Captain Brewster interjected, "we would like to take her with us on the boat to Portland. It would be best if we could keep everything as it is for now on the yacht until forensics do their work. You can pick her remains up there, after, if that's okay."

Greg reflected a moment before saying, "Very well, Captain Brewster. That relieves me of having to attend to my wife's corpse now. When we are finished here, I would like to go and be with Julia in the hospital."

"But of course. And thank you."

"Nicholas and Greg." Peters turned to address them. "I am sure you guys are pretty knackered after all you've been through. "Why don't we put you up for the night here in a little inn, and then in the morning, Agent Stewart and I can debrief you over a fine breakfast. Then we can all go to the hospital to see if the patients have anything to say and afterward, we'll give you a ride back to civilization. How is that?"

"That sounds perfect. You're right, Richard, it's been a long and stressful couple of days," Greg acquiesced.

"Jolly good then. I'll have one of these coast guard guys call around to the inns and see where they have four rooms, one for each of us."

"Thanks, Richard. Actually, sounds fabulous," Nicholas weighed in. "I, too, am ready to hit the sack."

"Well, consider it done."

Chapter 31

Greg woke to the sun streaming in through the window overlooking the picturesque village of Cutler Harbor on the north shore of the Little River. The quaint Little River Lodge—a white New England clapboard building with an inviting front porch—was poised high on a hill with a clear view of the port area where all the action had transpired the night before, and Greg could even pick out the *Rasputin* where Nicholas had so expertly moored the yacht.

As he looked out the window at the scenery below, he had trouble fathoming the recent changes in his life: he was now a widow, Anne was dead, and he needed to take care of Julia, plus, more immediately, it was important that he made himself available to be debriefed by the authorities. There was so much information he had to pass on to them on the arms smuggling and human trafficking enterprise that they—Nicholas, Anne, Julia, and he—had managed to break up. It was overwhelming. But at least he would have a lot of material for his writing, he told himself somewhat whimsically. Of course, only once he was able to digest it all. In the meantime, though, there was so much to do.

First, though—and he was glad he remembered this

as he went into the bathroom—he needed to call Julia's mother. He had promised, and, in fact, a call was overdue. But now he had some good news to report to her. At least about her daughter, that she was safe and free.

Greg found Julia's fixed line Vienna number in his contacts and pressed the dial button on his cell.

Just as he was about to hang up, the familiar voice answered in Russian. "Hallo? Elena Saparova here."

"Gospodja Saparova, this is Greg Martens. I am happy to find that you have arrived safely in Vienna."

"Oh, I am so glad you called, Gospodin Martens. I was wondering whether you were still alive. You and your wonderful wife do live such exciting lives."

Greg paused a moment before giving the old lady the good news. "Gospodja Saparova, you will be happy. We found your daughter. She is safe and free."

"Oh, thank God Almighty! Where is she?

"In a hospital nearby. Being checked out, just in case. But she is well. No one can harm her here."

"In a hospital! Why? What is wrong?" Greg sensed the heightened anxiety in the old woman's voice.

"Julia has been through a lot. I just wanted to make sure everything is all right and insisted she be checked out."

"Gospodin Martens, thank you. But where are you? I will come see her. I want to take care of my daughter."

"We are in America. In the state of Maine, way up in the Northeast corner."

"Why? What are you doing there with Julia?"

"It is a long story, Gospodja Saparova."

"Oh, I have so many questions."

"I am sorry, Gospodja Saparova, but they will have to wait. I have to go—"

"But before you do, you must let me know when I can see her. Here in Vienna, because I cannot go to

America. And please send my love to Anne. Your beautiful wife—she has been such a good friend to my Julia."

Greg could not answer immediately. He had to pull himself together to say what he knew he had to—it was still just too difficult to talk about it. Especially over the phone.

"Gospodja Saparova—Anne—she is—dead."

"Oh, Gospodin Martens, I am so sorry. I am so, so sorry." And Greg could hear Julia's mother start to cry over on the other side of the world.

As did he, standing only in his boxers, looking out the window in a hotel room in a small inn in Cutler Harbor, Maine.

✁✁✁

The tears were still in his eyes as Greg pressed the red button to end the conversation with Elena Saparova. He knew though, that before he went back into the bathroom to take his shower, he had to steel himself to make another call: one that would be much more difficult. To Anne's parents, in Dorset.

They had just been there visiting them, in their thatched hut on the Isle of Portland, right opposite Weymouth, before going to Vienna. Anne had grown up in the little village and loved going there, hiking the coast or into the Downs, and he had quite taken to the area as well. They had even talked about spending the coming year there since Greg was looking into taking a sabbatical from his professorship at Middlebury College in Vermont, where he now had a tenured position in the English Department. It would have been a great place to write his next novel, and they had talked a lot about how wonderful the time off would be. Anne had even taken him cottage hunting, and had suggested, snuggling up to him as they looked at a very cute little hut by the water, that this was where she would like to give birth to their first baby.

Now that was all not to be.

Greg sat back on the bed and scrolled down for the Rossiters' number.

"Hello. Eight, two, one, seven, five, eight." Greg recognized the kindly woman's voice. "Heather Rossiter here." He vividly remembered Anne explaining to him, with a little laugh, that her mother's quaint way of answering the phone, stating their number, went all the way back to the war.

"Hello, Heather. Greg here." He could not disguise the nervousness in his voice.

"Why, Greg! How nice you called. Where are you and Anne? Still in Vienna?"

"No, Heather." He hesitated a moment and then blurted it out. "Heather, I have some very bad news. Anne—Anne is dead."

No sound came back from the other end.

"Heather, are you there? Are you—are you okay?" He knew he was not.

"Anne—dead, you say? My daughter—my daughter…" He heard the tears, but they sounded very far away.

"Yes, Heather." He could not stop himself from crying too. "I am so, so sorry."

"How? When?" The old woman was sobbing, now uncontrollably, he could hear.

"Yesterday. Shot by a Russian gangster."

"But—I thought—she no longer worked with Interpol. I always told her—"

"She—she—was recalled. She wanted to help find a friend." And then he added, wanting to bring Anne back into the world of the living by sheer force of willpower. "She died in my arms, saying I love you."

"Where?"

"On a boat. Off the coast of Maine. I am now in the USA. Her body is on its way to Portland. I am going there later today to make the arrangements." He had to pause to gather his strength. "Would you like me to wait so you can come?" He was glad that he had managed to get all that out, even if not in one go, but without a sob.

There was another silence on the British end.

And then: "No, Greg. You know I can't leave James here by himself, and he cannot travel. William would go, but he is somewhere in Africa on business. It would probably be a week before he got there. I don't even know how to get in touch with him."

James was Anne's father, and he could only get around the house with a walker. William was her brother who lived in London but worked for a fund that invested in African renewable energy projects. It was unrealistic that he could turn around and drop everything.

"No, go ahead and—and cremate her. That was her wish. I will just have to remember Anne, my beautiful daughter as she was." She was crying again, Greg knew.

"Yes, my gorgeous wife—" He was, too.

"And Greg, do come and see us the next time you are in Europe. We love you as a son, you know that. Stay close."

He resolved to visit them soon.

His heart filled with the ache of love for them.

But even more so for Anne.

❦

Breakfast was on the porch, and the other three were already at the table, glasses of fresh-squeezed orange juice and a thermos of coffee in front of them.

"Greg, good morning!" Nicholas greeted his friend. "How did you sleep?"

"Good morning everyone. Like a log, I can assure you. And you?"

"The same. We ordered a full English breakfast for you, Greg, thinking you were hungry after missing a few meals yesterday."

"Excellent. I can smell the bacon, and I am salivating already." Greg was grateful that Labrecque was looking after his needs.

"Coffee or tea for you, Mr. Martens?" The good-looking proprietress he remembered meeting last night at check in, now with an apron around her waist, appeared through the screen door.

"Coffee, please. Black. And strong, if possible."

The eggs and bacon, fried tomatoes, hash browns, toast and home-made blueberry jam came within moments, and the four men tucked into the food as if there were no tomorrow. Greg remarked to himself that he was the only one around the table who did not work for an intelligence agency. But this entire-nuclear-smuggling-and-terrorist episode would not have come to a positive resolution if it had not been for him.

And, of course, Anne. *Oh, Anne, I do miss you so.*

He recounted to the American agents how Anne and he had been visiting Vienna when they had received a call from Julia's mother asking for their help in finding her disappeared daughter. Who had been kidnapped previously by the same arms and sex traders, and they had managed to find her that time as well. On that occasion, too, these merchants of evil were trying to use her to steal some nuclear material from Mayak and sell it to the Sons of Jesus terrorists. This time, though, they had come very close to achieving their objectives. And that if it hadn't been for Anne's perseverance and courage, and Nicholas' clear thinking and leadership these criminals would have succeeded.

"Greg, I know you're being humble, but you mustn't underestimate your contribution," Labrecque said. "It was you who connected many of the dots, and without your bravery, we would never have caught these guys and recovered the nuclear material. At the very least, it was great teamwork."

"Well, you can be sure that we are very grateful to you both. The entire nation." This from the FBI man. "And so, so sorry that you lost your wife, Greg. My—our—sincerest condolences."

"Thank you."

"I know it may be early to divulge this, but before you both came down to breakfast, Bernie and I were saying that we want to recommend you two for a Presidential Medal of Honor. Ms. Saparova, too, of course. And your wife, Greg, posthumously," Peters said. "That'll get you back over here at least, Nicholas. And we'll have a big bash for sure to celebrate," he added.

"That sounds like fun. And thank you. We know what an honor that is," Greg said trying to sound sincere.

"Yeah, I guess when we are finished here, I will have to get to Boston, probably, and catch a flight back to Vienna. After all, the fun is over, and I have to return to work," Labrecque said with a little laugh. "What will you do, Greg?" he asked his friend.

"I will be heading over to see how Julia is doing at the Down East Community Hospital in Macchias, and then I will go to Portland to see about—Anne."

"We'll take you both to Macchias. I would like to ask Ms. Saparova a few questions, too, if she is well enough. And of course, the Sons of Jesus guys who were taken there. Then, if you are ready, we can drive you to

Portland, and we can go our separate ways from there," the CIA officer said.

"Thank you."

"And then, Greg?" Nicholas asked, worried about his friend. "What will you do after Portland?"

"I promised to look after Julia until she is totally back to herself. I guess I will figure that out, how it will work. One of the advantages of the academic life is that the summers are generally my own—I can usually shift any commitments around."

"Lucky man."

"Come on, Greg," Richard said, folding his napkin and putting it on the table. "Get your stuff together. You too, Nicholas, let's get going. I might even drive you down to Boston if you'd like, old friend. At least we'll have some quality time to reminisce about the mischief you and I got up to in our youth."

"Excellent idea."

"Thank you, Richard. I am ready. This is all I have. My suitcase is still at the hotel in St. Pierre," Greg said, standing up. "But I'll meet you downstairs in five."

"Yeah, my bag, too, is back there."

"We'll make sure your luggage gets to you guys. Don't worry. It's the least we can do."

"I'll just check us all out and then follow you," the FBI man wrapped up. "This one's on America."

Chapter 32

At the hospital, Greg went straight to Julia's room while the others tracked down the two well-guarded but wounded Sons of Jesus terrorists. Julia was glad to see Greg and reached up to kiss him, then nuzzled up against his chest. She just wanted him to hold her in silence. A little later, she perked up when he told her that he had talked to her mother, and recounted his conversation with Gospodja Saparova word for word, including that she had really wanted to come and see her.

It was early enough, he realized, so he managed to get Elena on the phone. Seeing the joy on Julia's face made him happy too, despite the big hole he felt every time he looked at her, or looked away, or did anything. No, all the time. He missed Anne, terribly. But now he had to concentrate on getting Julia back on track, and then, afterward, he would have to figure his own life out. How to go forward without Anne…

They then talked about what had happened on the *Rasputin*, and it was Julia who said, "I killed both those monsters, Greg. Hetzel and Polyakov. The two men who raped me. And it was Polyakov who raped and killed Anne and did so many other vile things. He was the devil…the worst. The devil incarnate as you say. At least I got my revenge."

"Yes, you did. Good for you."

"But—but Greg…my life is ruined—"

"Julia, it was self-defense in both cases. They had it coming."

"I—I don't care—" And she buried her face in her hands and cried. "It was everything—all those things they put me through, the bastards."

Greg put his arms around her. "Julia, you have to try and forget. Put it all behind you. You need to rest up and get better, and then I will take you back home to see your mother."

"I don't know…I don't know," she cried. "I just want to die."

Greg had not expected this expression of despair from Julia and did not know how to respond. He just held her until she stopped sobbing and fell into a light sleep. He then gently lowercd her head back onto the pillow and quietly left the room.

❧❦❧

Outside at the nurses' station, Greg asked to talk to Julia's doctor. The woman at the desk paged Dr. Menzies, and Greg sat down in the waiting room. Here, the TV was on, although the sound was muted. But as Greg looked over, he immediately started searching for the remote: the screen was showing pictures of the devastation in Brussels. He found it and turned the sound up just as the announcer was saying, "…there are seventy-nine known dead and forty or so wounded in this terrible series of explosions. A video posted on Social Media claimed that the bombings were carried out by the Sons of Jesus—a group that has, up until now, been known to be active only in the USA, but seems to have forged links to European right-wing groups." Here, they showed the clip of the Sons of Jesus making their statement. "Separately, a caller claimed that the act of terror was carried out in alliance with a fringe element of a local far-right extremist group, Vorpoost...Interpol and local intelligence agencies are looking into the possibility that the Sons of Jesus group, which is known to have strong connections to a global network of arms merchants, may have provided the firepower, even as the local entity may have been the main one placing the explosives. Authorities fear that such alliances among extremist groups have raised the prospect of terrorist activity to another level..."

"I see you are listening to more depressing news."

Greg looked over as an attractive, dark-haired woman in a white frock appeared at the entrance to the waiting room.

"Mr. Martens?"

"Yes. Hello. Dr. Menzies?"

"Please come with me. So we can talk privately."

She led him to her small office, and it was here that Greg introduced himself as Julia's friend, and told the doctor her story: what Julia—what they—had been through over the last few days. At the end, he asked Dr. Menzies about Julia's condition, and what she thought would be best for her.

"Mr. Martens, thank you for filling me in on the history. That will certainly help us make sense of her condition and develop an appropriate treatment plan. And I am truly sorry for your loss. You, too, have been through a lot and need to be careful that you look after yourself. As for Julia, she has endured severe physical and psychological trauma, including rape and torture, terrible emotional and psychological abuse. She has killed at least two men, the ones who defiled her. One of them, the one who raped her just a few days ago and threatened to do so again, you say was, in fact, her first cousin."

"Correct."

"I must admit, I have never come across depravity of this magnitude before in my life. The poor girl's understanding of herself in relation to others has been completely distorted, and her sense of self-worth has plummeted. The only way she now can see of getting away from all the confusion, the terrible pain, and suffering, is by ending her life."

"Yes, as I said, she told me so a half an hour ago."

"I don't suppose you would know—but just on the off chance—did Julia use any birth control?"

"I have no idea," Greg answered, somewhat embarrassed by the question.

"There is potentially an additional danger here then, which she may have thought of—or perhaps, as a woman, sensed already—but if so, is too terrified to talk about."

"What is that, may I ask?"

"The fear that she is pregnant. With the child of her rapist cousin. Someone she saw as the devil incarnate."

"Oh my God!" This thought had not occurred to Greg, but he could see the terrible implications of it. "If she is, couldn't she just get an abortion?"

"I would definitely not advise it in her condition. But let's cross that bridge if and when we get there. I just wanted to alert you that this is something we need to be on the lookout for. We will do some tests at the appropriate time, but not yet. She should remain in our care for the time being. It would not be advisable to move her even by ambulance to another facility. I promise I will take the best care of her possible."

"Thank you, Dr. Menzies. I trust you. I need to go to Portland to make the arrangements for my wife, and then I promise I will be back."

"Very good, Mr. Martens. We will then figure out the best way forward together. Take care of yourself."

"Thank you, Dr. Menzies." Greg said, and then added as an afterthought, "Oh, I will tell my intelligence friends out there to spare her the questions. There is no need for a prying interrogation."

"I would not have allowed it in any case, you can be sure."

"Thank you."

☙☙☙

Back out at the nurses' station, Greg asked for Billy Crawford's room. It was one floor up, in a wing guarded by soldiers armed to the teeth with machine guns, grenades, and all the necessary military paraphernalia that might be needed to thwart any attempt to free the terrorist. Captain Brewster had ensured that his prisoners would have no chance of escaping or being sprung from the hospital.

Billy was awake and alone in the room when Greg entered. The rest and the care seemed to be doing him some good. He was slowly gaining strength, coming back to the land of the living.

"Hello, Billy," Greg greeted his former co-camper turned terrorist.

"Piss on you, asshole. Get the fuck out of my room…"

"Or else what? What, Billy? The place is teeming with American military and intelligence officers to make sure you stay put and face justice. The Brother Peter charade is over, my friend. For good. You will be tried for terrorism and locked up for the rest of your life. Your parents, your siblings, your friends and lovers—if you ever had any—the whole world will know that you, Billy

Crawford connived with your fellow Sons of Jesus sickos to destroy not just this country, but with the Brussels incident, it seems now other nations as well. Murdering many innocent men, women, and children along the way—"

"What do you know, dickhead? I said get the fuck out of here."

But Greg ignored his protests. "As you are aware, Billy, you too, came very close to dying just now thanks to your own depraved actions. And, in any case, is that the legacy you want to be known for and leave behind? A really great one, don't you think?"

"Shut up, fuck nuts."

"I am not finished. As soon as you are deemed fit enough to travel, you will be taken by my friends at the FBI and CIA to a detention center, where you will be interrogated. With this administration, I am not quite sure what methods they will use, but you can be sure that you will be put under...shall we say?...a lot of pressure to divulge who your co-conspirators are and everything you know about your Sons of Jesus outfit. And then, as I said earlier, you will be tried and put away to rot for the rest of your life in some stinking prison where you know what kind of stuff goes on."

"Oh yeah, you would know, you fucking queer."

"So, Billy, let's put the hatchets away, shall we?" Greg continued, ignoring the comment. "As you well know, my best friend, Adam Kallay—yeah, you remember him, don't you, Billy?—he was corrupted to try and get you guys some nuclear material and killed in the first of these damn heist attempts. Then my beautiful wife, Anne—whom I loved very much—is dead, too, shot yesterday by that beast, Polyakov. Your business partner...or shall we say?...partner in crime. He was the worst of the worst, that devil. He trafficked everything—arms, drugs, women and children for sex, body parts, you name it. The monster viciously raped both my wife and Julia—whom I think you actually quite liked, didn't you?—as well as countless other women. But, as you saw, Julia took her revenge on the reprobate and shot him dead. He deserved to die a dog's death, Polyakov did."

"I've had enough of your—"

"There was no hope for him. But for you, Billy, maybe there is. So here is what I have to propose to you. If you agree to tell us who, and where, your fellow Sons of Jesus brothers are, I can plead extenuating circumstances for you. The authorities may even let you go free, give you a new identity and forget everything—if you play ball, and give us all the details we ask for."

"Forget it, asshole. I am not going to rat on my buddies."

"Well, that's okay, because I am quite sure that your good friend and brother, Johnny Apostle, will spill the beans on you and all the others as soon as they start interrogating him. Then you and your friends will rot in prison, and it is he who will be given amnesty. You see, Billy, I am just offering you this special deal, because we go back a long way, you and I, don't we? Back to the Piarist Oddfellows Youth camp in Kentucky. You remember. But if you're not up for it, no worries, because the next man will give us what we need, and then, Billy, you will be shit out of luck. So think on that for the next few minutes, because once I am gone from here, that's it. No more opportunities for deals. The full force of the law, the full weight of history, will come down on you. And that will be a very heavy load to carry, my friend." Greg knew he was taking a bit of a flyer with this offer of a deal, but as he saw it, this was the best way forward. He knew Nicholas would back him up, and hoped the others would too.

"So—so, no prosecution? Forget all the Brother Peter stuff?"

"That's what I'm offering—but only for the next three minutes—in return for everything. The names and whereabouts of everyone active in the Sons of Jesus clan, the relationship with the Polyakovs and other Russians, all your activities so far, plans, contacts, everything."

"That is a hell of a lot, you prick."

"Well then, goodbye, Billy. And best of luck in prison." Greg turned and started walking toward the door.

"No, wait—Greg—wait a second." Billy's pleading voice reached him just as he reached for the doorknob. "I will do it. But not here. Not in this hellhole of a hospital."

"Good choice, Billy. I'll go out and tell my friends in the intelligence community what we have agreed and make sure they're on our side. We'll come back in, and we can then decide the next steps."

"Hold on, Greg. I also want full protection while I'm in here and on the outside. If I'm going to talk, they'll be out to get me."

⌘⌘⌘

Greg went out to the hall looking for Labrecque, Peters, and Stewart. He found them in front of the next door along, talking to a couple of the doctors.

"So, you'll be pleased to hear that Brother Peter has agreed to talk, provided you give him immunity and a new identity."

"Oh, did he now?" the FBI man asked, surprised that Greg had come to an agreement with Billy Crawford.

"Great, because we could not get anything out of the other guy," Richard Peters said. "Not even an acknowledgment that he belongs to the Sons of Jesus."

"Yeah, we were also just trying to go see your lady friend, but her doctor nixed it," Stewart added. "No interrogation, no questions, until she is much better."

"That's all right. She needs the rest now. I can fill you in on everything you might want to know from her," Greg said, then added, "But you better discuss how you want to handle Brother Peter. He won't talk here, in the hospital, and he wants assurances—and full protection."

"Well, the doctor was just saying that he might be able to release him to us tomorrow," Bernie Stewart said. "I am happy to stay on and take him to Washington under guard. This is now my business in any case. And I know you guys are keen to get on the road to Portland."

"Good, but let's just go back in so I can make the link for you."

"I am going to go and say goodbye to Julia while you do that. I don't want to see that asshole Brother Peter ever again." This from Labrecque.

Greg took Peters and Stewart back into Billy Crawford's room and introduced them. Stewart took charge and said he would return in the morning with a full complement of armed guards to take Billy to Washington, where he would be debriefed, and if he told everything he knew to the FBI's satisfaction, provided with a new identity.

Greg took his leave of this now-former terrorist, ancient co-camper acquaintance of his. "Okay, Billy. It's good luck to you from here on in. I know you made the right decision this time. You will help save countless lives."

"Bye, you dickhead. I was right back in the Oddfellows Camp when I wrote 'Greg masturbates' in red chalk on the outhouse wall. I know you used to be big on it, and probably still are. Especially now, that your wife is no longer around to jack you off."

Greg was seething when he heard this comment and wanted to kill the bastard. But, instead, he just continued the banter with the terrorist, saying, "And Adam and I were right to beat the holy living daylights out of you, and stuff your head in the shithole, you pompous bastard." Then, with a little laugh, he continued, "Goodbye to you. I hope our paths never cross again."

Billy's weak laugh cheered Greg as he followed Peters out the door.

But he still just wanted to kill the asshole.

Chapter 33

The drive to Portland was a little over three hours and thirty minutes, and Greg and the two intelligence operatives took the occasion to debrief each other and compare notes.

"Well, at least we have put an end to the Polyakov arms trading operation," Nicholas summed up after he and Greg had recounted everything that had happened over the last few days. "Thanks to Julia, who killed the boss and his fawning deputy, Hetzel."

"Yeah, but Boris, the brother, and Sergei's son are still around," Greg observed. "It seems that certainly the twin is heavily implicated. And as Julia recounted, the son, too, at least in that Syrian deal. It was very much a family affair, I think."

"You're right. Many of these FSB type oligarchs just think of lining their own pockets and of those around them," Richard contributed.

"I was actually thinking just now that Boris twice threatened Anne and me already. Both times, at the opera in Vienna. And now that Julia has killed his brother and we have put a serious dent in their golden goose, he may come after us with a vengeance."

"Well, for the time being, she is in good hands in the

hospital. Certainly safe, with Stewart there, and Brewster's men all over the place. And you're with us. We'll protect you, Greg, don't worry." This from Peters.

"The FSB Deputy Director is a very dangerous man. No doubt he is supporting other terrorist groups, not just the Sons of Jesus," Labrecque said. "I am sure once he gets over his brother's demise, he will want to rebuild the arms trading network somehow. It's too good to let go of, for sure."

"Well, it would give me great comfort if he followed his twin brother to the grave," Greg commented. "Julia and I will live in constant fear until he is gone."

"Too bad US law forbids assassinations. Otherwise, I'd see what we could do," Peters added, laughing. "It would rid the world of the source of a lot of evil. And dent the capacity of the Russians to create chaos."

"Yeah, that's for sure," Labrecque agreed. "I am not sure if you are aware, but, in Vienna, Interpol has been working to put together a file on the FSB Deputy Director's activities. Including his fondness for young women. And his regular supply of girls to the leadership. But for that to have any traction, there may need to be some régime change in Russia, since they are all so intertwined there, the mafia and the *siloviki*. They are one and the same."

"Unless we can use the material to expose them all, the bastards." Greg knew that this was no more than wishful thinking at this point.

⁙

With Peters at the wheel, they got to the US Coast Guard Northern New England Sector headquarters in Portland down by the harbor where Captain Brewster's office was just before five p.m. He was glad to see them and informed Greg respectfully that his wife's body was at the nearby Irwin Funeral Home on Cottage Road, less than ten minutes away.

"I'd be glad to have my driver take you over there, Greg, when we're done here."

"Thank you. I think I've decided to stay overnight, in any case, so I'll face that in the morning. I am just too exhausted right now, and need a good night's rest."

"I'll get my secretary to book you a hotel room then, don't worry. Nicholas and Richard, if you'd like, I can brief you on the details forensics have come up with after going through the yacht with their fine-toothed comb. But Greg, you don't need to hear all that, and I am sure you have recounted everything from your side to our two friends here. So why don't you go rest up. You certainly have earned it."

"Thanks. You will be able to reach me if you need anything more from me—"

"Before you go, the one thing I wanted to tell you, Greg, is that we will be confiscating the yacht from the dead Russian or whoever legally owns it. And after re-pairing the slight damage from the gunshots and spilled blood, we will look into selling it at auction. It should fetch a pretty price, that's for sure. The intention is that the proceeds from this sale will go to you and Ms. Saparova for the pain, heartache, and damages you have suf-fered at the hands of these criminals. And as a reward for bringing them to justice. The entire nation owes you the sincerest thanks."

"Wow! Thank you. I certainly didn't expect that."

"Why don't you come by in the morning so we can line up the appropriate arrangements?"

"Thank you, Captain Brewster," Greg paused before continuing. "I also wanted to raise something with both you and Richard, Captain. Julia Saparova, the young

Russian physicist who was kidnapped and abused by Sergei Polyakov and is now in the hospital in Macchias, is a Russian citizen who was working at the International Atomic Energy Agency in Vienna. So theoretically, she is here in the USA illegally, although clearly, it was an emergency and we were all involved in bringing her onto American soil. As you know, Julia has been key in this entire operation. However, she may need a longer period to convalesce and get back to being herself. I am wondering if you could help get the requisite papers to normalize her situation."

"Why, of course, Greg. Consider it done. As you know, the coast guard is part of Homeland Security, and I should be able to get that in place very quickly. Also, that reminds me, we found her passport with some other material on the boat that might be of interest to you or her. We can deal with that tomorrow, too."

Greg said goodbye to Nicholas and Richard, and the Frenchman expressed his regret that he wouldn't be at Anne's funeral. But he really needed to get back to Vienna, to brief the IAEA and then the officials at Mayak about everything that had transpired. He said he would be in touch with Greg in a few days.

"Of course, Nicholas, I understand, and don't worry about it. Would you also please make sure they know at the IAEA Julia won't be back to work…indefinitely?" Greg paused before continuing, "In fact, maybe never."

"Sure thing. And take care of yourself, old man."

"You too," and the two friends who had been brought together by Anne in the first heist attempt hugged. They had been through a lot together.

⌘

Finally checked into in his room at the hotel—Brewster's secretary had reserved for him at the Hilton Garden Inn in downtown Portland—Greg decided just to stay in and have a quiet night. He certainly didn't want to go out, and he could use the rest, he told himself. He flipped on the TV as he unwrapped the two pairs of underwear, socks, and shirts that he had bought himself on the way over with the money Brewster's secretary had advanced him. He found the BBC news, which he liked to watch occasionally to get a somewhat more international offering than what was normally shown on the US channels.

As he started to undress to jump in the shower, his attention was piqued by the third item, which was about the Brussels bombings. They showed a clip from a closed circuit camera that had somehow survived the devastation in the European Quarter.

The newscaster was saying, "…authorities now believe that this man—seen here depositing a lunch bag in one of the recycling bins in the main hallway of the Berlaymont Building—is one of those responsible for the act of terrorism. Instead of the remains of the man's lunch, explosives experts have determined that the bag contained a small time bomb, which was detonated remotely several hours later. Police are now looking for the man, and an international alert has been put out for him. Anyone with any potentially relevant information should call three, two, two, five, six, eight, six, two, one, or the one-one-twelve European emergency number."

As the short video clip was played several times over, Greg looked again and again and was astounded to find himself recognizing the hippy long hair and sallow face of Johnny Apostle. "Holy Shit!" he muttered to himself. "That guy sure gets around."

Greg got on the phone to Labrecque, who he knew was likely to be still in the car with his CIA friend on the way to Boston. "Nicholas, guess who I just saw on BBC news!"

"Greg, this must be important."

"You can bet your ass it is, my friend. The hippy Johnny Apostle was caught on one of the closed-circuit cameras in the European Quarter of Brussels dropping a bag into a recycling bin just outside the Berlaymont Building two days ago. Just a few hours before the bombing. You need to tell Richard."

"Are you sure? Time wise, I guess it is possible."

"Absolutely positive. You should watch it for yourself."

"Great. We are holding that fucker, so at least one of these Sons of Jesus assholes will do major time.

"Yeah. It's about time."

⁊⁊⁊

Greg took a taxi to the funeral home, enjoying the ride through a pleasant residential part of South Portland on a sunny morning.

Although he dreaded what would come next. In the waiting room—which he remarked to himself was decorated in the same manner as undertaker's waiting rooms everywhere—he did not have to wait long before a youngish man dressed solemnly in dark suit, white shirt and muted tie appeared, greeted Greg and introduced himself.

"Mr. Martens? George Irwin. I am so sorry for your loss, but indeed very honored to meet you. Captain Brewster briefed us on your wife. I will take care of all the arrangements for Mrs. Martens myself, you can be sure. She was a true heroine."

"Thank you."

"Why don't we go into my office so we can talk

more comfortably? Can I get you a coffee? Or some water?"

Greg sat on the leather couch in the spacious office with the Funeral Director opposite him, notepad and pen in hand. The coffees came within moments, just as Irwin was asking, "So, Mr. Martens, how can we be of assistance? What would you like us to do for your wife?"

"Well, I am sure Captain Brewster told you that I am not from Portland. What I would like—and I am sure Anne would have wanted—is a simple cremation, and then the ashes in an urn or a box that I can take with me back to Vermont, which is where we live."

"That is all, Mr. Martens?" The Funeral Director seemed disappointed that there would only be so very little business for him in this woman's funeral.

"Yes, Mr. Irwin, and I would like to get it done as soon as possible. I believe the body is already here, and as I will be the only one at the cremation, there is really no need to fix her up a lot—"

"But sir—"

"I think Anne would have liked a simple casket since we are doing a cremation, and equally, I would like an unpretentious container for the ashes if that is possible."

"Of course. In that case, let's look through our catalog." George Irwin came over beside Greg and flipped open a brochure that had been sitting on the coffee table.

Greg chose both quickly, and asked, "Could it be done this afternoon?"

"Well, let me just talk to my secretary." The Funeral Director left the office, and Greg reflected on the rituals associated with death and burial—neither he, nor Anne, had ever been very keen on them. Once you are dead, they had always said, you are gone, and no ceremony, no expensive casket will bring you back or make it easier for you. And he, as the only survivor in attendance would find more comfort in simplicity, he told himself.

"Yes, Mr. Martens, we can do it at three p.m. today, if that works for you. We'll need you to sign these authorization forms in any case. Of course, it will be a little tight to get everything ready, but we try to do everything we can to satisfy our patrons."

"Thank you, Mr. Irwin. Now could I see Anne before I go?"

"Certainly, Mr. Martens. Let me take you to where she is resting."

The Funeral Director led Greg down a hall, off which there were several closed doors presumably leading to private mourning rooms. Toward the back of the building, he opened one of these and ushered Greg inside with a, "Please, Mr. Martens."

As Greg entered and approached the table on which Anne's body was placed, covered with a shroud, Irwin asked, "Would you like me to leave you alone, Mr. Martens?"

Greg answered, "Yes, please," without looking around.

When the door closed, he gingerly lifted the sheet, and seeing his wife's lifeless but still beautiful face, he muttered to himself, "Oh, Anne! My darling, darling Anne, how I miss you." He buried his hands in his face, and, after a little cry of a few minutes, looked at the love of his life again then reached down to kiss her, saying, "Goodbye, my love. Thank you for our wonderful time together. May you rest in peace."

Greg then slowly pulled the shroud back over her and left the room. On the way out he poked his head in the little office of Irwin's secretary to say that he would be back at three.

❧❧

"Hello, Mr. Martens." The secretary looked up when he entered the coast guard office. "Captain Brewster has been asking for you. Go right in, please."

"Greg, I am so glad you're here." Brewster got up from behind his desk and came over toward Greg. "We were trying to reach you at the hotel, but you had checked out. Something has happened."

"Bad?"

"Well…not good." The captain put his hand on Greg's shoulder before continuing. "The terrorist Brother Peter was found dead this morning in the hospital in Macchias."

"Holy shit! How did that happen?" And then, hesitating a moment, Greg added, "Foul play, do you think?"

"Not sure. He was well guarded and had someone monitoring him at all hours. Stewart tells me he and my men are interrogating everyone in the place. "

"But Billy was getting better when I left him."

"It may just be a sudden relapse. Natural death from the wounds. But we'll do an autopsy, you can be sure."

"Julia? Is she…"

"She is okay. Still the same."

"Brother Peter and I had made a deal that he would tell all. Stewart was going to take him under guard to Washington today."

"Yes, I know."

"So, to me, it looks like it was those bastards who got to Billy. Somehow, they must have found out. I am quite certain."

"Or maybe they were just taking precautions. But let's not jump to conclusions."

"Well, if I may suggest, you had better make sure they cannot get to Johnny Apostle. He's the only chance to get information on these Sons of Jesus terrorists. And I guess that other guy in the hospital, if he makes it—"

"Johnny is already under lock and key in a very secure place. And the other terrorist is still in intensive care. We don't have much hope for him."

"I want to get up there as soon as possible to be with Julia. I'll go right after Anne's cremation this afternoon. Which is at three."

"Very good, Greg. I will have Lieutenant Casey go with you in one of our cars."

"Thank you."

"Greg—regarding Julia—as I mentioned yesterday, we found her passport on the yacht. If you can leave it with us for another couple of days, I will have them stamp a visa in there to legalize her stay," Captain Brewster said. "And I will just courier it to you, wherever you are."

"Thank you. That would be perfect. I will let you know where."

"And as for the proceeds from the sale of the yacht—which, unfortunately, may take several months to materialize—if you give me an account or accounts for yourself and Ms. Saparova, we can have the money transferred in there once the boat is sold."

"Thank you again, Captain. I think I will certainly want most of my portion to go into the two foundations we established with Anne. One to help the women and children abused by these merchants of evil—the Polyakov gang were also trafficking human beings, as I think you know—the other to help the people whose lives were destroyed by Russia's nuclear program right after the war and through to the present. But let me firm that up with you when all this is behind us. And I will need to talk to Julia about her share."

"That is very noble of you, Greg. In any case, there is no hurry, and you can think on it in the meantime."

"Thank you."

"Goodbye now, Greg. Casey will pick you up at the funeral home at three thirty."

"Goodbye, Captain."

❧❧❧

George Irwin led Greg back to the renovated barn behind the main funeral home where the crematorium was located.

He entered the small, sparse room and saw the unassuming coffin he had chosen sitting on the conveyor belt that would take it into the furnace, which was behind a metal flue at the end. Since he had not asked for any religious ceremony, only he and the Funeral Director were present.

After a few moments, Irwin asked, "Mr. Martens, are you ready?"

"Yes, sir."

"Anne Martens, née Rossiter, may you rest in peace." The Director pressed a button behind him on the wall, and Greg steeled himself as the guillotine-like door at the end started to lift and the coffin moved slowly along the conveyor belt.

"Goodbye, Anne, my love," Greg whispered to himself as he fought the tears.

And then the coffin entered the inferno, and Anne's body was consumed by the flames.

"Thank you." Greg turned around, wanting to leave the crematorium as fast as possible. "When can I have Anne's ashes?"

"Tomorrow, say around this time."

"I am sorry, I can't stay till then. Could you post them to me? My address in Vermont."

"Of course."

"Thank you. That's it then." Greg said, seeing Lieutenant Casey standing by a car parked right out front. "My ride is here."

He was worried about Julia.

Chapter 34

"Greg, I want to leave this hospital," Julia said for the second time. "Please take me away from here," she implored with those beautiful big blue eyes, a plea Greg had difficulty resisting.

Plus, he really could not argue with her. He didn't think she knew that Brother Peter had died in another wing of the hospital, although he couldn't be sure. Nurses did talk after all. More importantly, she certainly wouldn't know of his suspicion that somehow it was likely to be the Sons of Jesus or someone connected with them who had committed the crime. Or worse still, that it might even have been someone allied to Polyakov—and this thought had been gnawing at him all the way during the drive up from Portland—his brother Boris Polyakov, the Deputy Director of the FSB, for example. Or maybe some operative sent by Boris. Either entity could easily have found out by now that Julia was here too, and she could very well be the next victim after the terrorist who had agreed to tell all.

And the more he thought about it, the more he was convinced that Julia—and he too—could be in severe danger if Boris—who had threatened Anne and him in Vienna—was behind the Brother Peter death. Even more so, if somehow the FSB Deputy Director found out that it was Julia who had killed his brother. He and his agency had a very long arm.

His fear for Julia had become acute in spite of the added men that Lieutenant Casey had ordered stand guard outside her door night and day. It was not safe for her here. Her instinct to leave was totally justified.

"Okay, Julia. I agree. But Dr. Menzies has gone for the day, so the earliest we could get you discharged is tomorrow morning. I'll see if I can convince her first thing." Greg did not want Julia to know that he, too, was afraid. "In the meantime, I will get them to put a cot in here, so we can be together. I will watch over you during the night, Julia. But right now I do have to pop upstairs for a moment to talk to that FBI man guarding the Sons of Jesus terrorist. I'll make sure there is security outside your door the whole time."

"Thank you, Greg. You are such a good friend," Julia said, sobbing. "You give me a reason to want to stay alive."

∽∾∽

On the way up to the next floor, Greg had a sudden, crazy thought, *And what if Julia is, in fact, pregnant with the dead reprobate Sergei Polyakov's child, and what if Boris, his brother, who has no children, finds out? Julia's progeny would be the only grandchild of Beria in the Polyakov line, and Boris might do anything to get his hands on it. Kidnap pregnant Julia again, for example. A horrible thought. Just as well I am getting her away from here, where there seems to be a murderous mole. Before the time comes to do those pregnancy tests Dr. Menzies had mentioned, and this added danger might become a reality.*

⚜

"So, Bernie what can you tell me about what happened with Billy Crawford? As you know, he and I had a deal." They were in the upstairs waiting room with the TV off.

"Of course, and I had geared everyone in Washington up for our arrival. For some tough questioning of the bastard. But then, this morning, as you know the nurse in charge found him dead."

"What do they say? How did he die?"

"Well, it seems now they have confirmed that in his drip bag they found that the dose of morphine for the pain—Infumorph Five Hundred—had been increased. Doubled or tripled up. He died of sudden cardiac arrest."

"But wasn't he being monitored twenty-four hours? And didn't we have guards outside his door at all times?"

"Yes and yes, Greg." Stewart seemed a little impatient. "We have questioned all the people involved. No one admits to anything. It could have been a simple fuck-up. Shit like that happens in hospitals all the time, Greg."

"The coincidence, though, is too incredible." Greg was not prepared to give up the notion that Billy Crawford had been assassinated.

"Anyway, if it was murder, it would have been someone with some knowledge of medicine. Or at least drugs, and how to administer them through a drip bag. That's why we're questioning all the hospital staff."

"Could Billy have done it himself?"

"You mean suicide? Rather difficult, I would say."

"Just a thought."

"Greg, leave this to us." Again, Greg sensed impatience in Stewart's tone. "We will get to the bottom of it, you can be sure. It is my job."

"Okay, Bernie. But don't give up. I am positive Billy

Crawford was murdered. Most likely by the Sons of Jesus. To prevent him from talking. But there is another possibility too, that you should look at. The FSB."

"You're crazy. Here in northern Maine?"

"Well, as you know, Polyakov's twin brother is the Deputy Director of that agency. He personally threatened my wife and me in Vienna. Not once, but twice. They have a very long reach. And, similarly, they may have wanted to erase any embarrassing links."

"What are you getting at, Greg?"

"Well, Billy may have known of Boris's involvement in this heist attempt, as well as in other acts of terrorism. Like Brussels for example. And then all the sex trafficking, too. He got to be very close to Sergei, after all, and probably to Boris as well. Exposing any involvement by Boris could have caused a major international scandal, and would not have been to the deputy director's liking. Worth looking into, don't you think, Bernie? On the off-chance, if nothing else…"

"Hmm. I don't know. Rather far-fetched, in fact. But okay, I'll look into it."

"You will need to talk to Labrecque. He might be able to help. For example, he knows that Sergei Polyakov and Billy had been spending a lot of time together, also possibly with Boris. He told me Interpol has been building a file on the FSB Deputy Director. There were obviously links there. Just check into it."

"Okay, Greg. Thanks for the lead."

"Good luck, Bernie. I'll see you around."

"Goodbye, Greg."

∽∾∾

"Good night, Julia," Greg kissed his beautiful roommate for the night on the forehead. "Get some rest, because tomorrow we have a long drive to Vermont. It'll be just a little over seven hours in the car. I hope you're okay with that."

"Yes, thank you, Greg. I am game for anything to get away. You too, rest up. And Greg, you cannot imagine how happy I am that you are here. I—I—" Julia stuttered before finishing what she wanted to say. "—you are my only real friend."

But with lights out, Greg just lay there without sleeping. So much had happened over the last few days, and so much was happening in his life now, and so fast. He needed to think.

He simply could not let go of what he now was convinced had been Billy Crawford's murder. And the more he thought about it, the more he was sure that his hunch, that it was the Russians—most likely an FSB operative working for Boris Polyakov—who had assassinated the terrorist, was indeed correct. There were both professional and personal reasons for Boris to have ordered the killing to prevent Brother Peter from spilling the beans. Billy would have known about Boris' facilitation of the nuclear heist, as well as the extent of the payments to the Polyakov brothers, and probably had even met with him when Sergei and Peter had fled to Chechnya from Montenegro after that last sordid sex trafficking affair. Plus, Boris might have wanted to show the Sons of Jesus clan that he did not brook failure by any of his partners. Especially, a fiasco that resulted in his brother's death.

The conversation he had with Bernie Stewart kept gnawing at Greg, and he couldn't really figure out why. The FBI agent had seemed so passive about the notion that Billy had been assassinated, especially when he kept trying to talk about who might have done it. So dismissive that it might have been a murder.

Greg turned over in his cot, and it was then that the

idea hit him. *What if the mole—the assassin, is, in fact, none other than Bernie Stewart? A double agent, working in the Counterterrorism Division of the FBI. Certainly, an ideal place for a mole, if the Russians wanted to promote chaos in the USA. But surely FBI agents are well checked out, and unlikely to turn.*

What kept coming back at Greg was the matter-of-fact way in which Stewart had told him that Billy's morphine dose had been doubled up, and that it was probably just a fuck-up of the kind that happened periodically in hospitals. And, that in any case, they were questioning all the medical staff who might have known how to carry something like that out with relative ease.

Was that just a ploy to focus attention away from himself?

What should Greg do? He needed to be extra vigilant tonight, in case Stewart—or whoever—came after Julia since she was still somewhat incapacitated and in one of the rooms in the hospital building. But even once they left for Vermont, there was clearly some urgency, he realized, to expose the double agent, since the other Sons of Jesus terrorist was still in the hospital and could be the next target. Moreover, they could very easily come after them. Or send someone else working with the mole, whoever he or she was.

But what could he do? In the morning, talk to Richard Peters, Stewart's CIA colleague? Hmm…Although the agencies were often rivals, the two operatives worked closely together and seemed to be friends. Peters may find it hard to believe that his buddy was a mole. So maybe not the best idea.

Calling Labrecque would be good, although the Frenchman wouldn't be able to do very much right away. But it would make sense—he could certainly confide in his friend. For one, Nicholas could confirm whether Bernie followed up on his suggestion that they talk. If he did, then Stewart was more likely to be making a genuine effort to find the assassin. But more importantly, Greg felt that the Frenchman was really the best person he could talk to about his suspicion of the FBI operative. And, in fact—the thought just struck him—he could ask Labrecque to research Bernie Stewart's credentials, discreetly of course, especially to see whether he had any background in medicine. If so, that would be a sure sign that this latest hunch was right. But that would all take time.

He needed someone who could act immediately. And fast. Captain Brewster. Yes, the captain, he would call him first thing in the morning. Brewster would listen to him for sure. The captain had his men still in the hospital, and they could take Stewart aside and question him.

Greg looked over at Julia and saw that she was sound asleep. His thoughts turned to tomorrow, and how he would try to whisk her away. First, he would have to get a car. Casey or one of his men could take him to a rental car company. Things would work out, he told himself.

He must have dozed off, because he woke some time later to the sense of a presence in the room, by Julia's bed. He looked over without raising himself and saw what he thought was Bernie's silhouette.

His hunch had been right.

With a single leap, Greg was upon the intruder. With one hand, he twisted an arm back. With the other, he grabbed the hand holding a syringe and plunged it downward and into the assailant's thigh. The noise woke Julia up, and at the sight of the scuffle on the floor beside her bed, she screamed, even as the man started to twitch and gasp for air. The night nurse burst in, flipped the light on, and seeing the suffocating man on the floor, rushed over to him, while Greg tried to comfort Julia who was sobbing and shaking. Within another couple of minutes,

Lieutenant Casey and two of his men burst through the door—they must have been alerted by another nurse at the desk—machine guns pointing uselessly at the nurse and the dead man on the floor and at Greg and Julia on the bed.

The guns were lowered as Casey asked, "What's going on in here?" And then surprised at the sight of the victim, he continued, "Is that Agent Stewart on the floor?"

"Yes, Lieutenant. I saw this man come into the room—and I thought I recognized Stewart. He was holding that needle, and was clearly going to administer it to Julia when I grabbed his hand and plunged it down and into his flesh."

"It seems that it contained some potent toxin," the nurse said, standing up to get some rubber gloves. "This man is dead. Sudden cardiac arrest." She put the gloves on and knelt back down beside the corpse to pull out the syringe.

"Let us take it as evidence. We'll send it to our lab," Lieutenant Casey answered. "Just to be sure. Although fingerprints don't really matter—they would only be his and yours at this point."

"Just to let you know, I was starting to suspect that Agent Stewart could be a mole," Greg confided to Casey, "and that he was the one who killed Billy Crawford."

"Well, Mr. Martens, it seems that your intuition may have been right. But is Ms. Saparova all right? And you?"

"Yes, thank you. But could you leave some of your men outside until daybreak?" Greg said, glancing over at the clock. "I wouldn't mind getting a little sleep. Then, in the morning, if one of your men could take me to a car rental agency, we have a long drive ahead of us tomorrow. And I just can't be sure that there's no one else here who might want to do away with Julia and me."

"Of course."

But much as Greg tried to force himself to fall asleep, dawn came all too soon, with the bustling activity of the hospital.

ↄﬆↄ

"Well, Mr. Martens, if you and Julia are absolutely sure that this is what you want, I can't stand in your way. Especially after what happened last night. Horrible. But thanks to your quick thinking and heroic act, you are both safe. Unharmed, that is."

Greg had caught Dr. Menzies on her way into her office.

"We're just lucky."

"In any case, I'll need both of you to sign these standard documents absolving us of any liability, before I can issue the discharge papers."

"Of course, and thank you, Dr. Menzies. Let me assure you that this is not in any way related to the care you and your staff have been giving Julia. That has been great."

"Mr. Martens, will you be taking Ms. Saparova to another facility? I can certainly recommend ones close to where you live. Vermont, you told me?"

"I think Julia will be more comfortable staying with me until I can take her home to her mother." He was not so sure about the long term, but things had a tendency to work themselves out one way or the other.

"Well, Mr. Martens, you must be fully aware of what you are getting into. She is still this far away from a nervous breakdown—" And the good doctor put her hand out, thumb and forefinger almost touching, to illustrate the closeness. "—and she could have a relapse at any moment. If you are looking after her, you will especially

need to pay attention to any physical or emotional changes."

"Of course."

"We discussed briefly the prospect of her being pregnant with the progeny of her rapist cousin—that is of particular concern to me. We were hoping to do some pregnancy tests without necessarily telling her, but it is too early yet. For one, it would make it that much more difficult to treat the trauma, because PTSB drugs can have very adverse effects on a pregnancy. So there is very little we can do until we know for sure, to prevent the nightmares and the horrible reliving of the trauma that she will experience periodically. But, assuming she is pregnant, she is emotionally too unstable still, either to accept pregnancy and bring it to term, or else to handle an abortion. Either way, the suicidal, self-destructive tendencies could be reignited. So, Mr. Martens, that is all to say that you are taking on a lot…especially after what you have been through yourself. But since you insist, I cannot stand in your way."

"Thank you, Dr. Menzies."

"All that remains is for you to sign the papers and for me to wish you good luck."

Greg read the document releasing the hospital and its staff of any legal liability in the case of Julia Saparova, and signed on the dotted line. He followed Dr. Menzies into Julia's room.

"So Julia, you're sure this is what you want?"

"Yes. I do not want to stay here any longer. Especial-ly after last night. But thank you."

"Well, I'll need to do a few cursory tests before I can let you go, and you need to sign this document too."

"While you do that, Dr. Menzies, I will go and see if I can rent a car somewhere."

"Sure thing, Mr. Martens. I need maybe half an hour for the discharge tests."

∽∽∽

Lieutenant Casey's driver took Greg over to Alamo in East Macchias, and within half an hour he was back up in Julia's room. She was smiling, radiant to be leaving the hospital. They both said goodbye to Dr. Menzies, who had a rather anxious look on her face as she gave the Russian girl she had become rather fond of a big hug.

"Take care of yourself, honey. And good luck to both of you."

Chapter 35

Greg was glad to be going home to Vermont, although it was not without trepidation. Things would be different without Anne, in the lovely New England Victorian house they had bought just last year, outside Middlebury, with a picturesque view of the Green Mountains on one side and Lake Champlain on the other.

They would be very different.

And he was not sure how it would work out with Julia. How long it would take her to recover enough to be able to travel back home and be on her own again. Given what Dr. Menzies had said, there was no question, though, that she could not be left alone or undertake an arduous international flight back to Vienna, or Ozersk, for some time. The stresses would be too great.

And even more so, if she was pregnant…

In any case, Greg was glad he would have Julia's company for a while. She would help him recover. Get over Anne.

If he ever could…

All he knew was that he would have to give it time.

⁌⁍

The drive across Maine was beautiful, and Greg had a lot of time to think as he drove since Julia slept most of the way.

One thought that kept coming back was that—if indeed Boris Polyakov was coming after Julia and in fact, him—maybe going back home to Middlebury was not such a good idea. The FSB Deputy Director knew that Anne and he had been living in the Green Mountain State, so it wouldn't be difficult for him to find out the exact address. Although they had moved from Burlington, a little over a year ago when he got his professorship at Middlebury.

Boris could easily send someone to kill Julia there. And him. The FSB must have other agents in the US capable of doing just that. Not just Bernie.

But then where could Julia and he hole up?

On the other hand, Greg was really aching to get home. He still only had the clothes that he wore when he left St. Pierre, supplemented by the two pairs of essentials he had bought in Portland. But he was still wearing the same pants, the same sweater, the same shoes…And there was so much he had to do back home…paperwork, outside work, housework. Plus, he was aching to get back to his writing. He hadn't had much time for it since they had left for Vienna, and there was so much new material.

There was Julia, too. He was keen on showing her their place, and the more he thought about it, it would be there, on their hillside property with nature all around that he would have the best chance to help her recover and get back to being herself. And deal with a pregnancy, if…

Moreover, he was convinced that Julia would be a welcome distraction to help him start his own new life without Anne. Her good friend: someone he could talk to about her, and help him put her to rest.

He would just have to be on his guard all the time,

never let Julia out of his sight. And he would need to fortify the place somewhat. Yes, as soon as he got home, he would figure out some ways to make the place more secure.

❧❦❧

So when Julia finally woke up and stretched her arms above her head, asking, "Greg, where are you taking me?" he was confident in answering, "Home. To where I lived with Anne, near Middlebury, a small college town in Vermont. It is a beautiful spot, you will see. I am sure you will love it as much as we do."

Did, in Anne's case, he almost added, but there was no need to dwell on it. He had to move forward.

❧❦❧

"This is amazing." Julia sat up as Greg drove along the long curving driveway to the house after the almost eight-hour drive from Macchias. They had stopped in Middlebury at the Natural Foods Coop to do some shopping, and Julia had enthused over all the local products, the healthy organic options that were so missing in her native Russia. Even in Vienna, buying organic was not yet such a thing.

"I know you're going to love this place, Julia," Greg said, remembering his first evening together with Anne after they had moved in.

It had been a similarly balmy evening, with a gorgeous sunset over the Adirondacks on the other side of Lake Champlain. They were sitting out on the front porch, finishing the delicious wild Alaskan king salmon and assorted vegetables that Greg had grilled on the barbecue, sipping a Valmiñor O Rosal Rio Baixas Albariño he loved. He could not forget Anne's radiant smile, her easy manner as she had enthused about the garden, the food, the sunset—everything.

Just as Julia was doing now.

"I already do. And thank you for bringing me here," Julia said, before adding, with a bit more seriousness, "It is already helping me put the terrors of the last week or so behind me. I hope you, too, Greg will be able to heal."

"It'll take time for both of us, Julia. We will help each other, won't we? Now that Anne is gone, you are my—my closest friend." Greg said as he lit a hurricane light when the curtain of night had fallen on the stunning sunset. He poured the last drops of the Albariño he had brought up from the fridge in the cellar into his glass.

"And you mine."

They had Vermont blueberries with Ben and Jerry Vanilla ice cream for dessert, and after cleaning up, as it was a clear sky with a full moon, Greg said, "Julia, I have an idea. Let's take a blanket, and we'll snuggle up on the hammock down by the pond, listen to the frogs, and watch the stars come out." He had done this often with Anne, and this was one of the things he loved the most.

"Wonderful."

They held each other close as nightfall cooled the air down, and watched for shooting stars in the heavens of the Milky Way and the universe beyond. Greg shed a quiet tear as he remembered the many times he had done this with his beloved Anne, and Julia kissed his wet cheek saying once again, "Thank you, Greg. This is exactly the peace I need."

It was close to midnight and Greg was feeling the cold when he finally picked the sleeping Julia up from the hammock and carried her upstairs. At the top, he started down the hall toward the guest suite, but on second thought, decided that that might not be so wise: it was too far from the master bedroom for him to feel comfortable that he was keeping an eye on her. He had vowed to himself and to the memory of Anne that he would not let anything happen to their friend. In fact, once he had covered her up with the quilt on Anne's side of the king-size bed, he went back downstairs and fetched the pistol she had kept in the study, loaded it and put it on his night table. He did not want to be surprised by an intruder like he had been at the hospital. As he went to perform his ablutions in the bathroom, he told himself: *I will see what I can do tomorrow to improve security.*

Climbing back into bed, Greg looked over at Julia and remarked, *God she is beautiful.*

But so was Anne, and I am still in love with her...

☙❧

It was maybe three hours later that the nightmares came: Julia started screaming and thrashing about, and in her hysteric state, when Greg tried to hug her to calm her down, she seemed not to recognize him and beat his chest and face with her fist. But as Greg just held her tight, repeating her name and saying that he was there to protect her, at first, her screams changed to whimpers and then to quiet weeping. Finally, she calmed back down, and just lay there in his arms, still sobbing.

Eventually, they dozed. Hours later, with first light, Greg stirred, waking from a dream. An erotic one. He realized that he had an erection.

Julia must have too. She moaned and moved her hands to touch him there.

"Julia..." Greg was taken aback.

She snuggled even closer.

Then after a few minutes while he let her pet him, enjoying it and trying to overcome any guilty feelings,

Julia implored him in a whisper, "Greg, will you—will you make love to me? I want to feel how it is—to make love again. With someone I—I could love—To help replace those horrible memories. Once and for all."

"Julia—Julia, are you sure?" Greg still was not, even though his libido had been aroused.

"Yes. If—if you don't mind. With Anne—"

"I am sure Anne would approve of anything we do now," Greg said, already in the heat of passion.

And with that, Greg slipped off his boxers, she her T-shirt and panties, and Greg slowly and carefully entered her. They made love, Greg, climaxing first, but she, not far behind.

After the euphoria of orgasm, they lay in each other's arms, quietly sobbing, stroking each other. "This is all so sudden, so soon," Greg said.

Then, after a long pause, Julia said, nibbling on his ear, "Greg, maybe this is the best way for both of us to put our personal trauma behind us. This is how we can help each other start a new life."

"I guess we can look at it that way."

"And, it is much more than that. It is a fabulous experience. Thank you, Greg."

"And thank you, Julia." Greg turned his head so his lips were next to hers, and they kissed again.

Chapter 36

They were finishing a late breakfast on the porch, Julia looking radiant in Anne's cut-offs and halter-top after the therapeutic night and walnut waffles with maple syrup—Greg's specialty—he, too feeling energized after the nocturnal surprises, when the USPS delivery truck drove up the driveway. Greg signed for the registered package, knowing already in his heart what its contents were.

"Anne's ashes…I'm pretty sure."

Indeed, when he unpacked the carton and the bubble wrap, he took out a little teak box, a label with Anne's full name and address attached to it.

"Oh." This from Julia.

"We'll go to the nursery tomorrow and buy an apple tree to plant in Anne's memory, and mingle in some of her ashes. The rest I'll scatter around this property, which was our first real home together and which she loved so very much. That way, she will always be close."

"Yes. Dear Anne—"

৩৩৩

Greg spent the rest of the day making sure the alarm

system worked and ordering online a number of close captioned cameras to install around the property to catch any intruders. For the next few days, though, he resolved to be extra vigilant, and while in the house or on the property always to have a gun nearby. Just in case. He did not want to be caught off guard.

A morning swim in the pond—Julia managed to fit into Anne's bikini, and Greg remarked to himself that she was as stunning as his wife, though a bit taller and blonde, not raven-haired—was followed by a late lunch on the porch. It was when they were having a piece of dark chocolate for dessert that Greg's phone rang.

"Hi, Greg." Richard Peters was at the other end. "I just wanted to congratulate you on capturing the traitor."

"So, you heard from Lieutenant Casey?"

"Yes. I would never have believed it, though. I must say, the lab analysis of the syringe confirmed it. Stewart was about to inject Ms. Saparova with a concentrated dose of one of the most deadly toxins in the world. Tetrodotoxin, the poison found in the sting of the Blue-ringed octopus or in the Japanese fugu fish. The victim dies within seconds—suffocation, cardiac arrest. In the end, Stewart was hoist by his own petard, you might say, thanks to you. He deserved it, that's for sure. But it's too bad we couldn't get some information out of him."

"I am sure he was working for the Russians. Probably ordered to eliminate Julia. After Billy Crawford. The other terrorist could have been next. Or me. The command must have come from Boris Polyakov himself, the Deputy Director of the FSB, and twin brother of Sergei, the arms merchant. Revenge, since it was Julia who shot and killed him on the boat."

"I wonder what else Stewart was up to. I'll get the guys to look into his other operations. See if we can find what else has gone foul."

"Yeah, that's probably a good idea, Richard."

"Speaking of the Polyakovs, Greg, the one terrorist we got thanks to you who was still in good shape—Johnny Apostle—talked big time. Of course, with lots of encouragement from some of our colleagues, you can be sure. Eventually, he spilled the beans and told the guys that he was the finance man for the Sons of Jesus and that much of their funding actually came from Russia, arranged through Polyakov. Boris and the FSB that is. But then the deal was that the terrorists turned around and used the money to buy material for their bombs. From his twin brother's arms trading operations."

"Wow. That is a nice little business the Polyakovs had going for themselves. One doles out government money for state-sponsored terrorism, the other brings it back into their own pockets by selling them armaments stolen from the state—a double dip, if ever there was one."

"In fact, Johnny and Boris met up in Vienna, we are quite sure."

"Hmm. Interesting. Actually, I saw both of them there. Though not together. One at the opera, the other at my presentation."

"Johnny also told us about his involvement in the Brussels bombing."

"Yes, I suspected him of being there. After I saw the video from the close captioned cameras.

"Well, you and Ms. Saparova are still up for a Presidential medal, and I'll let you know when we have lined that up. But in the meantime, keep well, and look after yourself, Greg."

෧෨෧෨

They hung out below the stars as their second beautiful evening back home in Vermont turned into night, only this time Julia did not fall asleep on the hammock. When they had enough of stargazing, Julia suggested they go for a skinny dip in the pond. Refreshed by the spring fed water, they ran to the well-lit house holding hands. When they went upstairs, neither of them hesitated. They shared the double sink for their evening ablutions without saying much, and when Greg took his clothes off to get in the spacious shower, Julia joined him, surprising Greg as she kissed him with the water warming their bodies and their hearts.

From there, it was a quick step to making love again once the lights were out. This time more assuredly, both seeking to give, and to take, maximum pleasure. Not just to help forget the trauma of the past ten days, but even more so, to enjoy the present and to look forward to the joy of shared pleasures in the future.

⁓⁓⁓

But like their first night together, this one was not all honey and roses either. Julia's nightmares and the screaming and crying came back again in the early morning. Greg exercised patience and love to quell her fears, to comfort her, and bring her back to a balanced, happier state.

That night, as he lay awake thinking, with Julia in his arms, he resolved to contact Dr. Menzies if these episodes of hysteria persisted.

⁓⁓⁓

The next morning they went to the nursery, and Julia helped Greg choose a pretty little apple tree.

Pink Lady, the kind of apples Anne loved.

They took it back home, and Greg planted it in a prominent spot, where it would be seen from far and wide, and from where one could see the faraway mountains and the lake. He threw a small shovelful of Anne's ashes in the hole before positioning the tree's roots, saving the rest to scatter around the property later. Together he and Julia then carried an old bench that had been at another viewing point when Greg and Anne bought the property over to the tree and placed it nearby. "This will be Anne's spot and her very special tree," Greg remarked as they surveyed the result of the morning's labor of love.

It was as they were walking back to the house to prepare a late lunch that Julia felt the first wave of weakness and nausea. Greg had his arms around her waist but felt useless as she vomited on the grass time and again. When she came up for air, she said, "Oh, Greg, I am so sorry! I don't know what is wrong with me...I feel so weird."

"Come, let me get you up to the house. You need to lie down. I'll call a doctor." Greg feared the worst.

He helped her up to the master and had her get into bed, while he went back downstairs to call their GP. He left a message for the secretary to call back.

When he went to back to the bedroom, Julia was sobbing inconsolably. "Greg, Greg. I think I am pregnant. I know—I know that this is how you feel when you—you are with child."

"Julia, you need to see a doctor. We mustn't jump to conclusions."

"I just need a pregnancy test. I am convinced. I have felt weird ever since...in Ozersk." She melted into tears again.

"Now, now Julia. You were certainly not feeling weird when we were making love the last couple of nights."

"Yes, but I want to get an abortion if I am. I do not want to have the child of that rapist cousin of mine."

"Julia—"

"Oh God, I am carrying Beria's grandchild. I—I want to kill myself." It was all hitting her at the same time.

"Julia, if you are pregnant—think about it. The child could also be mine."

"It would be too soon to show up like this."

"No, not necessarily, Julia. You cannot get an abortion now. That would kill you. Let's just take this step-by-step. Fine, let's get you a pregnancy test. That is certainly easy enough, but it's probably still too early to be accurate. We may have to wait. I'll take you to see a doctor here, of course. But we will also call Dr. Menzies, who knows what you have been through." Greg didn't know what else he could do.

∽∾

The next morning, Julia was up early, slipping quietly out of bed well before Greg. She was in the kitchen already wearing her panties and one of Greg's shirts when he woke and came down for his morning coffee.

"I have decided. I will keep the child, whatever happens," Julia said, turning toward Greg as he poured himself a cup. "I will keep it and raise it, love it—for sure, it will be mine."

"Good. That's what I thought would make sense. If you are indeed pregnant."

"You know, Greg, the child will be more related to me than a normal child—if it were your child, for example."

"What do you mean?"

"Well, it will be half me because I'm the mother, but

then again an eighth me because Polyakov was my mother's sister's son. Five-eighths me, in all."

"Umm. I sort of see what you mean. Genetically."

"Of course, if it's yours, I would definitely want to keep it," Julia said, coming over and giving Greg a kiss. "But even if it's Polyakov's, I also want it because it is more me. Don't you see?"

"Well, that is a good way to think about it." Greg was glad for the outcome, however Julia rationalized it.

"Should I make some eggs? Scrambled or fried?" Julia asked as Greg sidled over to her, putting his coffee cup on the island.

"Julia," he took her hands in his, "I know this is all very sudden for both of us. And maybe all too soon. With Anne just gone. But—but will you—will you marry me? That way, the baby will have both a mother and a father. We can raise it together. And have a few more. I love you. The way I loved Anne."

"Greg." She leaned into him, as his hands moved to her chin, gently tilting it toward his. "Are you—" But her question remained unfinished, as they kissed passionately.

"Yes, Julia. This is what I want. And I am sure this is what Anne would have wanted too," Greg said, before continuing. "I want to be with you, protect you, love you for the rest of our lives."

"Oh, Greg, I couldn't be happier."

☙❧

They went into town to shop and decided to have a celebratory lunch at the Fire and Ice Restaurant. Julia ordered the Broiled Scallops, Greg the Roast Duckling, with a bottle of Perrier-Jouet Grand Brut Champagne, with sparkling cider for Julia. Feeling deliciously full and happy after the meal, they sauntered up Main Street and into The Vermont Book Shop, where Greg made sure that they had enough copies of his books on hand.

"Let's go home for a swim in the pond," Julia said. Greg was delighted to hear her say the word "home."

As he drove up the curved driveway, Greg sensed that something was not right. When he entered through the kitchen door, he saw that indeed, someone had been through the house, rapidly but methodically. Drawers were open, closets ransacked, papers strewn all over. Fortunately, he had taken his laptop with him.

"Julia, we will have to be very careful from now on," Greg said. "There has been a break in, and someone has searched through our things. They must know you are here. With me."

"Oh, Greg, I am so scared."

ဖာဖာ

It was timely therefore that UPS delivered the close captioned cameras from Amazon a few hours later that afternoon.

Greg set about installing them immediately around the property so that they would not be visible, but would make it pretty well impossible for anyone to approach the house without being filmed and an alarm inside going off.

Nevertheless, he had a gun within reach at all times the rest of the day, even while making and eating dinner, and he put one on his night table when they went to bed. He was not taking any chances.

They did not let go of each other for most of the night and talked about who might have broken in and searched through all their belongings—that is, mostly Greg and Anne's. Greg kept coming back to operatives sent by Boris Polyakov as the most likely.

The FSB did indeed have a long reach, and it did not seem like the kind of thing the Sons of Jesus would do.

⁂

It was just before three-thirty a.m. that the monitor Greg had placed on his night table started bleeping. Not just once, but several times in a row. Waking from his light sleep, Greg was able to discern three men approach the house from different angles.

Okay, you bastards, you're going to get the holy living shit scared out of you.

Greg had the advantage of surprise, since he knew from which direction the men were coming. He chose the one who had circled to the back to knock off first. He went to the glass door leading to the rear terrace and, seeing movement out there, threw it open and shot in the direction. He knew he had scored a hit because there was a loud scream and some wild shooting in the dark. Then quiet. He hoped that this intruder would not be the source of any more trouble.

He then moved to the patio on the side of the house facing the pond, from which direction he knew the next thug was approaching. Again, checking on the monitor to see how close the guy was, he waited behind a pillar until the man was five meters away, then opened gunfire. This interloper, too, went down. Greg did not concern himself with the third man, who he saw on the monitor was now running away from the house, but called nine-one-one, hoping that his friends from the local fire brigade would show up very soon, and take the two injured or dead assailants away and off his property for good.

Chapter 37

Greg went back inside, satisfied that for now the danger was over, and found Julia hiding under the covers. He had been thinking as he climbed the steps, formulating a plan. As he snuggled up beside her, he asked, "Julia, how would you like it if we went to Vienna? For a short visit. After what has happened, it would be good to get away from here for a while—even if it means going back into the lion's den. And you would see your mother. I know you are keen on being with her as I am sure she is with you. If we have time, you might also give notice on your lease, and tell them at work that you will not be back."

"Wow, that sounds great!"

"What with these intrusions, we will be no less safe there than here, I am sure. Plus, I would very much like to hear Jonas Kauffman and Irena Kokova in *Götterdämmerung*. At the Wiener Staatsoper. They were amazing in *Siegfried*. That would be another nice distraction for us."

"Oh, Greg, that would be the best. I would love to go back to Vienna."

"Are you sure you are up to it? The trip, I mean. We would have to leave this coming Thursday."

"Of course, Greg. I am feeling so much better now. I feel healed, with your love."

"You don't know how happy I am to hear that."

Then after a kiss, she said, "But, Greg, weren't you telling me that Kokova is—is Boris Polyakov's mistress?"

"Yes. And I am sure he will be there. At the performance. He knows me, and I am sure, by now, he has seen pictures of you, so we will have to be extra careful. I hope that will be all right."

But that was exactly one of the reasons why Greg wanted to go. He was hoping there would be at least a slight chance that he might confound the FSB Deputy Director into making him think that he was still in Europe. Also, to tell the Polyakov twin to his face to leave them alone, now that his wife and Boris's brother were both dead. They were even, and he was ready to call a truce. He would promise not to pursue the Russian if, in turn, he agreed to desist from coming after them.

"What I would most like to do is kill that bastard," Julia said, after a moment of reflection.

"Sure. So would I, of course," Greg agreed, without going into his plan to try and get the Russian to back off. "But that would be very dangerous."

"Still…"

"Okay, Julia. If you agree, I will call Nicholas to get opera tickets for us, and I'll book the flights."

"I am really looking forward to seeing my mother. We can all stay at my place."

"Are you sure she won't find that strange? Too soon for me to be with her daughter—after Anne."

"Well, if you didn't, Greg," Julia said, smiling as she stroked his chin, "I am sure my mother will be okay with it. She really likes you. We will just have to explain, won't we? She knows that we both loved Anne."

Greg was secretly happy that Julia was so enthusiastic about this plan. The last couple of days, he had found that she was less anxious, indeed more her old happy self. She definitely seemed to be on the mend, and even the mention of Boris Polyakov had not caused a setback. And remarkably, she had sloughed off the nocturnal attack.

Nevertheless, before he got in touch with Labrecque in Vienna and booked the flights, he called Dr. Menzies. She, of course, was delighted that Julia was healing, also, that although she was sure she was pregnant, Julia wanted to keep the child and was reconciled to the fact that it might be the result of the horrible rape she had experienced.

"In reality, Greg," the doctor said, "when I think about it, Julia's rationalization on the sound genetic grounds that the baby would be more related to her than if it were not that horrible Polyakov's is possibly the best way for her to think about it."

And regarding Greg's query whether it would be safe for Julia to travel back to Vienna, Dr. Menzies answered, "Yes, from what you tell me, I think it could actually do her good to see her mother and make the break with her former life. Greg, you will, though, have to keep a close eye on her, because a relapse is not out of the question. And that would not be good. For one, she might react very negatively after seeing the twin brother of her rapist. No doubt there is a strong resemblance."

"Thank you, Doctor Menzies." Greg was comforted to hear that the doctor supported their upcoming trip.

Chapter 38

Much as Greg loved being back in Vienna, he found it strange and painful to be there without Anne, and with Julia instead. The memories were still raw, the hurt tangible. He resolved to put it all out of his mind, not dwell on the wife he had loved so very much. Seeing how happy Julia was to see her mother again helped. He, too, was very fond of Elena.

But it was only when Julia appeared in her low cut, tight fitting navy blue dress ready to set out for an evening at the opera that he was able to switch completely to the present. They said good night to Gospodja Saparova, who looked with delight at her ravishing daughter, and took the elevator down the four floors, kissing the whole way down. The waiting taxi took them to the Staatsoper, where the patrons were already streaming in through the wide open doors.

They were ushered to their parterre row ten seats—Greg made a mental note to thank Nicholas for the excellent tickets—where they huddled close, flipping through the program before the lights were dimmed. Peter Schneider, the Conductor, came out to huge applause, and the magical music began, sending a *frisson* down Greg's back as Julia squeezed his hand.

Once the curtain lifted and the sparse Wagnerian scene was lit up, and the singers appeared one by one and started singing their resonant arias, Greg allowed the music to sweep him away. Kauffman was at his best, and Kokova's voice, was, if anything, exhilarating. Intermission came all too soon, and Greg felt withdrawal symptoms as the majestic music was replaced first by a moment of silence, then the dissonant din of clapping, and, as the curtains lifted, a murmur from the audience. It took him a minute or so to return to the moment, with Julia beside him.

"Unbelievable," was all he could say, as he took Julia's hand and the two got up to file out behind the row of formally dressed Austrian patrons.

Greg had trouble fighting back the memories of his last visit to the Staatsoper with Anne as he led Julia up the majestic stairs to the first floor Schwind foyer, with its gorgeous frescoes.

"Julia, I'm going to get me a glass of bubbly and you a soft drink while…"

"Wonderful. In the meantime, I'll find the ladies room."

"Join me back here at this pillar."

It did not take long for Greg to get a flûte of champagne and a Coke and saunter back to the appointed place, admiring several of the well-turned-out women in the audience along the way. Waiting for Julia, he was not at all surprised, though, when he saw a familiar-looking man approach him: Boris Polyakov. This was a déjà vu. One he had wanted to happen.

"Well, Mr. Martens. I know you are a great lover of opera, so I was indeed hoping to see you here. Despite your wife's unfortunate death—"

"Yes, and your brother's. I must say, it was a dangerous venture indeed."

"Someone is going to pay for that, you can be sure."

"Couldn't—couldn't we come to an understanding?"

Just then, Greg saw Julia approach from behind the FSB Deputy Director. Polyakov turned, his eyes following Greg's admiring gaze. She appeared to stumble, dropping her evening purse right in front of the Russian intelligence man, who, in a reflex motion, bent to pick it up.

Julia, seemingly trying to regain her balance, put her hand on his shoulder, brushing his neck on the way, as she said with a radiant smile, "Why, thank you. How gentlemanly of you."

Polyakov stood back up and handed the purse to her, muttering between his teeth, "My pleasure, of course, my dearest cousin. I am surprised to see you with this American. But take it from me, the two of you are as good as dead."

"I wouldn't be so sure," Julia countered.

"You may not be aware, Mr. Deputy Director, but Ms. Saparova is pregnant. With your brother's child." Greg thought he would throw that in. To confuse the bastard. To gain time. And maybe some semblance of protection for Julia.

"As for you, *cousin*—" Julia spat the last word at the FSB man. "—you will not see the end of *Götterdämmerung*. Goodbye and good riddance," she brazenly said as she grabbed Greg by the arm and pulled him toward the staircase. Greg looked back to see Polyakov turn white and clutch his throat, as they skipped down the steps.

"We're leaving, Greg," Julia said in a calm voice. "I just pricked the bastard in the jugular with a pin infused with some Tetrodotoxin. The same poison they tried to use on me. He will be dead in a few minutes. We must get away. Quickly."

Greg followed, not knowing what to think. "Julia, what do you mean?"

"Nicholas knows. He's outside with a chauffeur who will drive us to Munich. It would be too dangerous for us to fly out of Vienna."

"Julia, why didn't you tell me?" The enormity of what Julia had just pulled off suddenly dawned on him.

"You would have tried to stop me, for sure."

"It's very risky."

"I had to do it. For myself. And for Anne. And us. Rid the world of these Polyakov monsters."

They came out in front of the opera, on the Ring side, and, sure enough, Labrecque was just a few meters away, standing by a black car, looking very spiffy in his evening gear. They rushed over, and Greg said, "Why, Nicholas—"

Labrecque chuckled as he handed him a small canvas briefcase. "Greg, get in, and safe travels. We'll talk later. I have the rest of *Götterdämmerung* to attend to."

"You lucky bastard," was all Greg could think to say. And then catching Nicholas's *double entendre*, he added, "You mean there are more of these bastards? The twilight of these crooks. Good luck with them. And—and what's this?"

"Read it. It's the material we have amassed on the Polyakovs. It is all highly confidential and pretty damn explosive."

"How?"

"We'll talk. We might get you to publish some of it. It could compromise the entire Russian political elite. Maybe even bring them down. Goodbye now, Greg. You better get going."

"Bye for now. And thanks, Nicholas." All Greg could say as he climbed in beside Julia was, "Wow! What a night."

Chapter 39

"So, Julia, will you tell me what just happened there? Why did I have to miss the second half of my favorite opera?" Greg asked, tongue-in-cheek.

"Well, from your conversations with Nicholas and others, I figured that my vile cousin Boris would be there at the Staatsoper. To see his mistress perform Brünhilde in *Götterdämmerung*. He wouldn't have missed it."

"Yeah, I guess that was pretty obvious."

"And after the last time these creeps kidnapped and abused me, Nicholas gave me a small vial of that Tetrodotoxin—you know the same poison that FBI agent tried to use on me. Just in case…"

"It seems to be the toxin of choice for these agents. So you used that?"

"Yes, I put a special needle, infused with the stuff, in my purse, and on my way back to you from the bathroom, took it out, and—when I stumbled and my cousin went to pick my bag up—I stuck him in the neck with it. He didn't stand a chance, it was such a strong dose."

"You just took it upon yourself to kill one of the most important men in Russia, Julia."

"After what his brother did to me and Anne, and his father to my aunt, and all three, no doubt, to many others, he did not deserve to live. I said I wanted to kill him, and I did. Using their very own methods."

"There will be a hue and a cry, an international search for us if this gets out."

"That's why Nicholas gave you the file, Greg. Once you read it, he told me, and write an article or two based on it, they will leave us alone."

"I am not so sure. Rather, they might come after us with a vengeance."

"Well, read the stuff. And publicize their evil story. And then we will see. At the very least, it will tell the world how vile the ruling cadre in my country really is."

എന

There was a reading light in the back seat of the limo, so while Julia slept, Greg opened up the briefcase and started into the files. He finally finished as they approached Munich airport at the tail end of the four-hour trip, just before two a.m.

Since the flight to Montreal that Frau Huth had booked for them was not until four-fifteen p.m., they checked in at the Hilton and went straight to bed. They were both exhausted from jet lag and the events of the last two days.

It was over a late breakfast after a morning of making love and lying in each other's arms that Greg summed up for Julia what he had learned from the Polyakov files.

"These guys had it all figured out. They had the entire top echelon of the Russian government eating out of their hands. The Polyakovs supplied most of the top brass regularly with girls as a sideline to their human trafficking and arms trading operations. They catered to every perversion imaginable—and believe me, there are many weird people in the Russian elite—and arranged for parties with luxury items we can only dream of. This way, they could carry on their nefarious activities without being troubled. If anyone started getting out of line, they would use blackmail or even murder. It is the decadence of Rome under Caligula that they reinstituted big time in Russia."

"Wow. Unbelievable!"

"As for Boris, he was the worst of the lot. Besides being the mastermind and the puppet master, he was—just like his father, Lavrenti Beria—a raging pervert who would take pleasure in kidnapping any young woman he saw and using her in any manner he saw fit. His brother paled in comparison—no offense meant, Julia."

"I am glad I killed the creep—creeps. Both of them. And that sycophant, Hetzel."

"As we found out earlier, the Polyakovs provided for themselves and the entire operation by having the FSB finance all sorts of terrorists around the world through some slush funds who would then buy the nuclear and other arms from Sergei's operation, which then paid off whoever to get continued access to those armaments. The profits to the Polyakovs from this double-dip rip-off of the Russian state were staggering. And superimposed on all this, were the sales of women and children to anyone in the world who would pay, as well as drugs, stolen artifacts, and even human body parts. In short, they would trade in anything provided they were paid enough."

"Just terrible."

"Well, this is unfortunately what a system like the one in your country without any institutional checks and balances will give rise to. Human greed, cruelty, and ingenuity are limitless if given free range."

"So, Greg, what are we going to do about it?"

"I need to talk to Nicholas. To see what he and Interpol have in mind as to how I can best help to put an end to this by writing about it."

"What do you think?"

"I am thinking of doing two articles. First, one to expose in detail the Polyakovs for what they truly were: depraved and corrupt criminals of the worst kind. And then a second one a little later about their links to the Russian governing circle."

"Won't that be dangerous?"

"I am hoping that the first article will get anyone still interested in us off our backs. The focus will be on the Polyakovs, and as the others run away from and lambaste the dead who can no longer threaten them—or us—it might lull them into complacency. Then, when I hit them with the second article, everyone will be more concerned about distancing themselves from the mess, and each other, rather than targeting the messenger. But yes, it will be dangerous. However, we are already living in great danger, Julia. We can't deny that."

෬෧෬

Labrecque called as they were packing up in the hotel.

"So, Greg, you read the files?"

"Yes. Pretty damning, all right."

"Before we get into that, you probably want to know what happened back here in Vienna."

"Sure. Tell me."

"Well, since Julia acted at the end of intermission when most of the audience was already on the way to, or back in their seats, and Boris just collapsed right by the pillar you were standing near, very few people were aware of what happened. Eventually, when the body just lay there, without moving, the staff called an ambulance.

Needless to say, in the theater itself, the performance went on, and there was not even an announcement."

"Perfect."

"He was whisked away to the hospital, and it was not until after the opera that the Russians even learned what had happened. Kokova waited in triumph after her performance in her dressing room, and when her lover didn't show up, the diva went crazy. Eventually, she found out which hospital he had been taken to—the AKH—and showed up there, but by then the corpse had been put down into the morgue. It was almost two a.m.—"

"So right around when we arrived here."

"—but with her histrionics, she managed to get the local FSB Director out of bed—Boris Polyakov's driver must have been a local agent—who showed up shortly after. They tried to get the hospital to release the body to them, but the night staff would have none of it and told them they would have to wait until the following morning. It was only around eleven a.m. that the FSB man and Kokova watched as the remains of Boris Polyakov were loaded into a specially rented funeral car, to be taken, we think, to the airport."

"That's more than twelve hours after Julia stabbed him with the pin."

"And by the time they got back to Russia for an autopsy, much longer."

"Good. The more time elapsed, the less chance they will be able to conclude it was murder."

"But, Greg, what is really interesting is the telephone and message traffic that we have been monitoring since the Russians have the body. Kokova—who has canceled her further engagements in Vienna and back in Moscow—and her allies are blaming the powers-that-be and saying that they wanted to destroy the Polyakovs, probably because they had too much sensitive information on them. They are also alleging that, in fact, Sergei's death too, was somehow engineered by the Putin crowd. Of course, Putin and his gang are refuting this and putting the blame on Abruzov, one of the oligarchs who has recently fallen out of favor."

"Good. Just as I hoped. There's lots of finger-pointing, but none at us."

"Yes, and—"

"What I was thinking, Nicholas, is to write two articles. First, one—and I have already started this—exposing the Polyakovs and their entire operation. That will reinforce the penchant for all the powerful in Russia to distance themselves from them. And second—one maybe ten days later—to lay bare all their links to officialdom in Russia. Naming names. Giving the details of all their sordid dealings with the Russian elite. The supply of women, the lavish parties, and all that. The blackmailings and murders, an exposé of everything."

"That sounds excellent. We will have them fed to Associated Press, and published in all the main newspapers around the world. And get it up on all the social media."

"Good. I'll send you something when we're back in Vermont. And thanks for everything."

"No, thank you. And Julia. Tell her that we have twenty-four/seven security outside her flat, to protect her mother."

"Great. I was going to ask. We will get on to Brewster and Peters to get her papers to come and stay with us. She may as well be near her daughter. And in a safer place."

"Good. Let me know if I can help with that."

"Thanks. Oh, by the way, I don't think we told you, Nicholas, but we have decided to get married. You will be getting an invitation to the wedding."

"Wow! That's wonderful news. Congratulations! I can't wait."

Chapter 40

The articles were explosive in their effect. Interpol acted quickly, in concert with the CIA and local intelligence and security forces in many countries, to mop up the criminal Polyakov empire, along with many of its customers. On those that could not be reached by the arm of the law, serious sanctions were put in place by most OECD governments. Overseas assets were seized, travel restrictions imposed, wings clipped. A serious effort was made to locate and rehabilitate as many of the thousands of trafficked victims of the Polyakovs as possible. In this, the fund that Greg and Anne, and now Julia, had sponsored, and were administering, played a significant role.

One morning a couple of weeks after they got back to Vermont, as they were both finishing their coffees and checking overnight emails on their laptops, Greg was surprised to receive a call from the White House. The secretary asked if he would be kind enough to hold for a moment while President Landers came on the line.

"Greg—I hope I may call you that."

"Mr. President, I am honored."

"Greg, I would be delighted if you joined me at the White House on the fourth of this coming month to receive the Medal of Freedom. Also, on your former wife's behalf who I understand died in the act of apprehending these criminals. I am told she was key to the whole operation. A true heroine, she was. The American people—indeed the whole world—owe you their gratitude for helping destroy a violent gang of arms merchants and human traffickers and for preventing a major act of terrorism targeting this country. And Greg, I hear you are about to marry someone whom I would like to honor similarly as she was also instrumental in defeating these villains—congratulations to you both. If she is there with you, I would like to have a word with her personally, if I may."

"Of course, Mr. President. And thank you."

He reached the phone to Julia, who had perked up when she heard who it was, and said with a smile, "Julia, the President of the United States of America wants to speak to you." For a young woman who had grown up in Ozersk in Siberia, there couldn't have been a higher honor.

The congratulatory calls started coming in very soon after. First to call was Peters, their CIA friend, who had been the first one to suggest their nomination. "Well done, you two. I am glad it came through, although I never doubted it."

"Thanks to you, Richard."

"No, you deserve it. By the way, Nicholas is coming over and will be a recipient as well."

"Fabulous. Then we'll see him—"

"And we should have the papers all in order for Julia's mother to be here for the event. And stay, permanently, as a resident."

"Richard, we can't thank you enough."

It was as he was signing off from this call that the idea came to Greg. "Julia, let's set our wedding date for the Saturday before the White House presentation. We'll tell Nicholas and, that way, he and Marie Christine can be here to celebrate with us. And Richard just told me that by then your mom's green card will be in place. I know it's short order, but I am sure I can mobilize my family by then. And we don't need a blow-out event. It is really just for us."

"Good idea, Greg. I would like nothing more than that. We can all celebrate together."

⋐⋑⋐⋑

The wedding was at their home, by the pond. It was a beautiful summer afternoon, with a short ceremony presided over by Peter Spyrou, a Middlebury colleague of Greg's, and a reception deliciously catered by Jim Reiman, a local restaurateur and good friend of Greg's and Anne's. Julia was a gorgeous bride and Greg a radiant husband. Nicholas was the best man. Julia had her friend Elizabeth from Vienna come over to be her maid of honor. Richard and Captain Brewster were there too, with their wives. The two mothers sat side by side, both visibly full of joy and love. The feast was sumptuous, with champagne and wine flowing freely the whole afternoon, evening and night. Jim, a talented musician himself, had set up a sound system on the patio with the best of Motown to which they danced into the wee hours of the morning.

It was close to three by the time all the guests had left, and Greg and Julia collapsed into their bed. Although with the mothers sleeping in the two spare rooms they had to be quieter than usual, nevertheless, they took full pleasure of each other's bodies. Sleep only came to them finally when dawn started to creep over the windowsill.

❦

"I am deeply honored this day to present the Presidential Medal of Freedom to four people of exceptional bravery, who were instrumental not only in preventing a direct attack of potentially hugely destructive proportions on our country but helped put a stop to a very vile global arms trading and human trafficking operation. These four went way beyond any call of duty, risking life and limb to destroy the evil that threatened to kill many of our civilians." The president paused before continuing. "First, I would like to call up Ms. Julia Saparova. Julia, by the way, is an eminent nuclear physicist who until recently was working in a very important position with the International Atomic Energy Agency in Vienna. She suffered a lot at the hands of those criminals, yet showed tremendous strength and resolve to rid the world of them. Julia, please come up..."

Everyone applauded as Julia, looking gorgeous in a discreet navy blue dress and high heels—and bedecked with the family pearls that had survived the darkest days of Stalinism, and which her mother had given her as a wedding present—went up to receive her Medal of Freedom from the President of the United States of America. Greg, at the very least, found some irony in all this.

Next, it was Greg's turn, then Nicholas's. And last, but not least, the president cited Anne, asking Greg to accept it in her name. Then the president launched into a speech about their bravery: how Julia and Anne had been abused by the Polyakovs, and yet how they had managed to hold it together to destroy the evil enterprise of the twins. How, lamentably, Anne was killed trying to stop them, but Julia took revenge and killed the brothers. And now after all that, Greg and she had just gotten married and deserved the congratulations and gratitude of all Americans, and indeed the whole world.

The speeches finally ended, and champagne was brought out on silver trays to toast the recipients. Afterward, leaving the White House, Greg and Julia, Nicholas and Marie Christine and Richard Peters and his wife, Joanne, went over to the Old Ebbitt Grill for a meal. Once they sat down at the table, the conversation naturally turned to the affair that had brought them all together, and particularly the way in the end, that they had finally defeated the 'merchants of evil'. There were lots of accolades to Julia particularly since she was the one who had suffered the most and had, in the end, killed both the Polyakovs as well as Hetzel. In fact, Richard and Nicholas commented on how beautiful and radiant Julia looked after her terrible ordeal.

Sitting on the bench, Julia huddled close with Greg, and kissed him on the cheek before she answered their compliment, saying, "I am sure you will all be happy to learn that I am pregnant!"

"Wow! Congratulations, you two," Marie Christine said.

"We—Julia and I—are so, so very happy." Greg hugged his wife of three days. He was indeed happy, although he knew the child was not his.

"Yes, that is fabulous news," Nicholas added. "After all you two have been through."

❦❦❦

Greg rushed to finish the manuscript of *Twisted Fates* and sent it off to his publisher just a few days before Adam was born. The birth went smoothly, and mother and child were home the very next day. Greg and Julia were elated with the addition to the family, and any concerns about the child's conception were forgotten. Greg was particularly happy that the role of motherhood seemed to completely absorb Julia and the memories of the nightmare she had lived receded.

The publisher came back with a very favorable contract within three weeks. Such a rapid response, Greg knew was an extraordinary event in the publishing world. Of course, he was delighted to have another work appear in the public domain, so he accepted the same day. Another three months saw the book on *The New York Times* bestseller list, his third book now to have achieved such accolades.

Greg was now very happy in both his family life with Julia and his career as a writer. At times though, he could not help but miss his former life as a struggling author with Adam as his best friend, Anne as his lover and wife.

But life goes on, he told himself, *and we change and adapt.*

Christmas 2065

Epilogue

Christmas in Vermont was always magical, and everyone in the family loved the time together. But none more than Greg and Julia, for whom having son Adam and daughter Anne with her husband George, and their children Andrew and Lily, there together at their home, was always a time to be cherished. As every year, they opened the presents *en famille,* before dinner Christmas Eve with the tree lit, sipping champagne to accompany little *tartines* of *foie gras*, oysters, and skewers of shrimp in front of a roaring fire.

The last gift left under the tree was one wrapped in burgundy-colored paper and tied with gold ribbon, the same shape and size every year. The entire family had come to know full well that the package contained a delicious Sachertorte in a wooden box from Greg's and Julia's friends, the Labrecques, who were now living in Paris, but it had never been fully explained to them who these people were, and why they would be sending a present. The same thing every year. The iconic Viennese gift, a Sachertorte. Each Christmas, the grandparents had sloughed it off, saying, "Oh, one day you will meet them. They are great people, and we did some interesting stuff together. Remember, Andrew, we talked about the heist of nuclear material—you read about it in *Twisted Reasons,* remember. We first knew the Labrecques in Vienna, from where Sachertorte comes." Greg usually added something like, "Yes, I used to stay at the Hotel Sacher, right opposite the opera. One day we will all go and see a performance there and stay at that hotel—it is beautiful —and eat lots of Sachertorte. You'll love it."

This year though, Lily would not let it go. "Grandma, you have got to tell us why you keep getting this gift—this cake—every year from these same people. The same present every year. Why?"

Julia hesitated a moment, then looking at Greg, who nodded, answered, "Well, Lily, and Andrew, you are old enough now. And I don't think your parents know the full story either. Nor does Adam."

"No, I don't know what you're talking about," the forty-five-year old said.

Greg offered the De Luze XO Fine Champagne cognac around before he sat back saying "Well, where shall we start?" He and Julia proceeded to recount their adventures in great detail, particularly the role that Nicholas Lebrecque and Anne, Greg's first wife had played. They recapped how they had all met, which Greg had talked about in *Twisted Reasons*: first Greg and Anne, then an Interpol agent, when they were hunting for Adam Kallay, Greg's best friend from college, who got involved in the first heist attempt. That's when they had all met Julia, who was Kallay's girlfriend at the time. Then how Julia and Anne had both been kidnapped by the 'merchants of evil', but had managed to escape or get rescued. And how Nicholas, who was a colleague of Anne's at Interpol, had always been supportive back up as they fought the arms and human traffickers, and in fact had taken a leading role in finally defeating them.

They recounted how Anne, Greg's first wife—after whom Anne, their daughter and the children's mother, was named—was shot as they were stopping some terrorists from bringing enough nuclear material into the USA to blow up New York, Boston or Washington. And how Julia had in turn killed the main arms merchant, and how Greg had then taken care of her and eventually married her. And that Nicholas Labrecque was Greg's best man at their wedding. The kids just loved the entire story, which took a couple of hours after dinner, with the many side plots and questions that Lily and Andrew raised.

Finally, Anne looked at her phone and saw that it was well past midnight. "Andrew. Lily. It's time you went up to bed. I will be there too soon, and I'll tuck you in. But say good night and Merry Christmas now to Grandma and Grandpa and to your dad and uncle before you go. Give everybody kisses. It was a wonderful Christmas, thank you."

Greg was ready to hit the sack as well, so when George and Anne went up to look after the children and turn in themselves a few minutes later, Julia was left alone with her son, Adam, who was still sipping on the cognac Greg had offered the adults to finish off the celebrations. She admired him from across the room: what an intelligent and handsome man he had turned into. But, like any mother, she worried that he had not yet found himself a partner.

For a fleeting second, Julia wondered whether she should tell him the truth: that he was, in fact, the son of Sergei Polyakov—who had violently raped both her and Anne, Greg's first wife and her friend. And the grandson of Lavrenti Beria, Stalin's perverted deputy, who had kidnapped and abused her aunt, along with countless other women. He would certainly know who Beria was, since he had majored in International Relations, with a special focus on Russian affairs at the Kennedy School, and now worked as a Russian expert at the State Department. She was proud that he had taken an interest in his heritage, and in fact, spoke the language fluently, although glad that, so far, the terrible truth had not come out.

And that is how it will remain, Julia told herself. *The secret will die with me.* No need to disrupt the life of this fine young man. The twisted fates of Adam, Greg, Anne, Polyakov, Hetzel and herself had already caused too much hurt and suffering, she told herself.

Julia stood up, went over to Adam and gave him a kiss on the forehead, saying, "Good night, my son. I am so glad to have you here with us." And she knew that he would not fully understand her meaning, but that was just a legacy of their twisted fates.

The End

About the Author

Born in Budapest, Geza Tatrallyay escaped with his family from Communist Hungary in 1956, during the Revolution, immigrating to Canada. After attending the University of Toronto Schools and serving as School Captain in his last year, he graduated with a BA in Human Ecology from Harvard College in 1972, and, as a Rhodes Scholar from Ontario, obtained a BA/MA in Human Sciences from Oxford University in 1974. He completed his studies with a MSc. from London School of Economics and Politics in 1975.

Tatrallyay worked as a host in the Ontario Pavilion at Expo 70 in Osaka, Japan, and represented Canada in epée fencing at the Montreal Olympics in 1976. His professional experience has included stints in government, international finance and environmental entrepreneurship. He is a citizen of Canada and Hungary, and as a green card holder, currently divides his time between Barnard, Vermont, and San Francisco. He is married to Marcia, and their daughter, Alexandra, lives in San Francisco with husband David, and two sons, Sebastian, and Orlando, while their son, Nicholas, lives in Nairobi with his Hungarian wife, Fanni.

Tatrallyay's thriller, *Twisted Reasons*, the first book in the Twisted Trilogy of international crime thrillers was published in December 2014 by Deux Voiliers Publishing. The second book in the series, *Twisted Traffick*, was released in October 2017 by Black Opal Books. *Twisted Fates*, is the third volume in the trilogy. An international political thriller, *The Rainbow Vintner*, is also slated to be published by Black Opal Books in December 2018. Earlier, Tatrallyay self-published an e-thriller, *Arctic Meltdown*, available through Amazon.

He has also written two memoirs that have been published and a third one that is currently seeking publication. *For the Children*, the story of his family's escape from Communist Hungary and immigration to Canada in 1956 was published in 2015 by Editions Dedicaces, and a second memoir, *The Expo Affair*, the story of three Czechoslovak girls who approached him for help to defect at the world's fair in Osaka, Japan in 1970 was published in 2016 by Guernica Editions under their Miro-Land imprint. Together with *The Fencers*, his third book in the genre—about a Romanian-Hungarian fencer who approached him to help him defect at the Montreal Olympics—these memoirs make up The Cold War Escape Trilogy.

Tatrallyay's poems have been published in many different literary journals over the years. A collection of his poems, *Cello's Tears*, was published in May 2015 by P.R.A. Publishing, and another poetry collection, *Sighs and Murmurs*, was released in April of 2018. He is working on a third collection, *Extinction*. Tatrallyay's first children's picture storybook, *The Waffle and the Pancake*, will be published also in 2018 by Bayeux Arts.

www.ingramcontent.com/pod-product-compliance
Lightning Source LLC
Chambersburg PA
CBHW060950120726
47910CB00002B/566

9 781626 949393